Truth or Dare - Text copyright © Emmy Ellis

Cover Art by Emmy Ellis @ studioenp.com © 2019

All Rights Reserved

Truth or Dare is a work of fiction. All characters, places, and events are from the authors' imagination. Any resemblance to persons, living or dead, events or places is purely coincidental.
The authors respectfully recognise the use of any and all trademarks.

With the exception of quotes used in reviews, this book may not be reproduced or used in whole or in part by any means existing without written permission from the authors.

Warning: The unauthorised reproduction or distribution of this copyrighted work is illegal. No part of this book may be scanned, uploaded, or distributed via the Internet or any other means, electronic or print, without the authors' written permission.

TRUTH OR DARE

EMMY ELLIS

PROLOGUE

Rachel gritted her teeth and tried to smile at her students. She *hated* playing truth or dare. But the kids wanted to, and as it was their choice of a game as leisure time at the end of the school week, she'd have to grin and bear it.

She hadn't liked that sort of game when she'd been younger. The dissecting of human organs, though, that was another matter.

"Mrs Levington, can you help me a minute?" Darwin Gringley. A stupid name for a stupid boy.

A brilliant candidate for the Darwin Awards if ever there was one. Maybe that's why his parents named him that. They'd known he was thick as shit from the minute he'd been born.

"What's the problem?" She smiled and walked over to the long bench desk he shared with four others.

"I can't work this out." He pointed to a plump heart in front of him.

Blood smeared the white tray it sat on, bringing to mind the spatter and scuffs of it on the wall when she'd murdered her father last night.

"What can't you work out?" she asked, disguising her impatience as interest.

"It's not the same as the one Ben has." He frowned. "Look."

She peered from one lump of flesh to the other. Darwin was right, it wasn't the same, but he wasn't supposed to have noticed. She'd thought by him being at the end of the line when God had dished out brains that he wouldn't take in the differences.

"Perhaps this pig had something wrong with it," she suggested. "Ignore it and follow the rule sheet I've given you." What she didn't say was: *Just get on with it, you little bastard.*

She strode away, thinking the pig did indeed have something wrong with it. Her father was a giant arsehole, and she'd loved getting rid of him.

All the rage from her childhood had spilt out with every arc of her arm, blood spilling, too, from the puncture wounds she'd made in his flabby body.

A shiver passed over her, and she sat at her desk to watch Darwin cutting up a piece of a man who had given her a life of hell. Satisfaction wended through her, and the sight of the teenage lad's forehead scrunching as he worked incited a rush of self-importance.

I did that. Me. All by myself. I brought that heart to the table.

The damn thing was cold now, but it had been colder inside his body. She was surprised it even beat he was that cruel. But she'd become crueller, biding her time, and now look at him, left out in the open for someone to find in his favourite place. It had taken an age for her to drag him to her car. The fat sod was heavy and cumbersome in death. That was all the pies he'd liked to scoff, and the cakes that reminded her of Nan and her baking. God, she'd hated seeing him eat. It was like he couldn't get it in his trap fast enough, and meat or cream filling squirted out more often than not, oozing down his chin.

She shook the memory away. It wouldn't do for her to get angry here. In the classroom and at home, she played a part, of a teacher, a wife, a kind woman who wouldn't hurt anyone. That was a joke. Inside, evil lurked, waiting to come out when the time was right. How long had she hidden those urges? It had to be since she'd realised exactly who and what her father was. No little girl should be put through what she'd endured. A mean devil had formed within her, created by circumstances beyond her control, left to flourish with each instance of wickedness inflicted upon her, infecting some of her.

She'd known, even as young as she'd been, that she had to hide her desires beneath a mantle fit for a sweet girl, not someone as rotten as she was. Her two selves had resided side by side for years, and last night she'd let the demon free again.

And it had felt so good to be the one in control, not *him*.

"Mrs Levington, it's got all weird things inside it," Darwin whined.

She'd fucking kill *him* in a minute if he wasn't careful.

"What weird things?" She got up once more, her smile hurting her cheeks. It was hard work being a princess. *No, don't call yourself that. Never that.* She stood beside the boy, close, and bent over, fighting the need to punch him in the face.

"There's all these yellowy-white patches, see?" he said.

"That's cancer. Tumours." She sniffed. "Like I said, the pig had something wrong with it."

"I don't reckon this is a pig's heart." He scrunched his face up. "It's more like a human's."

He must have been paying more attention in previous classes than she'd given him credit for. And there was her thinking he gazed around the room like a gormless prat because he couldn't wrap his head around the lessons. No, he'd been taking it in all along.

"I'm going to show this to Mr Nichols," Darwin said.

She rested her hand on his bony shoulder and resisted digging her nails in. "No, you're not to bother him." The last thing she needed was the other science teacher shoving his oar in. Nichols would spot it as a human heart right away. "He's busy marking papers."

Darwin opened his mouth to say something else, but she couldn't allow him to harp on about this when the other students were listening.

"Right, everyone, that'll do." She clapped. "Hearts in the waste bin provided, please, because it's time to play truth or dare."

A cheer went up, and the room erupted in a plethora of sounds: stools scraping, trays screeching on desks, chatter coming out of smart mouths—mouths she longed to melt with a Bunsen flame so their lips merged together, preventing speech.

She hated children, especially boys.

"Don't forget to wash your hands." She kept her attention on Darwin to make sure he actually put the heart in the bin. She didn't trust the kid not to wrap it in paper, stuff it in his bag, and give Nichols a visit.

Thankfully, he dropped it inside.

"Clean the trays," she called, going to the corner cupboard to take out the treats she'd begrudgingly bought for them. Every week she did the same thing, a game and sweets. It put her on a higher level to the other teachers, giving the intended impression she was great. No one would suspect her of murder. *What, Mrs Levington, killing people? Never!*

She stifled a mad burst of hyena laughter and blanked her face in case anyone was looking her way. Today's offering was fizzy cola bottles, five packets for a quid in the supermarket, so she'd bought thirty-five and placed a bag in each child's place. By the time she'd finished, everyone was ready and seated.

She returned to her desk and sat.

"Okay, as usual, one question each to one other pupil," she reminded them. "We'll start with the back table and work our way to the front. So that's you first, Darwin."

She wanted to get his go out of the way. *God knows what shit he'll come out with.*

He beamed, showing his unsightly teeth, too long and large for his overly round head, which reminded her of an orange on top of a drinking straw.

"Okay," he said. "But can I ask you instead?"

"I suppose that would be all right." She cringed inwardly. *What was the little twat going to ask her?*

"I choose truth," he said.

Some girls giggled, and a few lads *oohed*.

Darwin cocked his head. "So, was that really a pig's heart?"

She nodded, let out a bit of that insane laughter. "Of course it was."

"Only, a pig's heart weighs more than a human's. Like you told us, a human heart is trapezoidal—I remember that because it's a weird word—and a pig's is more of a cone. The human atrium receives four pulmonary veins, but a pig's receives two. Mine was definitely like a person's. How do you explain that, Miss?"

Her stomach churned at the smug glint in his eye and his accusatory tone. "I assure you, it was a pig's heart. Okay, next person, next question."

"But, Miss, if we have a human's heart in class, won't you need to tell the police?" he went on. "Like, the butcher, he could have *murdered* someone. You buy the hearts, and he'd know we get rid of them after..."

"You're being daft," she said. "The butcher wouldn't murder anyone."

But I would.

"I'm going to tell my mum when I get home," Darwin prattled. "She'll know what to do."

The rest of the class either laughed or told him he was being divvy—after all, he was known for his dimwit behaviour and picked on because of it.

"You do what you think is best," she said.

But you won't get home. I'll make sure of it.

CHAPTER ONE

Darwin wandered down the back of the school towards the trees. Some kids, the bullies, gobbed off at him for walking across their footy game on the field, but he ignored them. He was always being shouted at, people saying he was a thicko, ugly, or a geek, but their yells didn't bother him. Not anymore. How could they when he'd heard them so many times? Name-calling failed to impact him now, thanks to Mum. She'd sat and talked to him when he'd finally confessed to being bullied, and her advice had worked: *Feel sorry for them, love. Once you do that, it won't hurt anymore. Bullies are sad people, taking their insecurities out on others. You're perfect as you are, never forget that.*

He hurried, wanting to get home fast so he could tell Mum about the heart. No matter what Mrs Levington had implied, it definitely wasn't a pig's, because she'd taught them all about that a fortnight ago—*and* she'd been specific about the differences. It had to be like he'd said. The butcher had killed someone. What else could it be when she bought the hearts from him? And why hadn't Miss taken Darwin seriously? Murder was a big thing, and it shouldn't be swept away like that. It could even be the bloke who worked on the meat counter in the supermarket. He gave Darwin the creeps with his leery grin and the way he nodded after everything he said, as if he knew something you didn't. Yeah, if it was anyone, it'd be him. He'd slipped the heart in the bag and thought no one would know the difference.

Well, Darwin had.

He was at the diamond-wire fence at the bottom now and climbed over, the tail of his blazer catching on the top. If a teacher spotted him not using the gate along the way a bit, he'd get detention, but in the two years since he'd been at Smaltern Secondary, he hadn't been caught. He entered the woods, the kids' voices behind him faint, whispers of *Mark, pass the ball, mate!* and *Kick it to me, will you?* and *Offside, you donkey!* Soon he'd come out on the cliff top, and then he could walk to the estate where he lived. Everyone else took the other route, through the streets, but he preferred being alone. He didn't have to listen to any jibes or whatever then.

He rushed between the trees, making it to the track down the middle, thinking of those lads who'd been held captive inside a hollow tree. It happened twice a day, him being scared by going through the woods to and from school. It was better than being harassed, though, so that was why he did it.

A crack came from behind, maybe the breaking of a twig, and he spun around, gasping, his heart thudding too hard. His skin went cold, clammy, and he glanced about, thinking someone had followed him off the field, wanting to shit him up as a joke. It wouldn't be the first time. No one was there, though, and he let out an unsteady laugh.

Just being silly again.

He came out on the cliff top and leant against a tree to stare at the sea. He loved it here. It reminded him of his real home in Italy. The small seaside town of Smaltern attracted loads of people in the summer, and for those months he got to play with kids on the beach—kids who didn't know him enough to pick on him. They didn't care if he couldn't read half the time or didn't understand maths, they just wanted to hang out and have fun.

He kind of wished it was summer all the time really.

Still, it wouldn't be long, and the hordes would descend, all the caravan parks bustling with people, the shops that sold sticks of rock, fudge, and holiday memorabilia crammed to the gills, as Nan would say, their dormant months of being closed out of season behind them.

He smiled at the thought of the hot days and the fun he'd have. Maybe James from last year would come back.

Another crack ricocheted inside the woods, and he turned to peer around the tree, his legs going weak. What was *she* doing in there? Mrs Levington swung a rounders bat at her side, and was that silver *nails* sticking out of it? Whatever it was looked weird, as did her face. It was all skewed, like she was well angry, and he'd never seen it like that before. What was up with her? Had someone pissed her off?

He stepped out so she could see him. "Miss? You all right?"

"No," she said. "There's a bloody fox in here. It keeps getting under the fence, coming onto the school field and pooing."

Was she going to wallop it with the bat or something?

"Have you seen it?" She stopped beside him and scanned the cliff top, her eyes narrowed to slits.

"No. Never seen a fox, and I come through here a lot." He shrugged. "You're not going to hurt it, are you?"

"Nope. I just need you to help me with something a second. Come on." She walked back into the woods, tromping down the track then veering to the left where the school fence ran parallel, barely visible behind the trees.

He jogged to keep up, squinting when she disappeared behind a thick trunk. "Wait up, Miss!"

Darwin came abreast of the trunk, and the end of the bat loomed towards him as if in slow motion. He registered it, frowning at why it was aimed for his face, and then it connected, sharp, agonising, those spikes or whatever they were digging into his cheek, going through it, the tips piercing his tongue. Blood filled his mouth, and he wrenched his head to the side to get away from the bat. He screamed as it tore his skin, a spike dragging against his gum on its way down and out.

"Shut up, you stupid little dickhead," Mrs Levington said.

Darwin's eyes watered so much he couldn't see, and he sobbed, clutching his cheek. Why had she hit him? What had he ever done to deserve that?

"It wasn't the bloody butcher," she snarled, "it was me. *Me!*"

He sank to his knees. What was she going on about? *What* was her?

"*I* killed and then took the heart." She came closer, appearing as a murky shape on the other side of his swelling tears, a shadow demon teacher, the bat held high.

Oh God, she'd *killed* someone? He'd dissected a *person's* heart like he'd thought?

"No," he said, holding his free hand up in case she whacked him again. "Stay away from me. Please. I won't tell anyone." Blood oozed between his fingers, running down his chin and throat. He choked on it, coughing, and then another wretched pain radiated from the side of his head, into his other cheek.

The force of the blow knocked him over, and he landed on the ground, grit digging into the back of his hand, his temple, his forehead. He squeezed his eyes shut for a moment, readying himself to scream again, then opened them wide. She was there, right there, holding the bat with both hands above her head, her legs planted far apart. She didn't look like Mrs Levington anymore but some nutter instead.

"No one can know what I did," she said. "Least of all you, Divvy Darwin."

The bat descended, and somehow, he knew when it struck that would be it, there'd be no coming back from this. He mustered his energy and scooted to the side, just as the spikes dug into the mulch where his head had been. She growled and yanked it upwards, then brought it down again. The weapon cracked onto his forehead, and for a millisecond he experienced the spikes going through his skull, the sensation of it, the agony, and, just as he thought of what would happen when the sharp tips pierced his brain, they did, and his world turned the darkest shade imaginable.

"Never seen a fox," Rachel mimicked, her breath coming out ragged.

Her lungs hurt, and it was all this gimp's fault. If he hadn't been so nosy about the heart, he'd be home by now, safe, and she wouldn't have the job of trying to get back to her car unseen. It was her presence in the woods and her mood she needed to conceal from people. They'd take more notice of an angry person, and she was raging, the other side of herself, and it always took a while for her to calm down and push that half away. If anyone said anything to her, even a simple "Good afternoon!", she was likely to rip their head off.

Rachel stared at Darwin. His chest didn't rise or fall, and her bat was wedged into his forehead. That would be a bugger to get out, but she had to. It was *her* weapon, one she'd made herself, and she couldn't leave it behind.

She planted her foot on his face, squashing his nose, and yanked. The spikes popped out, and she staggered backwards, almost falling. A quick glance around showed she was still alone apart from the dead kid, so she got to work using the cleaver she'd stashed behind a nearby tree and hacked at his chest. It took a while to break the ribs—hard work, that—and she was conscious someone could come along any minute, but she managed to cut through and slice out his heart.

She stuffed it in her pocket, blood seeping through the fabric, and ran the way she'd come, her bat hidden behind her. She'd left her car at the park, at the back of the public toilet block, and headed for it, praying no dog walkers ambled along.

They didn't, and she made it to the block. Pressing her back to the outside wall, she inched round to scope out the park. Mothers sat on benches while their children played, screeches and laughter fluttering in the air, no one peering her way. She flung herself into the loos, checking each stall was empty. A nose in the mirror over the sink gave her pause. She looked like *him*, her father, when he'd been in one of his rages, and she forced herself to change her expression so she was herself, Rachel, the nice lady everyone loved.

That's better.

She went into a stall and locked herself in, then cleaned the end of the bat in the toilet. Clumps of God knew what bobbed on their spiky moorings, coming loose and floating in the water, and she stared at them, wondering if they were the only bits of his brain that had actually worked.

She flushed the loo so it cleaned any remaining mess, mesmerised by the gushing, akin to the sea during a storm, all white spume and violent thrashing. Satisfied everything had washed off, she checked her clothing. Lucky she had black on—no blood visible.

She left the block and checked for anyone watching, then scooted round the back and stored the bat in the boot of her car. She drove to the outskirts, up high where the metal storage containers stood, and got out to stand on the cliff. The sea was calm today, and she imitated it, ensuring all the anger seeped from her, Nasty Rachel scurrying off and Nice Rachel taking her place. She was worn out, her limbs heavy, so she sat and dangled her lower legs over the edge.

One jolt, and she'd go down, falling, her life flashing before her, then she'd hit the surface. Maybe her back would break if she landed wrong, if she didn't torpedo feet-first. Either way, she'd be dead—she couldn't swim. Neither of her parents had been inclined to teach her.

The sun peered out from behind a fluffy white cloud, warming her skin. She'd have to get going soon, go home and put the dinner on. It was her turn to cook, so it'd be something easy like spaghetti or chilli. Jeff, husband extraordinaire, was the one who created the masterpieces on a plate. She wondered how she'd got so lucky, him being interested in her, then remembered he only knew Nice Rachel, and *she* was someone worth being married to. That was what he'd said anyway.

She sighed and pushed herself to her feet, then drove towards home. Jeff would be back about six. That gave her time to shove her clothes in the washing machine and have a shower. She'd get in her pyjamas and spend a nice evening on the sofa. They had previous episodes of *The Crown* to watch, so that'd be nice.

A left turn took her past where she'd dumped *him* last night, and her stomach lurched—fear or excitement, she wasn't sure. A police car had parked outside The Villager's Inn, and she wondered whether they'd found her father or there'd just been some ruckus or other in the pub that needed a copper to sort it.

She bit her bottom lip and checked out the scene. People sat at scarred wooden bench tables, drinking pints and smoking, and they didn't seem alarmed. She drove along, keeping her sights on the road ahead. Once she'd passed, she peered in her rearview. A large white van pulled up behind the police car, and then she had to take a right into her street, travelling to the end. She lived at number one, something she'd engineered because she'd always wanted to be just that—number one.

The problem was, during her childhood she'd been number five, the child no one took any notice of until her father wanted to play truth or dare, or blame needed to be dished out. Then she suffered.

But she wouldn't suffer anymore, not now Nasty Rachel had come out to play. She'd protect her, keep her safe from wicked people with wicked intentions.

She smiled, content, and left her car on the driveway, butted up to the garage door so Jeff could park behind it. That was the rule—he was up and out before her, beginning work at eight, and those early starts and dedication had paid off. He'd risen up the ranks and had taken on a new role recently, transferring from his other office to one in Smaltern. He was a good man, a kind man, and he'd protect her no matter what, she was sure.

But not me, Nasty Rachel said, her voice echoing in her head. *He won't protect me.*

Shaking off a shiver, she went in the house and hid the heart in the bottom of the chest freezer, putting a bag of oven chips and a packet of peas on top. The hearts she'd taken from the bin at school, she fed into the food disposal unit, then went into the garden to burn the plastic bag. Back inside, she stripped, putting her clothes on a hot wash. Naked, she walked upstairs and showered, getting off whatever parts of Divvy Darwin had landed on her skin and hair, then pushed him from her mind so the memory of him wouldn't spoil her evening.

Chilli, she decided, with garlic bread to dip into it. Jeff liked that.

Pyjamas on, she set about cooking, and the key twisting in the lock gave her a bit of a jolt. Jeff was early, something she'd have to get used to now he was able to work less hours and not be out there grafting on the streets. He spent most of his time behind a desk these days, getting more money for the privilege. Maybe they could afford to go to Malta this year instead of the Isle of Wight. That would be nice, wouldn't it?

"Hi," he said, coming into the kitchen and kissing her cheek.

She thought of the state of Darwin's and held back laughter. "Hello, love."

"Good day?" he asked.

"Yes, you?"

"So-so. Still finding my feet. People don't take well to new bosses telling them what to do."

"Well, you're almost the top dog now, so they'll just have to get on with it, won't they." She stirred the chilli, unable to understand how anyone could be upset that Jeff was their boss. He was the best. "So have people been funny with you again today?"

"Nothing I can't handle. I've introduced new procedures, and some of the others don't care for it. They've been used to doing it their way for a long time, so when the new boy comes in, they resist change."

"Poor you. Well, you're here now, so you can forget about it until tomorrow. Remember, no work talk at home." She didn't even do any marking if they were both in the house. That was another rule—when they were together, they were present, not off in their heads thinking about their jobs.

Jeff found that hard sometimes, he'd said as much, so if he was on a big job, she gave him some leeway. That shouldn't happen too often now, though. His position meant he'd stepped back from the grunt work and others did it for him. She hoped the same would happen to her when she climbed the career ladder. Headmistress had a nice ring to it. Mr Queensley, the current head, was retiring next year, and she intended to take his spot.

Jeff laid the table, and they settled down to eat, chatting between mouthfuls. He cracked the wine open, and they sat on the sofa side by side, *The Crown* playing.

Life was so good.

Nice Rachel sighed with contentment.

But Nasty Rachel itched to kill again.

CHAPTER TWO

Helena smiled at Andy across her desk. "Right, that's that then." She pushed the file away from her. "No more teenage gang."

"They were little shits," Andy groused, "wreaking havoc like that. I'm glad they're in youth custody. Might teach them some bloody manners and how to behave."

Helena didn't disagree there.

During the winter, six young males had strutted around Smaltern as if they owned the place, breaking and entering, intimidating the elderly, and one had egged another on to sexually abuse a middle-aged woman they'd dubbed a MILF. The whole episode had been aggravating, upsetting, and downright awful. Until they'd been caught. The trial had lasted a week, and now all of the ruffians were in a secure hostel. All right, they'd probably have games consoles and the like, but a stint inside would hopefully do them some good.

That or make them even worse.

"Well, they're out of our hair for now, so everyone can rest easy," she said. "Talk about a relief. How can so many kids be so evil?"

"You know my thoughts on that." Andy rubbed his rumbling belly. "The state of their parents says it all…"

"Hmm. They leave a lot to be desired, don't they. Do any of them even wash?" She shivered. "I don't think they have any remorse on behalf of their kids—I'd be gutted if it were me. They were just disgusted their lads had been carted away, as if it was rude of the judge to give them a sentence. Well, if you bring up hooligans, what do you expect? A free sodding pass because you don't think they did anything wrong?"

"God knows. Enough of them, there's more pressing matters at hand. I'm hungry." Andy winced. "Like, really hungry. Fancy going to the pub for dinner? Zach's working late like Louise, isn't he?"

Helena nodded. Her fella, the ME, had an old lady on his slab to attend to. Louise, the daytime front desk sergeant and Andy's girlfriend, was most likely pulling a double—a new fella was starting nights tomorrow, so she'd get her evenings to herself again. His name was Winston Collins or something.

"We may as well." She picked the file up and stood to put it in the cabinet. It was nice to slot it into place, knowing she wouldn't have to look at it again. Her phone rang on her desk, and she lifted the handset. "DI Stratton."

"It's me, guv."

"Hi, Clive. What's up?"

Clive, a PC, only ever rang her when there was a toughie he couldn't handle by himself. She didn't mind giving him advice—it was a joy to watch him grow in his role.

"Um, a body's been found behind The Villager's Inn," he said, sounding as if he didn't want to be telling her that when it was home time.

"Bloody hell." She sighed and scratched her temple, the short hair tickling her skin. "What is it, someone drink too much and fall over, doing themselves some damage?"

"No. I'd say it's murder."

She straightened at that and widened her eyes. "How so?"

"Looks like he was struck with something—his head's caved in on the top, and his face has holes in it. Rips an' all."

The image of that chased away her need for food. "Gross. Okay, we'll go there now. SOCO sorted?"

"Already in attendance."

"Thanks. You're there, I take it."

"Yep."

"Any ID on him?"

"Yes, a wallet. His name's Trevor Vakerby, aged sixty-two, lives at number seventeen Blagden Road."

She scribbled that down. "So quite close then. He's only a short walk away from the boozer."

"Yeah, it's his second home, apparently. Quite the pisshead by all accounts."

"Lovely. Still, I doubt he deserved to die. Right, see you in a bit." She replaced the phone and stared at Andy. "I don't even need to say anything, do I?"

"Nope. Looks like my gut's going to have to wait for a while to be filled."

"We're still going to the pub, just not our usual. The Villager's is our destination. I wonder why Louise didn't phone me about it." Helena powered her computer down. "Maybe she's too busy. Summer brings out the twats, doesn't it. Seems it's all that alcohol in the sun sending people mad. Come on." She took the page off her notepad and entered the incident room.

Her team were just packing up for the day.

"Sorry, you lot," Helena said. "We have a potential murder." She reeled off his name and address then strode over to add it to one of the whiteboards.

Evan Ufford groaned. "Ugh. I'm meant to be going to see my kids in a play tonight, then we're off to Wales for the weekend."

"That's fine, you can go. We'll cope without you." She smiled. "I know how much you've been looking forward to it."

"Cheers," he said then paused. "You sure you won't need me?"

"We managed before you joined the team, don't forget, and besides, you've had Wales booked for yonks. Sod off and enjoy yourself. As for you two…" She smiled at Olivia Vallier and Phil Keats. "Big bag of soz and all that."

"Have you been binge-watching *Miranda* again by any chance?" Olivia asked.

Helena laughed. "Bear with…"

"Bloody hell," Phil said. "Is it going to be like this for the foreseeable like last time, guv?"

"Might be." Helena winked. "Seriously, though, I need you to do the usual. The chief buggered off home a while ago, so you won't have him breathing down your necks, thank God." She couldn't stand him. Sanctimonious dickhead. "Off you go, Evan, before you get roped in."

He scooted out, waving.

"Rightio, we'll be off as well." Helena patted her hip to make sure her phone was in her trouser pocket. "Give me a bell with the next of kin and whatever."

She walked out, Andy behind her, and they went downstairs. At the front desk, Louise was deep in conversation with a rowdy drunk, who swayed on his feet and shouted at her that his geraniums needed watering and they'd wilt if he didn't get home soon.

"You should have thought of that before you necked half a bottle of Scotch and punched your friend," Louise said. "Now answer my questions before I get arsey."

"Gotta love her, haven't you," Andy said as they exited the building. "She's all masterful and stuff."

"Masterful?" Helena chortled and got in the car.

Andy joined her. "Yeah, commanding. In the bedroom, she—"

"No, no, and bloody no!" She started the engine. "I do *not* need those visuals, thank you very much." She was glad, though, that Andy had found love after his divorce from Sarah—and the less said about *her*, the better.

Helena nosed out of the car park while Andy laughed his head off. She headed up the cliff road. The Villager's Inn stood at the top on the little estate there, a mile away from the station. No matter how hard she tried, whenever she travelled this way, she could never stop thoughts of the three dead sisters from The Man in the House case entering her head. One of them, Emma, had worked at the pub.

"How's your love life anyway?" Andy asked, drawing her out of her thoughts.

"Like everything else—none of your business."

"Aww, spoilsport. And there was me thinking we were mates now." He opened the window, and his hair ruffled in the breeze.

Back in the day, Helena hadn't been able to stand Andy. He'd got slobby and dropped the ball at work, and she couldn't abide his lackadaisical attitude. Turned out he'd been going through it with his ex-wife—they'd split up, and he'd taken it hard. Helena had forced herself to back down from keep sniping at him, got him focused on going to the gym with her, and the rest was history. Now, they were pals as well as partners, but she'd never go so far as to chat about her sex life. Some things were private, for God's sake.

"We're friends, yes," she said, "but oversharing isn't my thing, you know that. There are two people in my relationship, and it isn't right for me to gas about what we get up to without Zach's say so. Do you think Louise would appreciate you telling me what she does between the sheets?" She glanced at him.

He'd gone red. "I didn't think of it that way."

"No, you usually don't until I pull you up on things. Just be mindful, all right?"

"Christ, you always make me feel like a little kid."

She barked out a laugh. "That's because you act like one sometimes."

"It's a good job I like you."

She smiled. He was joking about, and it was good to hear it. Life was great for them both, especially for her now two men from her past didn't feature any longer. They'd almost broken her, but here she was, still plodding on.

"I like you, too," she said. "I might even go so far as to say I love you."

He cleared his throat. "Pack it in. I don't do mushy."

"Yes, you do."

"Since when?"

"Mushy peas."

"Fucking hell, you *have* been watching *Miranda*. It's addled your brain. That's the kind of stuff she comes out with."

She cracked up and drove along the road The Villager's was on, sobering upon spotting the pub. "Enough now. We're here." She parked behind the SOCO van and cut the engine, assessing the scene.

A few people sat outside at the tables, mainly blokes with pints and fags. Clive stood at the side of the pub, in front of a six-foot wooden gate. Why hadn't he told everyone to leave? A couple of SOCO were talking beside Clive. Crime scene tape had been strung up, cordoning the seating off from the area closest to the gate.

"Surely Tom hasn't lost his marbles," she said, referring to the lead SOCO.

"What are you on about?" Andy unclipped his seat belt then reached into the back for booties and gloves, handing Helena hers.

"People carrying on as if nothing's happened. Drinking and whatnot."

"They might be witnesses." Andy sniffed. "We'll find out in a minute."

They left the car and approached the cordon.

Clive stepped forward to speak to them. "That lot there were in here last night with the victim. Everyone's been asked to leave the pub, but I told them to stick around until you got here."

"Fair enough, but wouldn't it have been better to get them off the property altogether? They could have stood on the pavement instead."

Clive shrugged. "There's been so many people here since last night, the scene's muffed up anyway."

"True." Still, she wished he'd insisted they move elsewhere. "Andy, will you have a quick word with them, see what they have to say, then send them home?"

"Yep." He ambled off to the tables.

She looked at Clive. "You have their names and addresses, yes?"

"Yes. None of them remember the exact time Trevor Vakerby arrived or went home—they'd sunk too many bevvies—and no one had a beef with him because he was apparently someone you didn't cross. He propped the bar up every lunchtime and evening."

"Christ, who has the kind of money to do that?"

"He'd just sold his business, one he bought a couple of years ago, though why he purchased then sold so quickly, I don't know."

"And that was?"

"The container place." Clive grimaced, most likely thinking the mention of that would upset her.

It didn't. Much. While she'd been locked up inside a container by a sex trafficker called Jason Uthway, treated abominably, and it had scarred her in more ways than one, she was well on the road to recovery and saw it as a short chapter in her story, not the whole book. If she let it mar the rest of her pages, she'd ruin the remainder of her life, and she wasn't prepared to give him the satisfaction of getting to her like that. Arresting him had gone a long way to making her feel better, and now he was behind bars, she could move on—providing her nightmares stayed locked up.

"Okay," she said, "so he had a fair few quid then."

"Vakerby got a loan and bought it for five hundred thousand, built it up, then it went for over a million when he sold it, so the pub landlord said."

"I bet it did. Lucrative business, that is."

Andy came over. "Well, that lot are about as useful as tits on a snake."

Helena snorted. "Clive implied as much, just not in that kind of way. Let's get going then. Where is he, Clive?"

"Go through the gate, walk down the side of the pub."

Her stomach contracted. She recalled what he'd said on the phone—head smashed in, rips on the face—and dreaded what she'd see. They signed the log with Clive. At the cordon, she slipped the gloves and booties on, then took a protective suit from a cardboard box and got dressed. Andy did the same, then she opened the gate and led the way out the back.

It resembled a garden, and she supposed it was, one used by the landlord. A patio, grass beyond, and a rotary washing line, pegs of many colours hanging from it. A plastic basket of dried, folded washing sat beneath.

Tom stood halfway down, in the doorway of a backless tent erected against a high hedge. "Ah, there you are." He lowered his mask. "I just came out for a breather."

The unmistakable sound of a camera being used filtered out to her, and the flash lit up the tent. Then the photographer exited, bent over, and appeared to be trying to control himself. If he was sick, she'd go mental at him.

Helena and Andy walked over the grass, which had no evidence markers dotted over it—odd. Tom went back into the tent, and Helena followed, Andy at her rear. A head and shoulders stuck out from the base of the hedge, as if his body had been stuffed there, and whoever had done it couldn't quite get the rest of him in.

"Um, how deep is the hedge?" she asked.

"About a metre," Tom said, "but his feet aren't sticking out the other side. We have another tent up round there. His legs have been bent at the knees so he's hidden."

As far as she could recall, a path ran down the depth of the pub, an alley shortcut folks used to get to the street behind. God, people could have gone down there throughout the day, assuming Trevor had been here that long, none the wiser that a corpse was to their left, out of sight.

"Who found him?" she asked.

"The landlord's wife. She'd come to get her washing in," Tom said.

Andy huffed. "So she didn't see a bashed-in head when she hung it up?"

"No, she said she was in a rush this morning and just pegged it up and went back inside." Tom raised his mask. "She'd folded the washing this afternoon, put it in the basket, and decided to have a moment to herself. She sat on that bench on the patio and stared across. First glance, she reckoned it was a deflated red ball—you know, kids fucking about in the alley, and the ball had come flying over. So she got up, went over there, and saw what it really was. Bit of a shock. She's inside nursing a vodka."

"Hmm." Helena faced Andy. "Can you go and ask Clive if he's let Zach know about this. I forgot to do it at the station."

Andy left, and Helena stepped closer. The top of Trevor's head had a hole in it, his blood-covered brain peeping through. Something had clawed at his cheeks—there were holes but also slashes, like an animal had attacked. But an animal couldn't stave a skull in—at least not any around here—so the only creature to have done it was a human. And that human was *angry*. This was horrific. His face wasn't recognisable as a face, his nose stamped on, pressed so far down the tip was level with what was left of his cheeks. His eyes had puffed up so much they resembled bruised apricots with slits down the middle, and those lips...well, two purple hotdogs came to mind.

"Blimey," she muttered. "He upset someone."

"Just a bit." Tom sighed. "I wouldn't normally move him yet until Zach's seen him, but the pics have been taken, and there's nothing been found on the grass here, so I reckon we can pull him out and see what the rest of him looks like."

"What, you want me to help you?" She stared at him, not liking that suggestion one bloody bit.

"Figure of speech." Tom glanced at the tent flap. "Ah, Zach's here."

Helena nodded at Zach, and he raised his eyebrows. They kept it professional at work. Andy came in after him, and Tom peered out of the flap into the garden.

"Can I have a hand here, please?" he called. "Moving the body."

Helena went outside while they did their thing. She glanced around. The garden was fenced off on the opposite side and at the bottom, the hedge forming the other boundary. Had the killer come in here to put the body there or had they done it from the alley? She strode to the gate and through to the front, pleased the drinkers had gone. She went round the side and down the alley, entering the second tent and startling the SOCO in there.

"Sorry," she said.

Plenty of leaves and a few twigs were scattered on the path, yet in the garden, only a couple were on the grass. She reckoned they'd pushed him in from this side.

She left the tent and spotted uniforms talking at the doors of houses in the street in front of the pub, so she trotted along the alley to check out the road behind. She peered down the side of the tent and caught sight of a uniform there, too, so the house-to-house avenue was covered—probably Clive sorting that out, bless him.

Back in the pub garden tent, she stared at Trevor. He was obese, so whoever had brought him here had to be strong, or anger had given them the strength needed. He was on a plastic sheet.

"Did you put him on that?" she asked Tom.

"Nope, it came out with him. Probably used to make it easier to push him under the hedge."

Ingenious. "Not the sort of plastic sheeting you tend to have hanging around, though, is it, so premeditation if it was bought for this specific reason."

"Mmm." Andy moved closer to the body. "Looks like cement dust is on it, so maybe someone who's having work done at their house?"

"Maybe." She stared at the blood on the material of Trevor's T-shirt. "There doesn't appear to be a stab wound or anything in that top. Can you lift it, please?"

Zach placed his own plastic sheet down and knelt beside Trevor. He raised the T-shirt.

"Oh, fuck me," Andy said.

Trevor's chest had a gaping hole, and his heart was missing.

"What the bloody hell?" Helena felt sick.

Zach pressed on, probably to get her mind off it. "Round-ended object used on the top of the head. Brain has puncture holes in it. These holes and rips in the face remind me of nails, as in, the type you hammer, not the ones on fingers."

"Goes with what Andy said," Helena mused. "Someone having work done. So what did they do, stab him with the nails?"

"No, they went too deep so needed force, and there are several close together, and all of them dragged down the skin, creating the slashes." Zach let out a breath. "I'd say they were attached to a weapon."

"Lovely." Helena sighed. "I suppose we ought to go in and speak to the landlord and his wife—if she's not too shitfaced on voddy."

Zach frowned as if to say: *Beg your pardon?*

She laughed, waved, and walked out, hoping the place had CCTV outside. It'd make their job a damn sight easier if it did.

CHAPTER THREE

Isla paced in front of the living room window, clutching her mobile. Darwin hadn't answered any of her calls, the damn thing going straight to voicemail. It was coming up to six o'clock, and he was always home by now, especially on a Friday. He liked to get his weekend started as quickly as possible. Was there some after-school club he'd mentioned and she'd forgotten?

She dialled Smaltern Secondary and held her breath, butterflies playing up inside her. An answering service message waffled in her ear about the school being closed, reopening on Monday at half eight. So no clubs, no staff there, unless they were ignoring the phone.

"What shall I do?" she whispered, eyes filling.

Darwin didn't have any friends until families came for the summer, so there was no one to contact to find out if they'd seen him since school finished. Lately, he'd been walking home through the woods, despite her warning him not to. Had something happened in there? The place gave her the creeps, what with those kiddies stashed in a tree that time, and she'd avoided it ever since. Still, she'd have to put her fears aside and go there, check he hadn't been beaten up by those wicked bullies and left injured.

Out in the hallway, she took Muppet's lead off the hook by the coat rack. No need to whistle him—the sound of the chain rattling had the daft sod bounding out from the kitchen towards her. She did love a Labrador. Such gentle creatures.

"A quick walkies," she said, grabbing her keys off the small table. "We need to find Darwin."

Muppet wagged his blond tail all the way down the road, and Isla hurried along, almost jogging she was that worried. A sinking feeling claimed her gut the closer she got to the cliff top. She rounded the corner and headed over the grass towards the woods she so hated. Maybe he was in the park at the other end, having a go on the swings. He'd always liked them as a littlun, God bless him.

She let Muppet off the lead, and he legged it into the woods, no sense of fear evident at all. Mind you, he didn't know children had been hidden in there, did he, so of course he wouldn't be scared. Isla followed, trepidation seeming to scour her stomach, bringing on a clenching pain. Muppet barked, the sort he used when something was wrong, and she knew then, knew he'd found her boy. Mother's instinct, call it what you like, but in that moment, her body went cold all over, and her scalp prickled.

Muppet barked again, and Isla stopped walking. She didn't want to see what the matter was, not if it meant having her suspicions confirmed, but at the same time, she had the urge to get it over and done with, face the shock.

She stepped to the left. Muppet's tail stuck out from behind a tree, the strands of fur hanging down, a golden bird's feather. Another bark, then a howl, and Isla dashed round there, her heart thrumming too fast.

And there he was, her boy, her lovely Darwin, splayed out on the ground with blood all over his face, deep gouges in his cheeks, holes in his forehead. His nose leant to one side, and his eyes, oh God, his eyes would never sparkle again when he was happy, would never see her coming towards him for a hug. They were lifeless. Staring. No soul in them whatsoever.

Her son was gone, at least the part that made him who he was, his shell left behind, discarded by some fucking bastard who'd taken a step too far in picking on him.

Isla screamed.

CHAPTER FOUR

The inside of The Villager's had the strong scent of hops, and it was getting right up Helena's nose to the point she kept having to hold back a sneeze—one of those ones where her mouth hung open and her face scrunched, only for the sneeze to retreat.

"We'll need to see that CCTV." She smiled at the landlord.

Ben Folton nodded, his bald head shining beneath the spotlight above their table. He was a meaty fella you wouldn't want to mess with and new to the area, having taken over the running of the pub last year. "It's in the office if you want to come with me."

She got up, leaving his tipsy wife with Andy. Ursula had knocked back two vodkas in the time they'd been talking and God knew how many prior to that. Helena followed Ben behind the bar and through an arch into a corridor halfway down. He entered a room and stood by his desk, which was neat as a pin and shiny oak. She joined him inside and waited while he woke his computer and accessed the correct file.

"I'm afraid it won't show you what you want." He clicked fast-forward to the previous night. "It doesn't span the whole of the front, just the beer garden so we can keep an eye on them out there—it's so they don't get silly and bother the neighbours. Anyone going down that path at the side alley…"

"It's okay. I'm interested in vehicles as well as people, and they might have parked in view then dragged him along."

"Poor old fucker. No idea why they did that to him. I mean, there's talk he's a bastard, but he was always okay with me. I take as I find." He pressed the PAUSE button. "That's stopped at six o'clock for you, so it's still light out. Fancy a coffee?"

"That would be lovely, thanks." She sat at the desk.

"I'll leave you to it then. Back in a mo."

She set the recording to play, the camera facing the street. People and cars flickered by, folks' arms going up and down while they drank at the bench tables, the speed manic. Ben returned with coffee, likely from their posh machine on the bar, and left her alone again. Andy came in, standing behind her, and she was glad he didn't speak when she needed to concentrate. This first watch was to get an idea of the activity before she viewed it at a more leisurely pace.

The time zoomed along to after midnight, the houses opposite with no lights on, no people walking, minimal vehicles, which wasn't surprising at that time. Come ten to one, though, headlights speared the darkness, two brilliant-white cones, a vehicle parking to the left, but she couldn't see it. Whoever it was must have clocked the camera mounted above the pub's double doors or it had just been fate that they'd chosen that spot. She set the tape to play slower. The headlights went off for five minutes, then they switched on again, receding with the driver going backwards.

"They know about the camera," Andy said. "Otherwise, why reverse?"

"I thought the same thing. I didn't spot any shadows or anything to indicate a body being dragged down that alley, did you?"

"No, but the techs might. Watch it again."

Helena rewound then played. "They've gone nowhere near the front of the car. Let's hope someone saw something from the houses, despite it appearing that no one is awake. We'll check with the uniforms in a bit." Her phone jangled, and she accessed the message. "That's Olivia. Next of kin is a son, George Vakerby. Twenty-three Blagden Road—same street as George."

"I'll go and get Ben," Andy said. "We'll need a copy of this recording."

He left, and Helena watched it again, peering close, but when the headlights snapped off, everything went that weird grey mixed with black. At the start of the path, something flickered, a brief sense of movement, and she jolted.

"Hang on a minute…"

She paused, brought the screen up larger to zoom in, then played it again.

"That's a fucking foot."

The back of a boot up to the ankle was there for scant milliseconds, the front hidden in darkness. She rewound, played again, then paused. Strained to see if she could make out anything else about it and came up with thick soles, a deep tread, possibly black leather. Andy walked in with Ben, and she pointed at the monitor.

"Can you print that out for us?" Andy asked Ben.

Helena got up and moved out of the way. "And we'll need a copy of this footage, please."

She drank her lukewarm coffee while Ben did as they'd asked.

"How's your wife now?" she said.

"She's calmed down." Ben tapped the mouse. "How long will…will the body be there?"

"Hopefully it'll be gone by the time you wake up tomorrow, although the tent might remain, as might the crime scene tape. We'll need to come into the pub as well, process it. Again, maybe by tomorrow you can reopen, but I'd say it's more likely the day after."

"I'm going to lose a lot of trade. Friday nights and Saturdays bring in the most." He handed her a memory stick while his printer whirred. "Selfish of me to think that way, but with the winter months only being the regulars, and summer just starting—this is the first weekend of holidaymakers visiting."

"I know, and I feel for you, but I feel for Trevor and his family more." She smiled tightly. "Your money loss is nothing to their loved one being dead."

"You're right. I'm an arsehole." He passed over the image of the boot and a memory stick.

"Thanks for your time," she said. "We'll see ourselves out. If you recall anything else, let us know. I left my card on the table out there, don't forget."

Back in the rear garden, she sighed and recalled she hadn't got a time of death estimate from Zach. She popped her head in the tent and asked him.

"Between midnight and one," he said.

"Okay, that matches with the CCTV we've just watched." To Tom, "Come and look at this."

He walked over and stared down at the image. "Right, we'll watch out for any footprints—not seen any so far, though."

"Thanks. Here's the footage that needs sending in." She gave him the stick. "We're going to speak to uniforms, then we're off to see the next of kin."

She put the boot image in her pocket and strode to Andy who stood by the gate, and together they entered the front beer garden. Clive turned and smiled. They signed out of the log and, on the pavement by the car, took off their protectives and popped them in an evidence bag. She tossed it towards Clive, who caught it and put it in a cardboard box behind the cordon.

"Split up," she said to Andy. "I'll talk to the uniforms in the street behind, you do the ones here."

Helena put fresh booties on and walked along the alley, scooting down the side of the tent and continuing on until she stood at the end. The uniform she'd seen earlier was leaving a house opposite—the one he'd been at before. He must have either been asked inside for a cuppa or the resident had seen something for him to spend so long there.

"Ah, glad you're here," he said.

"How are you getting on, Edwards?"

"A lady saw something. I was just about to ring you."

He'd gained a fair few wrinkles since he'd started this job. The poor sod looked knackered, and she'd swear it wasn't the sunlight playing tricks, but was that grey hair at his temples? He was only thirty-odd, for God's sake.

"I'll go and talk to her. Saves me hearing it twice." She walked up the garden path and rang the bell.

An elderly woman opened up, wrapped in a teal cardigan despite the heat of the early evening, and Helena supposed you got colder as you aged. Or maybe it was the shock of realising what she'd seen was related to a murder. That'd do it, bringing on chills the likes of which she'd probably never felt before.

"Hello, I'm DI Helena Stratton. My colleague said you noticed something with regards to the scene back there at the alley. Would you mind going over it again with me?"

"Of course not. Saying that, I do mind, because it's frightening me now, but I'll do what I can to help. It's not been safe here for a long while, what with all these murders going on the past couple of years. I'm surprised anyone comes here for a holiday." She stepped back and allowed Helena entry, then led the way to a living room. "Would you like a cold drink?"

"That would be great, thank you." While the coffee had been welcome at the pub, she now had a thirst on.

"I have some cans of Coke if that's any good to you. I don't drink it myself; it's for the great-grandsons, you know."

"Wonderful." Helena stood by the window while the lady shuffled out. She stared across at the alley—this was the perfect spot to see something going on. If the tent wasn't there, the view would be of the alley itself and the house at the end over the road in the street The Villager's was in.

"Here you go."

Helena turned and took the can, plus the glass that had some poured into it. "Brilliant. What's your name, love?"

"Katherine Yeats, but you can call me Kath. Everyone does." She lowered into a chair by the window and grabbed some knitting from a wicker basket down the side. "I've got a great-granddaughter coming. A pink cardigan, because she'll be arriving in the winter. Them scans are amazing, aren't they, telling you what you're having before it's born."

"How pretty." Helena sipped, and the bubbles popped at the back of her throat. "Do you mind if I sit?" She indicated the sofa.

"Oh my goodness, where are my manners? Yes, you park your bum. I'm not used to having people here who I don't know. Everyone's family or friends, and they know to make themselves at home without me saying so."

Helena sat. "So, if you could tell me what you saw?"

Kath's knitting needles clacked as she worked at high speed. "Well, like I told that nice chap, Mr Edwards, I'd got up for a wee at five to one. I shouldn't have had that last cup of tea at nine. Anyway, I always sleep with the curtains open—something I continued even after my Colin passed away; we always did it as a reminder of our honeymoon. We went to Cornwall and got woken by the sun every day, and we wanted to recreate it forever." She tittered. "Funny, the things you do. Anyway, where was I? Oh yes, I walked past the bedroom window, and if you look out there, you'll see there's a streetlamp right next to the alley. There was enough light for me to see someone down there. Crouching, they were, in front of a lump." She paused knitting, her bottom lip quivering.

"Are you all right, Kath?"

"Yes, it's just that now I know it wasn't a lump, was it, but a man."

"Did you know Trevor Vakerby?"

"I did. We went to school together—God, that's some years ago now. So I watched for a while, thinking they were fly-tipping, or that the landlord was doing something or other with the hedge. People tend to leave the beer garden and throw their empty bottles in there on their way home, and as he finishes late—I've seen the pub lights on well after three some mornings—I reckoned he'd been busy and must have come out to clear the bottles while he had a moment."

"What did you think the lump was?"

"A black bag." She carried on knitting. "Whoever it was pushed it into the hedge, and then I thought: *That's a bit weird. Why are you doing that?* I went to the loo, and when I got back, the person was gone, as was the 'bag', and they must have got into a car, because the headlights were on."

"How much of the car did you see?"

"Just the front part. So, around ten inches of it. The rest was hidden by the house on the other side of the alley."

"Could you make out a colour?" That was a big ask, considering there wasn't a lamppost at that end and the CCTV had been dark.

"It was light, I know that much, so white or yellow, something like that. Could have been silver or that gold so many have these days."

"That's very helpful, thank you. Did you go straight back to bed?"

"I did, and I stayed awake for a while, thinking about why the bag was put in the hedge. Now I know it was Trevor... They were hiding him, weren't they."

"I'm afraid so." Helena drank some more Coke.

"I thought about going along there this morning, having a look, but my daughter came round to take me into town—a surprise, which was lovely. We had lunch, which was also lovely. Fish and chips sitting on the seafront. A gull nearly stole my chip from my hand, the cheeky bugger."

Helena smiled. "They are a bit brazen, aren't they."

"Big, too. I'm sure they weren't that large years ago. Seems the fast food they steal has made them into giants." She gave a watery smile. "You know there was talk about Trevor, don't you..."

Helena perked up. "Talk?"

"I didn't tell Mr Edwards, and I suppose I should have done. Trevor was a nice enough lad when we were kiddies, but as he got older, he went in with the wrong crowd. God, he turned a bit nasty, going round starting fights and causing a bit of trouble. I'm sure it'll be on that database thingy you use."

"Yes, it will be. Go on."

"Well, he married Sheila, and there was gossip of him knocking her about. A bit of a slap here, a punch there, and she never did do anything about it. They had five children, and according to their neighbours, there was always shouting or crying."

"Did anyone report it?"

Kath shook her head. "You didn't in those days, and especially not with the reputation Trevor had earnt himself. You tell on him, he'll come and have a word with you, that was what we all knew, and his 'word' wouldn't be pleasant."

"I see." A bully then.

"The kids...well, they had bruises sometimes. Black eyes, split lips. The story goes that they fought with each other, the children, and as that was normal, everyone round here tended to ignore it."

"So did anyone ever find out whether the kids had been hit by the parents?"

"Not for certain, and it'd never have been Sheila, but Trevor..."

"I understand. Do all the children still live around here?" She knew about the son, George, but Olivia had yet to pass on anything about the others, nor that Trevor had previous.

"Didn't you know?" Kath dropped her knitting in her lap and rubbed one eye. "There's only two left—a son and a daughter. The other three, lads, were killed in a house fire when they were young."

"Oh, that's awful."

"It is. Happened at Trevor's mother's. She had them for the night, see. The other two got out, but the smaller lads and their nan..." She closed her eyes for a moment. "That was when Sheila finally lost it. She couldn't handle the fact she was out at the cinema with Trevor while her littluns perished. She cliff-jumped a month after."

What a bloody tragedy. "That's terrible."

"I know. They live down Blagden. You'd think the remaining two children would move away, wouldn't you. I mean, if my dad treated me like that, you can bet I wouldn't stick round once I was old enough to leave home."

Helena poured the rest of the Coke into the glass and finished it off. She placed them on the coffee table, a chill sweeping over her. A bad home life, terrible goings-on. A motive for murder. Had one of the remaining children bumped him off? And why hang around Blagden? Like Kath had said, if you had an abusive upbringing, you'd move, wouldn't you? Then again, the minds of some abused people could be moulded in such a way that despite the horrors endured, being close to the parent who dished it out was sometimes preferable to going it alone. Better the devil you know.

"Is there anything else you think I should be aware of?" She thought about Ben the landlord saying Trevor was a nice enough bloke to him. How could two people have such a different view of him? *Ben's relatively new around here, though. Maybe he only saw what Trevor wanted him to.*

"I don't think so." Kath gazed out at the alley and shuddered. "Do you think someone did it for the money?"

That had crossed Helena's mind. The sale of Trevor's business at such a high profit was a massive incentive to get the inheritance if you were his son or daughter—payment for abuse endured. She'd be looking into those two.

"Who knows, eh? I'll be off then," Helena said. "Thank you for your time—and the Coke."

"That's all right." Kath smiled. "If you could see yourself out. It's the hips…"

"Of course. I'll pop my card on the table here in case you remember anything else that may help."

"I'll have a think."

Helena smiled and walked out, ensuring the door was properly shut by pressing on it. If it wasn't one of Trevor's children who had done this, whoever it was could be out there planning random kills. She'd hate for Kath to become a victim.

Edwards approached her. "Nothing else from any of the other houses."

"Thanks. Kath had quite the story to tell."

Edwards frowned. "What, more than the body being put in the bush?"

"Just a bit." She left it at that, said goodbye, and squeezed past the tent again to meet up with Andy.

He stood by the car. "Blimey, I thought you'd bailed on me."

"I got talking to a woman." She told him what had been said.

Andy grunted. "That puts an interesting spin on things."

"It does. I'll give Olivia a quick ring, let her know what's going on, then we'll go and visit the son. After that, we'll nip to the daughter—*then* we'll finally get our dinner somewhere and go back to the station." She glanced at her phone to check the time. It was already past seven. "If we're lucky, we'll get to the pub before they shut the kitchen down at ten; otherwise, it's a takeaway for us."

"I'm not complaining, anything will do." Andy got in the car.

Helena took her booties off and walked over to pass them to Clive, then she drove round the corner into Blagden. Ben had said Trevor left The Villager's about eleven, walking, and he'd arrived close to five—he'd eaten there, sausage and mash, and sunk about seven pints, although Ben wasn't sure on that as Ursula had served him, too, but she couldn't recall what he'd had. So they had one pissed-up man, weaving down the streets, possibly so inebriated he couldn't see or think straight.

And someone had been waiting in the darkness, ready to kill him.

CHAPTER FIVE

George Vakerby stared at them on his front doorstep, his hair thinning on top, and with his glasses, plus a moustache that was so long it obscured his top lip, he reminded Helena of Dr Hawley Crippen who'd killed his wife in the early nineteen hundreds. She hid a shudder, telling herself a resemblance did not a murderer make.

"DI Helena Stratton and DS Andy Mald." She held her ID up. "We'll need to come in."

He jammed his hands on his hips, revealing sweat patches on the armpits of his light-blue T-shirt. Could he have enough strength in him to haul his father, who was considerably bigger, out of a car and down that alley? Perhaps. People managed incredible feats while riled with anger.

"What's this all about?" His cheeks flared red.

"Your father," she said.

"What's he bloody gone and done?"

"Inside is best." She smiled and gestured for him to move back.

He sighed and took them into the kitchen, the room outdated and nothing like how she'd imagined it would be, seeing as the hallway had modern laminate and fancy wallpaper which still gave off the scent of being recently hung. In the corner, a roll of plastic leant against the wall, and her stomach clenched. It wasn't the same colour as what had been beneath Trevor, but the fact that it was there set off alarm bells.

Andy cleared his throat and glanced at her. She raised her eyebrows.

Pots of paint stood around the bottom of the roll, as did a small bag of cement, open on one corner. The floor had no carpeting or tiles, and a fresh patch of cement was by the back door. He was obviously doing the place up—but why now, around the time Trevor had sold the container business? Had he gifted his children some money?

"Come on then, out with it." George wiped sweat from his forehead.

It was warm, she'd give him that.

"Would you like to take a seat?" She indicated the rickety table and mismatched chairs—pine, mahogany, and white-painted, as if he'd collected them one by one from a charity shop.

He huffed and sat on the pine, the wood creaking beneath him. "Look, I'd planned to get the painting done in here tonight, so if you could get a move on... To be frank, if Dad's got himself in the shite, he can get out of it on his own."

She wondered if Trevor had been just as blunt and imagined he had. "Where were you last night, Mr Vakerby?"

"What time?" He frowned.

Why does he need to know that? "After midnight."

"In here, this room. I was sorting the floor—it had a ruddy great crack in it." He pointed to the new patch. "I finished scraping off the wallpaper an' all. Why, what's that got to do with my old man?"

"Do you have anyone who can verify that?" Andy asked.

"Yeah, Steve was helping me. He's from next door at twenty-two."

"When was the last time you saw your father?" Helena's stomach rumbled.

"Sounds like you need a burger, missus." George pressed the side of his finger to his chin. "Yesterday, ten to five and thirty-four seconds. He walked past—I was putting up new curtains in the living room at the front, which is why I asked you what time you needed to know about. My father was a stickler for us saying our exact movements as kids, and I can't help but revert to that when asked where I've been. Anyway, I'd say he was probably going to the pub." He grimaced. "Second home for him nowadays."

"Right. Did you see anyone else out there after midnight?"

"Not bloody likely. Like I said, me and Steve, we were out here by then. We worked until two-oh-three, and the second hand was at twenty, then we called it a night. Steve was narked because he hadn't expected it to take so long—the wallpaper removal—and he had work early this morning. All right for some, he said, because I have the day off."

"We know about your father's business sale," she said. "Did he share any of that money with you?" She glanced round the room for emphasis and: *I want an answer for this lot.*

"You're joking. He's a miser, and I wouldn't want his cash anyway. I've always said that when he dies, if he leaves us any, my portion is going to local charities."

Now he'd touched on death, she said, "I'm sorry to have to bring you this news, but your father's body was discovered earlier."

"Body?" He sat up straighter.

"Yes, he was murdered between midnight and one o'clock."

"Bloody hell..." He rubbed his temples. "I'm not sure how I'm meant to feel."

"What do you mean?"

"Well, he was a wanker, wasn't he. Always hitting me, shouting and whatnot. He got worse after my brothers died, saying me and Rachel—that's my sister—should have saved them, but we were nippers, so how could we? The fire was too strong in their room—they'd bunked in with nan—and Rachel and me were sleeping in the living room." He let out a shuddering breath. "I hated him, to be honest, and once I left home, I didn't have anything to do with him, even though we live in the same street."

"We heard about the fire—and your mother," she said.

"It was awful. She didn't have the strength to stand up for us while we grew up, not against a pig like him, but Rachel's always said our mum should have walked out with all of us, and if Rach ever had any kids, she wouldn't put them through that. But the thing was, if Mum protected us, he hit her—and I'm talking a proper beating up. She had broken ribs once or twice. Now he's gone...is it mean that I'm relieved?"

"I can imagine that's a natural reaction if you've had a difficult childhood." She smiled to show him she didn't judge. If his neighbour gave George a solid alibi, she'd be able to scrub him off the list. "Where does your sister live?"

"Down the road at number one." He shrugged. "Now, fair warning, she might cry when she finds out. Rachel's a gentle person for the most part, always looking for the good in everyone, no matter how much of a bastard they are. She made excuse after excuse for our dad, yet she was the one he took shit out on the most. Suppose it was because she was the youngest, the weakest. She still visited him at his house once she moved out—the one we grew up in. Sorry, but you won't catch me in there. Too many bad memories."

"Can I ask why you both remained in this street if things were painful?"

George shrugged again. "As a kid, Rachel said she wanted to buy the house at number one when she was bigger, so I hung around, too. You know, in case she needed me. I bought this one when I was nineteen, cheaper back then, and I had a good job. She still lived with Dad, being that much younger than me. And she waited, got her wish for number one once it went up for sale, and by then I was well settled and didn't want to leave. I'm doing it up after a few years of being skint—I lost the good job and got a crappy one, but I'm in a new one that pays better now."

Helena jerked her thumb at the roll of plastic. "Is that the only colour you've ever bought of that?"

His eyebrows met in the middle. "Eh? What's that got to do with anything?"

"If you could just answer the question," Andy said, voice gruff.

"I've had that blue one, plus transparent."

"Is the transparent all gone then, so you bought the blue?" Andy again.

"Well, some dickhead nicked the see-through stuff—it was in my shed—and Steve brought this one round. It's so I can cover the worktops when I'm painting. They're new; I don't want to wreck them. I'll get on and start painting once you've gone. Tomorrow I'm replacing the cupboard doors for those high-gloss ones."

She couldn't begin to imagine what it had been like for George growing up—nor any of his siblings—and she empathised with his need to keep busy. She'd done the same after she'd been snatched by Uthway's lackey and kept in the container. And there was a thought. She'd no doubt have to go back up there to speak to the new owner, ask if he got along with Trevor or if there was a grudge—and see where she'd been locked up.

Maybe I'll send Phil and Olivia instead tomorrow.

"You have my sympathy," she said. "We'll nip along to see your sister now. Do you want to come with us?"

"No, she'll have her fella there, she won't need me. We don't see each other much. She has her own life, as do I."

"Do you need any company? Is there someone we can call to come and sit with you?" She didn't think Dave Lund, the Family Liaison Officer, was needed, but she didn't like the idea of George suffering by himself if he was hiding his true feelings.

He shook his head. "Cheers and all that, but no ta. I can always rope Steve into coming round if I need him. We're, um, we're seeing each other."

"Well, I'm glad you can rely on him."

He appeared shocked she'd been accepting of him and Steve, but what the hell did it have to do with her what he did in the bedroom?

"Um, it's just hit me what you said." He blinked. "Murder. Was my father found at home or something?"

"No, at the pub."

George frowned hard. "I don't understand…"

She decided to tell him. He'd find out through the grapevine soon enough anyway. "He'd been put in the bush in the alley down the side."

His mouth dropped open. "What? That's just weird. Are you sure he didn't fall in there?"

"No, he was placed."

"And how do you know it's murder?"

"He had head and facial injuries not linked with natural causes."

"So he finally got a good kicking himself then after pissing off the wrong person." He let out a wry laugh. "I always hoped someone would punch him, give him a taste of his own medicine. I didn't have the guts to do it myself. He made sure I didn't like violence. Me being the recipient of it saw to that. Giving him a punch wasn't something I could do when I knew what it felt like."

"It was more than a fight," she said. "We haven't established what the weapon actually is as the injuries are quite specific, but it was murder, no question."

"I don't want to hear any more." He got up and walked to the sink. Splashed his face with cold water. "I'm surprised Rachel doesn't already know."

"Why do you say that?"

George leant over the sink and retched. Whatever he'd eaten came up, landing with a splash-thud, and Helena turned away to heave behind her hand. The sounds kept coming from him, though, and she couldn't stand it any longer. She moved into the hallway, where the air was fresher, a breeze coming through the open living room window to her left.

"Are you all right now?" Andy asked George.

Helena stared at the curtains. They still bore package lines, rectangles where they'd been folded around a sheet of cardboard. So he hadn't lied—the curtains were new and recently hung.

"Okay, we'll be off then," Andy said.

Helena called goodbye and stepped outside, glad to be away from the stench in the kitchen. She waited on the pavement while Andy closed the front door, then they stood outside number twenty-two.

"I don't think it's him," Andy said.

"Me neither," she agreed, keeping her voice low. "And what do you think he meant when he told us he thought Rachel would have already known by now?"

"No idea. Maybe because if she visited him, she'd have seen he wasn't in and got worried?"

"Sorry, but if my dad beat me up, I'm buggered if I'd go round his house if I didn't have to."

"He probably had a mental hold on her, even after all this time."

"Hmm. We need to ask Steve about the alibi."

With that done, Steve confirming that he had been there all night until just after two, she strolled with Andy and stopped outside number one.

Two cars sat on the drive, and the one closest to them was familiar, although she couldn't for the life of her figure out why. She shrugged and walked to the front door, raising the posh brass knocker and letting it fall. It bounced three times, creating tinny raps.

A woman answered in her pyjamas, her hair crumpled on one side as if she'd been resting on it. "Hello?"

Helena raised her identification. "DI Helena Stratton and DS Andy Mald. Can we come in?"

"Oh, are you here to see my husband?"

Why the hell did she ask that? Is he likely to have broken the law? "No. Rachel, is it?"

"Yes…"

"It's about your father."

"Oh no. Has he upset someone?"

I'd say so. "It really is better that we come in."

Rachel stepped back and pointed to the kitchen at the end of the hallway—the place had the same layout as George's. "If you could go in there. My husband's fallen asleep on the sofa. Hard day, I expect."

A far cry from George's, this kitchen was high-end and expensive-looking, with all the mod cons. The dining half had a lovely white table, chairs, and sideboard, and a massive canvas of a fox in the woods hung on the largest wall. It was a tad creepy, to be honest, the fox's eyes bright amber, its teeth bared, blood dripping from the top of its head. A bird, half crow, half owl, rested by the fox's front paws, mangled, beaten. The woods themselves were like those on the cliff top, and Helena had to look away.

"Oh, don't mind my art," Rachel said. "I'm not at all good at it, but my husband thinks so. It was him who put it up there."

"It's great," Helena lied—although the artwork was, the subject wasn't.

"You're very kind." Rachel smiled. "Please, have a seat. Would you like a drink?"

"Not for me, thank you," Helena said.

Andy opted for water, and Rachel took a small bottle from the fridge and handed it over. Then she closed the kitchen door, and they all sat at the table. Rachel appeared worried, her face a little pale, and she wrung her hands.

"Can you just tell me outright," she said, "because prolonging things brings on my anxiety, an issue left over from childhood."

"We understand." Helena smiled. "Your brother gave us the general idea."

"You've been to see George?"

"We did."

"What on earth's happened?"

Helena was about to ask her where she'd been last night, but the faint shuffling of footsteps from the hallway stopped her. She'd wait until the husband came in, then tell them together. Probably best, because if Rachel was delicate like George had implied, she'd need the support. Silly of Helena not to have thought of that before.

The man came in, stood in the centre of the kitchen, and stared at them. Rachel shot to her feet.

"Sir?" Helena said.

"Helena, Andy?" The new chief, Jeff Levington, shook his head as if they were a mirage.

What the fuck was he doing here, and why did it seem like he'd just woken up?

Oh, you're kidding me. He's married to Rachel?

Helena glanced at Andy, who gave her a what-the-fuck? look.

"Um, we're here on business, sir," Helena managed, turning the chief's way. "And you might want to sit down."

CHAPTER SIX

Isla had sat beside Darwin for ages now, unable to move or get her phone out to call the police. If she did that, they'd take her son away from her, and the next time she'd see him would be in a coffin. Then this would be more real than it already was, and she couldn't handle that at the minute.

"A bit longer won't hurt," she said to him, stroking his hair back, some of it stuck on the dried blood of his forehead. "Then I'll let you go. Just not...yet."

She wished he could see her one last time, but of course, that wouldn't happen. He was gone, his light, his soul, and she took comfort that he was here in spirit, standing right beside her, stroking *her* hair back the same way.

She *felt* him. Here. Now.

Isla concentrated and almost, almost believed his ghost fingers rested on top of her head.

"There was so much I hoped for you. I took it for granted I'd see you grow up into a man. You'd meet a lovely lady and get married, have kids, and there'd be no more bullying." She sniffed, held his cold hand, rubbing circles on the back of it with her thumb. "I'm going to find them, you know, and do to them what they've done to you. I don't care if they're kids, they shouldn't have gone this far. They're going to understand the pain you went through."

Even while she said the words, she knew she wouldn't follow them through. She couldn't hurt a child, but the urge was there, so hot inside her, to the point it seemed to burn. So she imagined doing it instead, how she'd smack them on the forehead and cheeks with whatever made those horrible holes and rips on Dar. How she'd scare them until *they* wanted to walk through these creepy woods so they weren't taunted to and from school.

"I told you not to come here, didn't I, love? I said it was a dangerous place."

Muppet got up from lying at Darwin's feet and sat beside Isla, his head on her shoulder. He whined, as if to say: *Enough. Go home.*

"No. Enough is sitting here with him forever. Enough is never sitting here at all, and Darwin would have come home for his dinner. Enough is hearing him laughing. Things will *never* be enough for me now."

Muppet seemed to understand, and he flumped down, resting his chin on Darwin's thigh. Isla stared at the blazer, the school shirt, the pocket of it where he'd had a pen inside and ink had seeped through. She'd told him off for it, moaning that she couldn't get it out, even with a scrubbing brush and Vanish, and now she wished he was alive so he could make the stain worse, and it wouldn't matter, wouldn't be a big thing.

There was a large patch of blood there, too, and she didn't want to look beneath his shirt to see what had been done to him. Too painful.

She sighed, more tears coming. Her eyes were so sore, and her whole body ached. Was that heaviness grief? Would she carry the weight of it forever, or would it ease at some point like people said?

Muppet's head shot up, and he growled. There was a rustle behind her, footsteps, and Isla wailed—this was it, *too soon*. Someone had come, had seen them, and she'd have to give up her boy.

"Go away, go away, go away," she whispered.

"Oh my God, are you all right?" A woman, coming closer.

Isla ignored her.

Then there she was, the lady, in her skinny jeans and long white T-shirt, a small dog in her arms. Darwin liked those. Pugs. That was going to be their next dog when Muppet bounded over the rainbow bridge. Fitting then, that one should be here now.

"Shit, shit!" The woman pulled a phone out of her pocket and jabbed at the screen.

Isla wanted to scream, to tell her *no, put that phone away, I want just five more minutes...forever with my son*. But she didn't do that. She stared ahead at a tree, studying the intricacies of the bark, wondering how many years it had stood here, majestic, tall, reaching for the sky.

And then she sensed it. Darwin leaving. His spirit fingers left her head, and the warm cocoon she'd imagined around her lifted, drawing back, a cold, lonely presence in its place, the kind that said: *He's gone. Let him go.*

But she never would. She'd keep him locked in her heart, and in her mind, she'd see him every day, giggling, playing with Muppet, eating his favourite sweets, fizzy cola bottles. She'd keep him alive in there, playing on a film loop, so he wasn't really gone.

I love you, Ma...

She swallowed the lump in her throat. "I love you, too, my boy. So much."

CHAPTER SEVEN

Rachel stared between Jeff and his colleagues. Were these the two who'd given him the most gyp since he'd taken over from Damien Yarworth? The whiners, the ones who'd acted like brats because he wanted more structure at work? She didn't know, he'd never told her their names—the rule, they followed the rule of no work at home—but she reckoned she was right, although the woman DI seemed nice enough.

But she could be like me. Deceptive.

She pushed Nasty Rachel away—God, she'd nearly come right out, ready to say something cutting, but that wasn't advisable, especially not in front of Jeff, let alone the police. They had to see the other side of her: the worrywart, the kinder-than-kind teacher, the person she thought she'd be if she hadn't lived such a horrible life until she'd left home. This was all Nice Rachel was, the one who hadn't been tainted, a nugget of who she could have been. It was soothing to be her.

"Sir, will you sit down then?" the DI asked.

Helena, wasn't it?

"What's this about?" Jeff spoke in a voice Rachel hadn't heard before.

It must be his work voice. So he has two sides to him, like me.

That was interesting, how she'd gravitated to someone with double the personality inside them. *Birds of a feather flock together.*

Nasty Rachel snorted; Nice Rachel disguised it as a cough.

Helena turned to her. "Please, you'll need to take a deep breath for this, love."

Well, someone who called you 'love' wasn't the type to cause trouble for Jeff in the office, so the woman was all right in Rachel's book. She sat, as Nice Rachel would, lowering onto a chair and glancing worriedly between the police and her husband. Funny, but she didn't see him as the same as them, but he was. A copper. People Nasty Rachel ought to fear.

"I'll stand," Jeff said, all gruff, folding his arms.

"Fair enough, sir." Helena sighed and faced Rachel. "I'm sorry to have to inform you that your father's body was found earlier."

Rachel pulled her anxiety from the old days out from where she'd hidden it. She trembled, pressed a hand to her chest, and took short, sharp breaths, mimicking a mini panic attack—she'd had enough real ones to know how to do it, same as George had. Jeff was by her side in an instant, as she'd known he would be, and Nasty Rachel tittered at how easily he'd been fooled.

What a gullible twat.
Don't call him that.
I'll call him what I like.

"Let me deal with this," he said and sat beside her, clutching her hand tight.

She nodded, meek, vulnerable.

"Spell it out, Stratton." He rubbed his thumb back and forth over Rachel's skin.

Helena widened her eyes. "In detail?"

"Yes. My wife deserves to know everything."

"It's distressing."

"Get on with it, will you?"

Helena raised her eyebrows. "This is on you then, sir. Trevor Vakerby was found late afternoon at The Villager's Inn. His head and shoulders were in the private rear garden, the rest of him folded in the hedge. We believe he was pushed in from the pathway in the alley down the side of the pub—a witness has given an initial statement."

Nasty Rachel jolted, gasped. *A witness?*

Oh God, Nice said.

You stupid little cow. Look what you've done. You should have been more careful.

It wasn't me last night, it was you. It's always you.

Helena went on. "He'd been struck on the head, cracking his skull, exposing part of his brain. His face was damaged by a weapon that must have had spikes on it—his skin was torn and punctured. He'd been stamped on the face; his nose is caved in. CCTV footage shows a vehicle arriving at twelve-fifty, although only the headlights were visible. We captured a still of someone's boot. The witness saw them at this point. By one, they'd deposited the body and driven away. The vehicle is light in colour, and going by the height of the headlamps, it's a car or small van."

Rachel glanced up at Helena through her tears. "What...who would want to do this?"

Helena raised her eyebrows again, as if she knew things—things she had no business knowing. "We're aware of some of your family history and—"

"Now hang on a second," Jeff said. "Trevor's behaviour was Trevor's, nothing to do with Rachel. I'm fully aware of what he was like."

No, you're not.

"As you're *also* aware, sir, we have to look down all avenues, no matter how upsetting it is, and you being involved doesn't make any difference in how

I'll conduct this inquiry. I won't be allowed to report to you now anyway, so at present, as a family member, you're a suspect—you know this, too."

"Fucking hell," he muttered. "Go on."

"We've spoken to George and know some of what life was like for Trevor's children. We know you, Rachel, tried to find the good in your father, despite what he was, but you have to admit that his treatment of you, your brothers, your mother, and others, isn't acceptable. Someone was angry with him—angry enough to kill. While you may wish to hold him in high regard for whatever reason—perhaps it's your coping mechanism, and I understand that—you must know that other people can't cope in the same way. We need to find out as much about who he upset as possible so we can arrest them."

"I...I understand." Rachel nodded. "But I don't know who'd want to do this. George is too afraid of him, as is everyone else, and I...I still love my father. I don't expect anyone to get that...but I can't help my feelings. As for others...I didn't ask him who he'd had spats with once I left home. I visited him and kept things light." *Liar, liar, liar.* "What he did was none of my business. I can't help you, sorry." She rested her head on her arm on the table, curling her hand around to hide her face. Pretending to sob, Nasty Rachel smiled.

Prats, the lot of them.

But not Jeff.

He's just as much a fool as the other two, buying into my bullshit.

She thought of herself as a child, and the tears came easily then. She lifted her head. "I...I need to be alone."

"Sorry, but we have to ask some questions," Helena said.

The man, Andy, took a notebook and pen out of his pocket. Rachel had envisaged this moment, but never had she taken into account that she'd have to speak to them beyond this. She'd thought Jeff would step in, not allow them to hound her, but going by Helena's speech earlier, Jeff wouldn't even be on this investigation. How had she forgotten that? She *knew* it wouldn't be ethical for him to remain involved, yet Nasty Rachel had insisted it would be okay.

Why did I listen to you?

"Okay." Rachel smiled, a full-on sad one. "I'll...I'll do whatever you want."

"I'm sorry, darling." Jeff. "If I could prevent this, I would, but Helena's right. I have to step out of this."

"It's fine, truly," she simpered.

Helena sat opposite them. "Where were you last night, Rachel?"

At my father's, killing him, then in Jeff's car, the alley. "In bed."

"Can you vouch for that, sir?" Helena asked Jeff.

"Of course. We went to bed about nine-thirty—busy days. Rachel dropped off before me, so I read for a while."

"What did you read?"

"*Rage* by Netta Newbound."

"Good, is it?"

"Brilliant. What has this got to do with—?"

"You know why I'm asking—I may want to check your Kindle details, see if it proves you were, in fact, reading."

"This is ridiculous. Like I'd have anything to do with this. I am *not* a suspect."

"As I said earlier, you're a family member, therefore, you are. Where did you get up to in the book?"

"I'm at the part where a body is discovered at the bottom of a garden." He winced. "God, I realise how that sounds…"

"What time did you fall asleep?"

"Half ten? Somewhere around there."

"Thank you." She turned to Rachel. "Do you need a Family Liaison Officer to talk to?"

"Of course she bloody doesn't," Jeff said, "she's got me. I can tell her how the investigation process works and what to expect next."

"Is that all right with you, Rachel?" Helena asked.

This woman was playing it by the book, and although it meant Jeff was being undermined, both Rachels liked it. She was being treated the same as anyone else in a murder investigation, and it was refreshing not to be the odd one out. All she'd ever wanted was to be equal.

"Yes, that's okay, but if I feel it's too much for Jeff, I'll give you a ring to organise someone to come here."

"It won't be too much," he said. "I can handle this."

"If it was at work and another family, I'd agree with you," Rachel said. "But it's me, my family, your family now, and it's too close to home."

"I feel the same." Helena nodded. "But we'll leave it up to you, Rachel. It was *your* father after all." She gave Jeff a pointed stare.

Maybe she is one of the work brats and is grabbing the chance to push Jeff out. Either way, I don't care. She's on my side, and I respect her for that.

Even if it means going against Jeff?

Even then.

Rachel knew, deep down, she was a complex person, but she had to follow what she felt was right, what gave her the most peace. Right this moment, Helena was in her corner, wanting what was best for her, and that meant more than Jeff would ever know. She'd never told him the whole horror of everything, just the bare bones to give him an idea that she was fragile, wounded, and needed taking care of. Needed to be his number one. And she was. But she was enjoying being Helena's number one, too, and she'd soak up the feelings that produced for as long as she could.

Needy bitch.

Leave me alone.

"As you're unaware of who may have wanted to do this to your father, we'll leave it there." Helena stood.

"Thank you, for everything." Rachel held her breath, waiting for Helena to say she was just doing her job, dashing the happiness Rachel experienced at being her number one, but the woman didn't, and relief poured into her.

"Do you have keys to your father's house?" Helena asked.

"I don't, sorry."

"That's okay."

"Truth or dare?" Rachel blurted.

Shit. What a big-mouthed cow you are.

"Excuse me?" Helena said.

Rachel waved her hand as if batting the words away. "It's just something Dad used to play with us." She smiled to make out the memory was pleasant, when it wasn't, it so wasn't. "It popped out, sorry."

"That's okay." Helena smiled. So kind. Caring.

Rachel risked getting attached to her, clinging on, sucking all the detective's sympathy into her bones. She blinked, and a tear escaped. "Thank you for being so nice."

"It's the least I can do." That smile again. Genuine.

And then she was gone, along with the man.

Some of the light went out of Rachel's life.

She dipped her head and fake-sobbed. Jeff stroked her head, and she let herself go back in time, to when her father had done the same. Except the action hadn't been anything to do with love or comfort.

"Truth or dare?" He stood in front of her, fists clenched.

From her place on the edge of the single bed in her room, she darted her gaze to the door, figuring out if she could get around him, open it, and escape before he caught up with her. But where would she go? Who would save her? And leaving would only delay the inevitable. She may as well play the game, get it over with.

Truth resulted in admitting she'd done something wrong. Dare meant doing...that. And she didn't want to do that, but going down that route ensured she wouldn't be slapped or punched, kicked, locked in her room and starved for twenty-four hours. Telling the truth meant she'd have to remember everything, right down to the smallest detail, including the exact times she'd done things. She'd already memorised them out of habit, but what if she got confused and it came out wrong? He'd say she'd lied then.

Half past three and five seconds, she'd come in the front door after school. Thirty-one minutes past, she'd entered the kitchen. Mum had taken a batch of pies out of the oven, too many, as if her three brothers were still alive. She'd placed them on the wooden board on the worktop at thirty-two. Thirty-four saw Rachel alone, Mum rushing off upstairs after sobbing that she'd cooked seven instead of four, that she'd forgotten her babies were dead.

Rachel had stretched her hand out to steal a pie. She knew it was wrong, knew she'd be punished, but Nasty Rachel had egged her on.

If she ate the pie, she'd be her father's number one for a little while.

Warped, to hate his attention yet crave it. Odd, to complain to herself about it but instigate it at the same time. She'd muttered that if she was the one getting today's punishment, it meant George would be free, but that wasn't solely it at all.

She wanted her father's interest.

Life was so confusing.

She'd eaten the pie at twenty-five to four.

"Dare." She looked up at him.

He stroked her head with one hand while pulling down his zip with the other. "That was the correct answer. Good girl, princess."

She disappeared inside her mind, thinking of when she was bigger, an adult, and how she'd get him back for all this. For sending her contrary, wanting yet hating, purposely doing wrong so she'd be his sole focus. George would be home soon, at quarter past four, but this would be over by then; he'd be none the wiser. Mum was in the next room, probably having a nap, or crying into her pillow for the boys she'd failed to protect, or maybe listening to the grunts her husband made with the daughter she'd also failed to protect. She had to do that, Rachel supposed, or Mum would be his number one, and she didn't like that. It seemed she always chose truth, because bruises and broken bones followed her time with him, and Rachel wondered why Mum hadn't worked it out yet, that dare was less painful. Maybe that was why he had to come to Rachel for the dares because Mum wouldn't do them.

She'd never understand her mother. Or him.

One day, she'd make sure they were both dead.

It hadn't been long since her brothers had died, so Nasty Rachel formed a plan to make Mum kill herself. If it happened around now, it'd be put down to grief, the perfect cover.

Then all she had to do was wait to kill her father. If Nice Rachel would allow it.

When he left the room, she knelt on her bed and looked out of the window. A slatted wooden path ran down the middle of the back garden, a decorative banister rail either side, and on the right-hand one, a crow perched, seeming to hunch over to protect itself from the cold. Mist swirled, and she imagined herself at the far end of the slats, walking into that mist and disappearing, never to be seen again.

The urge to run away was strong. To vanish.

The crow turned to look up at her with its beady, flickering eyes. She thought of the fox in the woods, and how it always came out to see her if she waited long enough, leaving its lair to watch her from behind a tree trunk. She envied that fox its freedom, its ability to roam without consequences, and maybe one day she'd become just like it, untethered, liberated, able to do as she pleased.

Until that day, she'd remain here. Frightened yet excited. Full of hatred yet brimming with love for a man she despised.

The crow cawed, and she cawed back, and it flew away, into the mist.

Just like she would.

CHAPTER EIGHT

Helena got in the car with Andy and phoned Tom, letting him know some of his officers were needed at Trevor's house. Then she sat for a moment to gather her thoughts. She'd been insistent that the chief step back but was a hypocrite for doing so. During the Uthway case, once she'd become more than the SIO, involved on the other side of it, nabbed and taken to the container to be 'tested', used, a decision made as to whether she was good enough sexually to become one of his sex slaves, she'd escaped and begged the former chief to be allowed to continue as lead. She'd put so much into the investigation so far, and to hand it over completely would have upset her. He'd given her the same speech she'd just given Levington, minus the bit about being a suspect, but had relented, saying she should walk away the minute she got too emotional.

Why hadn't she supported the same thing with Levington?

Because she disliked him, hated the changes he'd made at the station, and wanted to get back at him for ruining what she felt was a well-oiled machine. His new cogs had added time they didn't have—reporting to him what seemed like every five minutes was a pain in the arse. How pathetic was she, though?

"Nice one regarding Levington," Andy said. "That gets him off our backs for the duration. We can move on with this case and show him how we managed before he came along in his smelly size tens."

"I was just thinking the same thing, and how childish I am to have done it. We promised we'd behave now, do what he wants, yet I grabbed the chance to push him out."

"That's because he's a dick. Look at how things are these days. You have to give him a ring every second you make a decision, and he usually vetoes it."

"I didn't get hold of him once we knew there was a body this time, though, and you can bet he'll be seething about that."

"But he'd gone home."

"I know, but he went on and on about how that didn't matter, that we must ring him if something happens when he's not there."

"Well, he'll just have to accept that's not possible in every instance. Sorry, but I'm going back on my promise to behave." Andy grinned. "He's new to being a chief, so he needs to see how it actually is. He was the top detective where he was before, so he knows damn well how things work from our end, how we don't always have a moment to check in. We're chasing a suspect, going hell for leather, and then have to think: Oh, hang on a minute, we need to tell the chief." He sighed. "Sod off!"

"I know, I feel the same. Maybe I should have a one-to-one chat with him after this, explain things a bit better. Anyway, we need to get back to the station, check in with Olivia and Phil. What I wouldn't give to be Evan now, sitting there watching a play."

"Err, pardon me, missus? Going back to the station? Haven't you forgotten something?" Andy lifted his eyebrows.

"Um, no..."

He patted his stomach. "This. It's crying out for food, woman."

"Ah, yes. Shall we go to the chip shop and take it back with us? I'm worried that if we eat in a pub now, with so much info we need to discuss between us, we'll get behind."

"Yep, that'll do. I'd eat a scabby donkey at the minute."

"No need for that."

She drove them to the chippy, got their food, four cans of orange Fanta, then raced to the station, cheeky in putting on the blue lights so they got there faster. Louise wasn't behind the front desk, probably in the loo, so Andy couldn't have his usual little chat with her. In the incident room, Olivia and Phil had their heads bent, working on their computers, and didn't look across as Helena and Andy entered.

"Not interested in some dinner then?" Helena asked.

Phil glanced over. "Ooh, chips. Too bloody right, I am."

Helena handed out the packets and cans, and they all tucked in, Olivia still pecking at her keyboard between mouthfuls.

"Will you stop?" Helena asked. "Five minutes to rest and eat isn't going to make any difference. You've done a full day, plus this overtime."

"I know, but I didn't want to lose the flow. I've found—"

"Tell me once we're finished," Helena said. "If Andy has to stop halfway through his dinner and go back out, I'll never hear the last of it. He's mentioned being hungry a fair few times this evening. One more, and I'll have a mare."

"Nice chips," Andy said. "I like the crispy ones."

"My favourite are soggy," Phil said. "Because of the vinegar."

They continued in silence and, once everyone had filled their boots, Helena collected the food wrappers and put them in a carrier bag, tying it up so they didn't stink out the room any more than it already was. She took a sip of Fanta.

"Okay, what have you got?" she asked Olivia.

"The chief's involved." Olivia looked well chuffed with herself for finding that out.

"Yep, we had that shock not long ago when we visited Trevor's daughter." Helena put her can down. "Levington walked in the kitchen, and I didn't know what to think. Anyway, I told him he can't be involved, and while he didn't like it, he agreed, so I'll be reporting to the superintendent in the meantime, which is a big relief, because he likes being left alone unless it's necessary for him to step in." She went on to explain their evening so far, writing on the information board as she went along.

"The chief and his wife have white cars," Phil said. "Not that I'm saying Levington did it."

"I'm not discounting him just because he's a copper," Helena said. "We can't. While I doubt very much the chief or his wife killed a man, we can't ignore the fact they might have. As for the remaining son, George, I don't think he did it either. While he had the plastic sheeting, it's the wrong colour."

"You said it was stolen." Olivia rolled her pen back and forth across her desk. "Could it be that whoever killed Trevor nicked the clear stuff so it'd look like it was George?"

"Highly likely." Helena added that to the board. "So it'd be someone who knew where he kept it—Rachel, Jeff, or Steve, George's neighbour and boyfriend?"

"Could be any number of people," Andy said. "A neighbour who saw George put the roll of plastic away from a back window—that person might have had a run-in with Trevor, seeing as they live in the same street."

"True." Helena wrote that down. "Okay, so say it isn't the family. What have we got from Trevor's previous crimes that will give us a direction to go in?"

"That's me." Olivia picked up a sheet of paper. "Lots of fights back in the day, before he married Sheila mainly, but there are a few after. There are other things, like him threatening people while he was drunk, but no one pressed charges—probably too scared to. An anonymous call was made to social services after the three lads died in the fire. Again, nothing came of it. To the outsider, the family presented as one suffering with grief, and the social worker closed off the ticket."

"What about Sheila's family?" Andy suggested. "They still around?"

Olivia shook her head. "No. She was a single child, and her parents died shortly after she married Trevor."

"So no one from that quarter with a beef," Andy grumbled.

"We could talk to all the neighbours and people involved with his previous tomorrow," Olivia said. "I don't mind getting out there and doing that."

"I've already done a search on all their addresses and cars," Phil said. "A lot of them have moved away, so that narrows it down for us. Seven people remain in Shadwell, and only two have light-coloured vehicles, so we could start with them first, then speak to the other five."

"Okay, you go with Olivia first thing, Phil." Helena jotted that down on a fresh board. "I'd rather you were together in case one of them is the killer. What about Facebook? Anything there?"

"None of them are on it—I mean Rachel, George, or Jeff." Olivia picked up another piece of paper. "Here we are. The ones on it from Trevor's past are the two with light vehicles."

"That seems too easy," Helena said. "It's pointing to the same two people."

"It might well be cut-and-dried." Andy burped. "Bloody Fanta. So gassy."

"Gross," Helena muttered. "Phil, what about CCTV on the estate?"

"Nothing except outside the pub, unless residents have their own."

"I'll just give Clive a bell." Helena got her phone out and jabbed at his number. "Hi, it's Helena. Is there a uniform still in the street?"

"No, guv. They had to leave—got called away to another incident."

"Okay, then maybe you know the answer to this: Did they clock any private CCTV?"

"No, I've already asked them. Same for the street behind."

"Right. Thanks." She ended the call. "We're shit out of luck on cameras, so we—" She stared at her ringing phone. Louise. "Bloody hell." She answered, cringing. "Hello?"

"Hi. Sorry, but there's something you might want to go and see."

"What's that?"

"Another body, although it's a kid this time."

"Oh no. Where?"

"In the woods where that hollow tree is."

Helena shivered. The Child in the Tree case had done a number on her—she'd never forget it as long as she lived. "What's the score?"

"A lad, Darwin Gringley, thirteen, found by his mother."

Helena frowned. "How would she have known to look there?" God, she hoped they weren't dealing with a woman who'd killed her own son.

"He walks through to get to and from school. Walked, I should say. She got worried about six when he didn't come home, and according to Edwards, she sat with her child for a while, not ringing us, nothing, and a lady walking her dog found her sitting beside the body."

Helena closed her eyes for a moment. The image of that was bloody *awful*. Heartbreaking. "We'll get down there now. SOCO there?"

"On their way, and Tom isn't happy being pulled from The Villager's, but what can you do?"

"He'll get over it. Anything else I need to know?"

"The boy has similar injuries to Trevor Vakerby: his cheeks have tears in them, and his forehead has holes."

"What?" Who would want to kill Trevor and a kid? It was a stretch to say the deaths weren't connected. The wounds were the same. "Where's the mother now?"

"At home. She had a Labrador with her. Edwards felt it best she be removed from the scene."

"Good. Her address?"

"Thirty-seven Minter Gardens."

"Right, cheers." She slid her phone in her pocket. "We have another one, and it seems to be connected to Trevor, only this time it's a lad. Darwin Gringley, thirteen, Minter Gardens, number thirty-seven. Write that on the board. Let's find this connection, please. Andy, we need to go."

She drove them to the cliff top, over the grass, and parked at the tree line beside a SOCO van and Zach's car, memories of the children in the hollow tree swarming her mind. They put protectives on and signed in on the log with an officer Helena had forgotten the name of. A woman and a pug stood close by.

"She the one who found them?" Helena asked the uniform.

"Yes. I've taken a statement of sorts. Basically, she was walking her dog, spotted the mother sitting beside someone on the ground, went up to them, saw the blood and the state of the boy, and rang the police. She didn't see anyone around prior to this, coming in this end from the estate."

"Okay, give Andy her name and address, and we'll talk to her another time if needed, but for now, get her to go home—obviously offer her some kind of support should she want it."

She dipped beneath the cordon strung between two trees and walked into the woods, heading for the cluster of people a few metres in—SOCOs, another uniform, Tom and Zach deep in conversation.

"What have we got?" She avoided looking at the dead lad. She wasn't up to that at the minute.

"His heart's missing." Zach sighed.

"What the fuck is that all about?" Anger coursed through her. She held her breath and stared down at the boy. "This is just terrible. Thirteen years old. What a waste."

His face was a similar mess to Trevor's, but he didn't have a hole in the top of his skull. She imagined the spikes in his forehead had done the damage, piercing his brain, ending his short life. His shirt was pushed up—maybe Zach had forgotten to lower it again—and the state of the chest was worse than Trevor's. It had been hacked, a wonky square cut away, the heart missing. She supposed the killer had limited time here, being in the open. Perhaps the location of Trevor's murder was enclosed, with no reason for anyone to drop by, hence his chest mutilation being that much neater.

"What does a child have to do with Trevor?" Tom asked. "That's what I want to know. Did he have a gripe with the boy's mother? Was this some kind of payback?"

"Ideas are welcome," Helena said, "because I'm at a loss here. What could a kid have done to warrant this? Has anyone found out what school he goes to?"

"Through there, Smaltern Secondary," Tom said. "I managed to get that from the mother before she was taken home. The scene's buggered, by the way. She sat here for ages with her son, and their dog was with them. We'll just have to take that into consideration and work around it."

Helena mused on Mr Queensley, the headmaster, and the fact she'd have to go and speak to him about what kind of person Darwin was. She'd need to do it at his home tomorrow, Monday would be too late, and she doubted the blustery man would appreciate her and Andy turning up on his doorstep, but that was tough.

Andy strode up to them and gawped, wide-eyed, at Darwin. "Christ Almighty…"

"And to think he was just walking through here after school," Helena said. "Someone had to know he used this route and waited."

"They were damn lucky not to have been spotted," Zach said. "With summer almost here, there are more people out walking. He died at around quarter to four, so he was by himself until his mother arrived just after six."

"Nobody with their dogs here at all, no one spotting him prior to the woman arriving?" Helena said. "That's just pure luck. Either that or they came through and kept their sights ahead. He is behind a tree after all." She thought about how far the park was at the other end. Five minutes on foot, so quite a way. No one would have seen anything from there, but they'd put a press release out asking for anyone there today to come forward if they'd noticed something strange. "Any tyre tracks in the grass on the cliff top when you got here?" she asked Tom.

"None."

"So they came through here either from the park or via the gate at the end of the school field," she said. "I'm amazed no other kids came home this way."

"There are boot marks." Tom pointed to the area around Darwin's feet. "We have a partial in the mud, although it isn't anything that tells us what size it is or whether it was a man or woman—the imprint is average, not deep, not shallow, so they're maybe twelve to fourteen stone."

"That could be any number of people." She thought about George, Rachel, and Jeff. All of them were in that weight range, Jeff and George maybe slightly more. "Fuck it." She turned away, staring out at the tree line, the *shush* of the sea calming her a little. "Why are the hearts removed?" she whispered. "Come on, think. Why would someone want to do that?

She didn't know, but she sure as hell intended to find out.

CHAPTER NINE

"Work came home," Rachel said, annoyed that had happened, their rule flouted by two detectives. She'd direct her anger at the man, though, Andy Mald, not Helena.

The worktop digging into her backside hurt, so she moved to sit at the dining table.

"I know." Jeff carried on making coffee. "Although this is slightly different. It involves us personally, so of course work would intrude."

He'd spoken in his placating tone, the one Nasty said meant he was humouring her or treating her as though she was thick.

"Are you going to do as Helena said and not work on the case?" That was another annoyance. She needed Jeff in the know so he might tell her how the investigation was progressing. To go out for meals and chat about it had been her plan—it wouldn't be at home then, would it—and she'd know whether she had anything to worry about.

"She's right, I need to step away, but it won't stop me keeping an eye on what's going on." He added Sweetex to their cups and stirred.

Rachel sighed quietly with relief. Everything would go as she wanted it to after all. She rested her chin on her folded hands on the table and thought about that bloody kid. Darwin, an unexpected and unwanted addition to her kill list. She was surprised Helena hadn't mentioned it. Perhaps they hadn't found him yet, and wasn't that a bit odd? People walked their dogs in the woods all the time in good weather—why not this evening?

Maybe the fox came out with its family and dragged him away.

That would solve a lot of hassle if they ate him.

No DNA evidence from her, only bones left.

If only.

"Here you go, love." Jeff placed a coffee on the table for her and sat with his hands wrapped around his cup. "How are you feeling? About your dad?"

"Oh, terrible." *Ecstatic.* "I can't believe he's gone." *I loved every second of killing him.* "I know he wasn't a nice man, but he was my dad. You only get one of those, and no matter how he treated me, I still have to have respect." *Hatred more like.* "It probably sounds like I need therapy." And she did. There was a lot she needed to purge, but telling a stranger wasn't her cuppa. Telling anyone at all wasn't either. Jeff only knew what she wanted him to. There was a lot you could imply with minimal words, a sage nod, and downcast eyes.

People took from these interactions what they wanted. Everyone liked a bit of drama to ponder over, didn't they, even when they said they didn't. A nose into someone else's horrors always made your life look better, sent you to bed with a smug smile that you weren't in that situation, thank the good Lord above.

At least, she thought that was the way of it.

"It'll take time to process everything," Jeff said. "You know, coming to terms with the life you had with him, his death leaving you without that conversation you really needed to have. Questions have been left unanswered, I imagine."

She nodded. "Maybe he thought I was the naughtiest, and that's why I got punished a lot. Some parents do that, pick on the weakest child."

Jeff didn't know about truth or dare. She couldn't bring herself to tell him. All he thought was her father had hit her, had ruled the home with a cruel fist, and expected them to remember all the minute details of their days should he ask. George had backed that up last Christmas after one too many eggnogs.

She wondered whether her brother knew about the dares and what she'd had to do. Mum knew, but she'd chosen to keep quiet, to let it happen.

And she'd paid for it.

George would, too, if she ever found out he'd left her to suffer.

"I feel so sorry for the child you were," Jeff said. "I'm surprised it didn't turn you into a terrible adult."

"No, I'm quite normal, whatever that is."

But I'm not, Nasty said.

She sipped her coffee. "You can either let it break you or make you stronger." God, she sounded like one of those drippy Facebook memes. *Embrace your past, forgive it, and have a brighter future!*

Her future was looking bright enough, thank you, without forgiving anyone. No, the person she planned to kill next could shove forgiveness right up his arse. He didn't deserve it.

They drank their coffees, Jeff casting worried glances her way every so often. He was such a good man, one she'd earned, but lately, Nasty Rachel had been saying some mean things.

I've spotted he's a bit controlling, she'd said. *Look at how convenient it is that there was a no-work rule at home once you started doing well at the school. It was fine to chat about it before then. He's jealous.*

That wasn't true. Jeff was the chief, for goodness sake, much higher up on the career ladder than her, so what was there to be jealous of?

You saying you want to be a headmistress. You'd be kind of on the same level then. A man can't take being one-upped by his wife. It's all that masculinity shit.

Well, that was ridiculous. The English teacher's husband earnt less than her, and you didn't see him harping on about it. He was just glad she was doing what she loved and getting paid for it. No, Nasty was wrong. Bitter that Nice had a good life now, forgetting the old for the most part—until Nasty had brought it to her attention again.

The problem was, the two sides of her didn't have a clear line down the middle anymore. They were merging, and Nice didn't know whether her slightly mean thoughts were average behaviour or whether Nasty was slipping them in when she wasn't being vigilant.

It was so difficult to work it out.

"Something wrong?" Jeff asked.

"Apart from the obvious, no. Why?"

"You were frowning."

"No, no, absolutely fine." She'd need to watch out for her face giving her away. It seemed Nasty was taking over *that*, too.

"Would you like to talk about anything?" he pressed. "I know you don't like it, but perhaps now you need to."

"No, best to plod on with a smile."

"Shall I leave you be?"

She nodded. "Yes, please. I just need a little time."

He rose. "I'll be in the living room then."

She smiled her insipid smile, the one that garnered the most sympathy, and waited for him to leave. He closed the door, and she silent-laughed, getting all the hilarity out of her so she didn't mess up by giggling in front of him later. She pinched her cheeks hard, to feel an emotion other than this overwhelming sense of drowning in happiness—it was alien, something she'd only ever felt when she'd met Jeff, and back then, she'd welcomed it.

Stop this bloody nonsense, Nasty snapped. *What if he comes in and catches you wetting yourself?*

"I'm sure you'll take over if that happens," she muttered. "Bossy bitch."

She got up and stared out of the glass in the back door. Jeff had put a wooden walkway with banisters down the side of them when he'd first moved in, like she'd asked, no questions, no prying as to why she wanted something the same as her childhood home when George couldn't bear anything remotely similar.

They were different people, her and George.

As were her other brothers. The golden children. The ones who'd never put a foot wrong, even when they did. Their father had been besotted with them.

Which was why they'd had to go.

The triplets sat in a line on Nanny's sofa, scoffing toffee popcorn while watching a film about some silly fairy who kept bumping into trees in the forest because she couldn't fly properly yet. They found it hilarious, but Rachel hated it. Why did Nanny always cater to them? Rachel and George had to suffer watching this rubbish every time they stayed here, although it looked like George was enjoying it, too, despite his age.

Some people never grew up, apparently.

Rachel drew her legs up on the comfy chair and ate some salted popcorn. The triplets had been given the nice stuff, Butterkist. That wasn't any surprise, and Rachel should be used to it by now, but Nasty said it wasn't fair, they should all be treated the same way. True enough, but try telling Nanny and Dad that.

The triplets had stupid names. They all rhymed, giving them even more exclusivity, as if being a trio wasn't different enough. It was as if they were one person in three bodies, and that just gave Nasty the creeps.

Barry, Harry, and Larry.

Please, *Nasty said.* What a load of old shit.

She felt emboldened by think-swearing. It gave her a sense of being naughty without anyone ever knowing.

Shit, piss, bastard, fuck.

A bit of a manic giggle escaped.

"See, you do *like it," George said. "I knew it!"*

He was on about the daft film, wasn't he. What a moron.

"I was laughing about something else actually," Nasty said, all snide. Nice felt guilty so rushed on with, "Sorry to snap."

George ignored her and carried on watching the telly. He had salty popcorn, too. She supposed she should feel closer to him because they were cast out most of the time. But she didn't. She had her own worries consuming her, so taking his on as well, and her being younger than her siblings, she shouldn't have to carry his burden.

Hers was heavy enough.

Nanny came in with a plate of cupcakes, ones she'd baked earlier and had been busy icing in the kitchen since they'd arrived with their little carrier bags containing their pyjamas and clothes for tomorrow. Nanny was going to take them all to school. Well, not George, he was old enough to walk by himself.

The triplets got the first pick of cakes, as usual, choosing the ones with buttercream on them that Nanny had piped into a swirl like a Mr Whippy. Theirs had Jelly Tots on them, too, and then came George, who took the one with royal icing and a strawberry in the middle. Rachel was left with a smear of buttercream on hers and no extras whatsoever.

This is so crap.

Anger burned.

The fairy's wings glowed on TV, where she was concentrating hard to fly. They were so hot they set the leaves of a nearby tree alight, and the fire spread, fast and consuming, and all the while, the fairy fluttered in the air uselessly, crying that the forest would be destroyed.

It was.

Nasty had a little think about that. Everything was black, ruined, no longer existing. The fairy had managed to fly at the last moment, fleeing the tortuous flames, but what if she hadn't *flown away?*

She'd be dead, *Nasty said.*

What would it be like without the triplets and Nanny?

Would a fire kill them and wreck this house?

Nasty thought about that all the way up to bedtime. The triplets had blow-up beds on the floor in Nanny's room, of course they did, all crammed in together for warmth, but George and Rachel had the cold living room on the cruddy camp beds. She stared at the dark ceiling, listening to the creaks of the floorboards where everyone was getting settled upstairs. Nanny's voice filtered down—bet she was reading those brats a story.

After about half an hour, all was silent apart from Rachel's breathing and George's snores. She got up, the camp bed groaning, and stood still to make sure it hadn't woken George. Nasty crept out and into the kitchen, Nice knowing this was so wrong, what she was doing. On the worktop, in a shaft of moonlight coming through the window over the sink, were Nanny's fags. Nasty reached for them, taking one out of the packet, and she held it up, wondering if she could suck on it like Nanny did and make the end glow. She picked up the Bic lighter, a blue one, although it appeared grey in the gloom, and clicked down the little red ledge.

A flame stood tall and proud.

She put the cigarette between her lips and lit the end. Sucked. Coughed up a storm and almost put the damn thing out in the sink—George might wake up and catch her. But that was all right, she'd say she was trying her hand at smoking, and he'd just take it off her, and no more would be said about it.

Composed now, she put the lighter down and stared at the orange fag ember. The scent of burning curled around her, and to get away from it, she held her arm low and walked upstairs, imagining the smoke following her in wiggly, ghost-like streams. Nanny's door was shut, so she opened it to check the layout of all the beds. Nanny's double in the middle, one blow-up either side, and one at the bottom. The rug that was usually there had been rolled up and propped against the wall beside Rachel.

She pushed the cigarette down the circular hole in the middle and took a pace back onto the landing. Waited until a different burning smell weaved out, acrid and strong. She closed the bedroom door, so they'd all bake, same as inside an oven, and returned downstairs. Got on the camp bed. Drew the blanket over herself and waited again.

The fire alarm didn't go off as Nasty had expected, and Nice got a bit worried. How long should she leave it before waking George? She glanced out of the doorway. Flames crept down the stairs, licking at the banister rails, tasting but not eating them. Not yet. They weren't hungry enough, but Nasty imagined, with the whoosh of noise upstairs, that it'd be starving soon and gobble the whole house up.

Nice panicked and leapt out of bed, rushing to George's and shaking him, shouting, "There's a fire. Wake up, there's a fire."

He bolted upright, sniffed, eyes widening at the fire reaching the step before the last one, then he jumped up and dragged Nice out into the hallway. A boom-pop echoed above, and she wondered what it was, but George didn't seem to care, not with the orange tongues lapping at the carpet in the hallway now.

"Quick, we have to get out," Nice said.

"But Nan, the boys..." He dithered.

"Leave them," Nasty ordered. "We can't get up there now."

He dragged her through to the kitchen, crying, to the back door, fumbling with the key, finally twisting it, opening up. A rush of freezing air hit her. They launched out into the garden, then round the side alley, bursting into the front garden. Nasty turned to the door. A lovely orange glow, just like in the fairy forest, lit up behind the opaque glass in the top.

George tugged her into the street. "Stay there while I get help." He dashed to the neighbour next door.

Nice stared at the glow, and in her peripheral, it flickered at the edge of the living room window. She wondered why Nanny and the triplets hadn't woken up, their skin and hair and eyes and everything burning, why they weren't screaming to get out.

Nasty shrugged.

She remained there, with George and the neighbour beside her, a blanket around her shoulders, until a fire engine rumbled down the street and came to a squeaking, hissing stop outside Nanny's. Then she had to move so the men in their uniforms could put the flames out, and when they did, she could still see them burning inside her mind.

She'd never forget it.

Nasty smiled.

CHAPTER TEN

Helena drove towards Isla Gringley's, dreading the upcoming conversation. Andy burped the last of the Fanta gas out of him, and she stopped herself from biting his head off about it. No point in sweating the small stuff, even if it got right on her nerves. Him seeing Louise hadn't quite got his bad habits under control.

Her phone rang.

"Answer that for me, will you?" She pulled it out of her pocket and passed it to him.

He tapped the speaker option. "Yep, it's Andy. Helena's driving."

"Tom here. You might want to go to Trevor Vakerby's."

"Shit, we're just on our way to the lad's mother's."

"My team have found a few things you'll be interested in. They'll be there a while, so it's up to you which place you visit first."

"Okay, thanks," she said, holding back the sarcasm, as it *was* up to her which one she visited, not him. Or maybe he hadn't meant it that way. "So we get no clue as to what we'll be walking into?"

"That'd be a no. Bye for now." Tom hung up.

"He's mardy because of being pulled from The Villager's, I bet." Andy dropped her phone in his lap.

"Hmm. Do me a favour and ring for the FLO to go round Isla's, will you? Tell him we might be a couple of hours, maybe less if we're lucky."

"Poor Dave. Bet he's enjoying a nice evening at home."

"Which is more than can be said for us."

Andy got on with making the call, and Helena did a U-turn to go to Trevor's. What had they found that would warrant a visit rather than just saying what the issue was over the phone? She cruised up to the kerb in Blagden just as Andy finished talking to Dave Lund. A peer through the windscreen at the gawking neighbours standing out in their coats talking to uniforms told her the arrival of the SOCO van and officers pouring from it had been too much of a lure, drawing them out of the warm to have a good old nose.

A fascination with someone else's misery.

She took her phone from Andy and slid it away, then got out, going to the SOCO van for protectives. Clothed from head to foot, they approached the uniform outside Trevor's, who stood on a rough cement step in front of the door. Log signed, they entered, and the stench hit Helena straight away. Dried blood, and lots of it somewhere.

A SOCO popped his head out of the living room at the end of the hallway. Kalvin. "Ah, hi. We're in here."

Helena walked in and blinked. Blood was everywhere, on each piece of furniture as far as she could tell, spatters, lines, blobs, arcs, drenching the room in the red paint of the dead. Evidence steps had been placed strategically so as not to disturb the blood in various places on the grey carpet. A large patch, on the cream rug in the centre, seemed particularly obscene, so stark with the lighter backdrop compared to all the rest.

"I take it he died there." She pointed at the rug.

"Yes, and it's also where I suspect the heart was removed," Kalvin said. "If you look at the shape of the more prominent bloodstain on the rug, there's a line of sorts on the left, probably where the body was. Blood dropped down his side and onto the fibres. There are also splashes there, perhaps from the hacking it would have taken to open a square in his chest. Mind you, I say hacking, it was more of a neat chop, four slices in all. The square is just there." He pointed to the windowsill.

There it was, skin-side down, next to a stack of yellowing newspapers and unopened bills that must have been there for ages. The mountain-shaped, jagged flesh had dried, the texture having the look of chorizo slices. Why put it there? Or was it just a convenient place to dump it, nothing more than that?

She moved over a couple of evidence steps to better study the rug. There was also a thinner line of blood on the other side, a clear space between that and the large splodge, indicating Trevor had indeed been there. How had the killer incapacitated him—a wallop with the nailed instrument? Was he dead before the heart was taken out? Did the bastard who'd done this stand over him to chop out the square or squat?

Evidence might be found on Trevor, and Helena could only hope for that. A fibre. A spray of spittle from speaking fast in anger. Something, anything, but most probably nothing. Killers these days had too much access to forensic programmes, watching at their leisure on how to kill someone and get away with it.

"His bed is undisturbed," Kalvin said. "So either he went to bed, got up when he heard a noise, and the killer made it afterwards, or he didn't even manage to get to bed."

"Estimated time of death indicates he could have stayed up late," Helena said, "so that fits. No sign of forced entry?"

"No. He must have opened the door, despite the hour." Kalvin shrugged.

"It bloody stinks in here." Andy coughed. "I'm going for some air."

A convenient excuse to avoid admitting he couldn't handle seeing this mess. But it was nothing compared to other cases they'd worked—a body in the bath; one found at the bottom of the stairs, stabbed to death in a frenzy; another left out on a picnic blanket for anyone to stumble upon; Jayden Rook, a lad she'd never forget, dead in the park beneath the slide.

Apart from the blood, this place was tidy, clean, which brought to mind the fact that Trevor had been house-proud and there might not have been a struggle. Or if there was, the furniture had been put back, if it had even got knocked over. There were no indents in the carpet, though, where the coffee table beneath the window hadn't been replaced properly, so she was going with no fighting here.

If you let someone into your home at that time of night, they were either family, a friend, a neighbour, someone you at least recognised, or the police. As George, Rachel, and Jeff hadn't set her radar off, was it like someone had said, and a neighbour had come to exact their brand of revenge? What did the heart—or lack of it—mean? That Trevor didn't have one? As in, he was heartless in the emotional way as well as literal? And where was that heart now?

"Has the whole house been searched?" she asked.

"Yes. All rooms other than this are clear."

"So no heart lying hidden under the bed or anything then?"

"Afraid not. I'd say he knew the killer. You don't invite someone into your living room like that late at night. You'd keep them on the doorstep if they were a stranger, the chain on for safety. I would anyway."

"I agree."

But who was it? Which one of the many people Trevor had upset had done this to him? Was the grievance recent? Or had it been left to fester for years, and something triggered the person, sending them round here in a rage? What did Darwin have to do with this?

"Then again," she said, "if you're Trevor and you go around with a chip on your shoulder, would you think you couldn't handle whoever knocked on your door? Surely he'd have attitude, like: I'll deck you if you try anything."

"Maybe. I'm not that way myself so can't imagine thinking like that."

Another SOCO came to the doorway. "Um, sorry to interrupt, but can you come and look at this? I need to get the evidence to digi as soon as possible."

Helena followed him into a small room off the hallway, beneath the stairs, that might have been intended as a broom cupboard when the architects had drawn up the plans. It was a mini office now, a narrow desk at the back, just enough room for a chair in front of it. A poster on the far wall gave her the jitters. Some clown, teeth all pointed, yellow, blood dripping from them and down its white-makeup chin. Lips bared, red, and at the bottom, the title of a film. Should that be something to worry about? The state of Trevor's mind? She shrugged it off. Lots of people liked horrors.

The monitor was on, a documents folder open and containing seven lines of yellow files. Each one had a girl's name, and her stomach flipped. If this was what she thought, it made more sense. Child abuse, a father or mother finding out and coming round to kill him, too angered to speak about it calmly. And who would be calm? She imagined she'd do the same if she had a child and someone did things to it that they shouldn't.

No file was labelled Rachel, but that didn't mean anything. He could have given her a code name. Pictures of her could be there.

She sighed out, "Oh God. Is it...?"

"I'm afraid so, although not as bad as some I've seen."

She was relieved, but that didn't take away the trauma the girls had been through. She thought about Tracy Collier from Serious Crimes, and how her own father and his friend—a policeman, no less—had used her. The case had been massive when he'd been found dead, and word had it that Tracy was looking into the cold cases of the girls who'd been through what she had at the hands of her dad and the copper, John. She wanted to pin those cases on him if she could, and who'd blame her?

Were these images as horrific as those were?

She took a deep breath then stepped forward, sitting on a paper sheet the SOCO must have placed there. A wiggle of the mouse to find where the cursor was, and she clicked on the first file.

She didn't need to look at many photos to get the gist of it.

Bile burned her throat.

She checked them all, searching for Rachel.

None of the images had faces.

"Excuse me for a moment." She left the house, glad of the fresh air, and stood beside Andy in the street. "He was a fucking paedo."

"What?" He gawped at her, eyes wide.

"Hmm. Files on his computer. We're going to have to speak to Rachel again, see if he did anything to her. While there's no file with her name on it—they have girls' names on them—and there are no heads visible to recognise anyone, he still might have…" She swallowed. "God, could you condemn her if she killed him for doing *that*?"

"Absolutely not, but she'd still have to serve time. Adds insult to injury, if you ask me. You get abused, finally snap or grow strong enough to want justice for yourself, and you get put away for it, when really, killing them prevents any other kiddie getting hurt."

"Murder is murder, no matter the reason—unfortunately. Whoever it was did any kids he touched a favour."

"This is a nasty web."

"It is. A sad one, too. I need to go back and talk to that SOCO. I bolted and left him there." She returned inside. In the cubby office, where the SOCO sat at the desk looking at something with lots of data on it, she said, "Sorry about that. The mind goes haywire. It gets a bit much."

"It does. Look, this is all his download history. The image names correspond with him downloading them, so I'm guessing these are for sale on the internet, not taken by him...you know, not him snapping pictures of girls here in his home or somewhere else."

"So he might not have been active in the community, just in private. Someone who is interested but hasn't had the balls to act it out. That's something, but these pictures have been taken regardless, so these girls are in danger whether it's Vakerby or not."

"Digi will get to the bottom of it. I'll have this taken away now. The sooner they can dive into it the better."

"Okay." She walked out and let Kalvin know she was leaving. Log signed, she stripped off her protectives, bunging them in an evidence bag and passing it to the uniform on the door.

Andy did the same, then she called the uniforms in the street over from the houses they were asking questions at.

"Anything?" she asked.

"No one saw or heard a thing," one said. "At that time of night..."

"Yep, I know, most are in bed. Thanks." She led the way to Rachel's, dragging her heels a bit. The things she needed to ask her weren't something she looked forward to. Abuse was a harrowing thing, and it lived on in the mind, as though it was still happening. It had an ugly face, an even uglier smile, and a tendency to want to warp your thoughts and continue to ruin your life.

She should know.

"This will go down like shit posted through a letterbox," Andy said.

"I know. Levington isn't going to be pleased we're turning up again, but that's not our problem." She knocked on their door, staring to her left at their cars. Each were clean, the tyres with nothing unusual in the treads—like debris from the forest floor. The driveway beneath was spotless.

Levington answered, his eyebrows high. "Have you found them already?"

"Afraid not, sir. We need to come in and speak to Rachel again."

"What about?"

Helena gave him a pointed look, and he stepped back without a word. She waited for him to close the door and take them to his wife, who sat at the kitchen table nursing what appeared to be a hot chocolate.

"Hi, Rachel, sorry to be back so soon." Helena smiled. "Sad to say we haven't found the person we're after yet, but we've been to your father's house. I need to ask some personal questions." She glanced at Jeff then back to Rachel. "Would you like to do that with us on your own, or do you want your husband here?"

"On my own," Rachel whispered.

Jeff didn't seem to mind, so maybe Rachel liked being alone sometimes and he was used to giving her space. He left the room, closing the door.

Andy stood by it with his notebook out, his foot against the bottom to prevent the chief coming back in.

Helena sat opposite Rachel. "Some of these questions may be difficult to take, so I apologise in advance if they upset you, but we need to ask them in order to find out why your father was murdered, all right?"

Rachel nodded.

"Would you prefer me to just ask bluntly?"

"Yes, please."

"Okay. Did your father interfere with you when you were a child?"

Rachel's eyes glazed with tears. "W-what?"

"Did he sexually abuse you?"

"No! Of course not! He wasn't very nice to me, and he told me off a lot, smacked me, gave me a punch a few times, but never *that*."

Her response was so full of indignation, Helena couldn't force the issue without coming across as a bitch, but in her line of work, what people thought of her sometimes had to go by the wayside. She was conscious of the chief, though, possibly loitering in the hall, his ear pressed to the door.

"There's no shame in admitting it." *Although it's bloody hard.* "And I fully understand blocking such trauma out. But what you say won't be repeated to anyone outside the police force, so please, think of all the other little girls."

Rachel's head snapped up, and pink flushed her cheeks. "All the *others*?"

"Unfortunately, images were found on your father's computer. It's clear they aren't all of the same girl."

"Oh God..."

"We think they were downloaded from the internet, not taken by him."

"He shouldn't have them, no matter what." Rachel shook her head.

"I know, but they're there and must be investigated. Were you aware of them?"

"*No*! If I knew, I'd have told Jeff. Yes, I stuck by my father through a lot of things, but not that, never that. How many...?"

"How many girls? Quite a few."

"I don't know what to think."

"It's a bit of a shock, isn't it. Now, did you notice whether any girls went to his house alone at all?"

She shook her head. "Once I'm at home, I shut the world out—I don't nose through the window like *some* people." She shuddered. "In the day I'd have been at work. At the school. Any kids going to my father's should have *been* in school."

Helena thought of the lad in the woods. "Do you know Darwin Gringley?"

Rachel frowned, as if the question was so out of context she had trouble processing it. "Yes, I teach him science. What has he got to do with anything?"

"He was found dead in the woods earlier. He has the same wounds as your father. Did Darwin know him?"

Rachel gasped, a hand to her chest. "Why would he? This doesn't make sense."

"It doesn't, but we'll make it so that it does eventually."

A tic flickered beside Rachel's eye. The poor woman had had enough by the looks of it. She sipped her drink, hand shaking. No surprise. This news was enough to send anyone wobbly.

She lowered her cup to the table. "What...why would someone want to hurt Darwin? He's a nice enough lad, although he has suffered with bullying since coming to the school. Not many friends." She shook her head. "So sad."

"His heart was removed, like your father's."

"P-p-pardon? Why?" Her eyes flicked to behind Helena, then down to the table.

Helena turned to peer over her shoulder. Just a small chest freezer. "We don't know. When did you last teach him?"

"The final lesson today. We were dissecting..." She swallowed. "God, this is going to sound awful—hearts. He kept saying the one he had wasn't a pig's, that the butcher had killed someone and given me a human one. Of course, that was just silly, because it *was* a pig's, I checked it once he'd opened it up and called me over to look at it. Everyone laughed at him—they're used to the things he comes out with." She smiled wanly. "I suppose if he were alive, he'd say the butcher had come after him for what he'd said to me. That's the sort of mind he has. Great imagination, very good at writing stories, although he tends to drift off inside his head at times, not paying attention."

She'd spoken of him in the present tense, but that didn't indicate sod all. Sometimes people did that, until they'd accepted the person was deceased. Then 'was' and 'had' came out instead of 'is' and 'does'.

"How did he seem when he left the lesson?" Helena asked.

"His usual self. We'd finished for the week and played truth or dare, as usual. And, also as usual, each class member had a bag of sweets—fizzy cola bottles. I provide them as a precursor to the weekend, and there are children who don't get many, what with their parents struggling financially, so it's a nice thing to do, giving them a treat."

"Truth or dare?"

"Yes, you know, like I said to you before. The game my dad liked playing. You choose one or the other, and someone asks you a question for truth or gives you something to do as a dare. The kids tend to pick that game over any other. I suppose it's because I Spy and the like aren't interesting at their age."

"So he left the class happy, didn't seem worried about going home?"

"No."

"Do you know which way he walks?"

"I'm afraid I don't have a clue. Once they leave my classroom on a Friday, I pack up, stay for about twenty minutes ensuring next week's lessons are mapped out, then go home. Perhaps his mother or the head can tell you that."

"Yes, we're going to see her now, and Mr Queensley tomorrow." Helena stood. "Well, we need to go. Again, sorry to bring bad news. I hope you manage to get some sleep tonight."

"Oh, I have tablets. I take them every evening, an hour before bed, then I'm out of it until the morning. I've had problems sleeping since I was a child. I need to have one soon, actually."

Helena smiled and walked out, bumping into Levington.

He pounced on her immediately. "What's going on?"

She wasn't going to tell him the business regarding abuse, because if Rachel was denying it through shame, she didn't want him knowing his wife's pain until Rachel decided to inform him. "One of your wife's students was murdered in the same manner as her father. We needed to question her about him so we get a picture of who he was before we visit his mother."

"Christ, what's happening here?"

"I don't know, sir, but if you let me past, I'll have a good go at finding out."

She left, getting in the car with Andy, and drove to Isla's. The woman was inconsolable, no help at all, and Dave Lund said he'd phoned the doctor to get her a sedative.

With nothing else that could be done tonight, Helena phoned Olivia and Phil, telling them to go home, then dropped Andy off at his place. By the time she reached hers, she was dead on her feet and cursed herself for that thought. Not exactly appropriate, was it.

CHAPTER ELEVEN

George got up and, out of sorts, roamed the house for an hour, tidying. He had to do something to get the taste of his father's death out of the air. It was tainted, smelling of his childhood, of everything bad he'd endured. A dark cloud of brokenness, sharp words, and the need to run away.

It was no good. He was going to have to see Rachel. Putting it off wasn't doing him any favours—he was just getting antsier by the minute, and that wouldn't help his blood pressure. The doctor had managed to even it out with prescription tablets and advising George to watch his salt intake, do a bit more exercise, and George didn't want all that hard work going to waste. Mind you, hearing his father was dead hadn't exactly kept his heartrate level, and thoughts of his childhood were adding to the stress levels, too. His vision was blurring every so often again, and the headaches had come back.

He walked up the balmy street, wondering what sort of reception he'd get. Since the fire, Rachel sometimes got stroppy; she wasn't always the same quiet, kind, and caring person she'd been before that. It was weird to hear harsh words pop out of her mouth on occasion, when usually they were gilded with sweetness. Everyone had bad days or moments, he got that, but with Rachel, the bad felt wrong. It didn't suit her.

Nervous, George tapped on her front door, his stomach doing that weird spasm it did when Dad used to belt him. He was glad the bastard was dead, so how would it feel to talk to Rachel when she'd be upset? Probably the same as while he'd lived—George gritting his teeth and letting her delude herself their old man was some idol. Except he wasn't, never had been, except in his sister's mind.

Jeff answered, standing in the doorway, a barrier between George and his sister. Nothing new there. Why was it always him at the door? George liked the bloke, but he was a bit in your face, and there were times George wanted to speak to her alone, but it was difficult to find private moments when they all worked. Plus, Jeff loitered, as if he didn't trust George not to say something about their upbringing, upsetting Rachel. The last time he'd managed to discuss it was Christmas, and while Jeff had put up a hand to stop him, George had blundered on, needing the release the eggnog had pushed him to get.

A waft of baking came out, sweet and a reminder of Nan. Rachel must be keeping herself busy. She baked a lot when things were getting her down. George remembered Nan's gingerbread men and smiled, although there was talk of them being called gingerbread people now, what with all that politically correct business going on. You could barely say a word these days without someone being offended.

"Ah, it's you." Jeff gave one of his stern policeman glares. "Rachel's a bit groggy this morning." His facial expression said: *You're not coming in.*

What? Their dad had been *murdered*. How could they *not* speak to each other after finding out? How could Jeff deny a brother and sister their chance to talk about it?

"I need to see her, what with the circumstances." George folded his arms, ensuring *his* expression said: *Move out of the fucking way.*

Jeff sighed. "Don't you go upsetting her."

"I won't be doing it on purpose, but we need to discuss things—there's a funeral to sort. She may well get upset, but it's not just her who went through shit. You don't know the half of it, mate, so don't come all holier than thou with me."

Jeff stepped back, frowning. Was he wondering what that meant—was he asking himself *what* he didn't know? Had George planted the seed that Rachel kept secrets? She'd confided in George, when she'd first started seeing Jeff, that she couldn't fully open up to the man. A bit odd, that was, considering they were married now. Did she still have that problem?

George went inside and poked his head in the living room. Rachel wasn't there, so he wandered into the kitchen. There she was, sitting at the table, a batch of cupcakes on a plate in front of her, all swirled high with pink buttercream icing and various treats stuck to them. Jelly Tots, Smarties, strawberries, and those weird sweets that always came with the Christmas hamper when they were nippers, orange and lemon slices covered in sugar.

They'd had similar cakes the night of the fire.

She didn't look 'groggy'.

Jeff must be lying. He doesn't want me here, spoiling his perfect life.

"All right, sis." George moved to the table and sat, feeling a bit big and cumbersome, even though they were of similar slender builds. He didn't fit in this house, a clumsy oaf among an upper-class twat and a regal-looking sibling.

"Hello, George. What do *you* want?"

The way she'd said that... So she was in an arsey mood then. Great.

His heart throbbed in a set of three manic beats.

Jeff came in and went straight to the kettle. "I'll make us some tea, then we can chat."

We? On your bike.

George bristled. "Err, I want to speak to my sister alone."

He wasn't having Jeff hanging around, taking over the route of the conversation, steering it where *he* wanted it to go. He'd put umpteen spanners in the works if he had the chance. George would then go home without getting a few things off his chest, stew about it, and make himself poorly.

"It's fine," Rachel said, nicer now. She smiled at Jeff. "I can make the tea."

"If you're sure..." Jeff raised his eyebrows—they had some kind of weird code between them that only they knew.

It gave George the creeps.

Out Jeff went, closing the door, but George reckoned he'd earwig. Well, there was shit to be said here, and if Jeff heard stuff Rachel didn't want him to know, that was tough. Since George had found out about their father's murder, he'd been bombarded with memories of the past, ones he'd locked away in order to survive as an adult, and one thing in particular stood out. To do with Rachel.

She got up and made the tea, her body all stiff, and George held back until she was sitting again.

Once she was, he sipped his drink, trying to work up the courage to ask *that* question.

"He's apparently a nonce," she said.

It was like she'd read his mind.

Startled, he placed his cup down and forced his thoughts and pulse to stop racing. "What was that you just said?"

"Dad. A pervert." She inspected her nails. "Lots of images downloaded on his computer. Girls."

Why hadn't the police told him that? "Oh. Right." He'd suspected it for years but had never seen any kids going to the house once him and Rachel had moved out and left Dad alone. Then again, George always averted his attention from the place where he'd grown up, so it didn't prod a memory and set him off.

"Is that all you have to say?" she asked. "Are you not upset that he had it in him to...to want *other* girls?"

Why the stress on 'other'? "He shouldn't have wanted *any* girls." He wondered if she realised what she'd actually said.

"Exactly." Pause. "Any girls."

"Were you one of them?" It was out, in the open, and he couldn't take it back.

"What?" She stared at him. "You think...?"

"I don't think, I know, and I didn't do anything about it back then. I didn't want him to hit me. I let you...let him...to save myself. I'm fucking sorry, Rach. I'm no better than our mum."

If it were him, he'd be angry that someone knew and didn't step in to stop it, but she appeared embarrassed, livid maybe. Her cheeks went red, and she pressed down on a cuticle with a thumbnail.

"I allowed it to happen," she said. "If his attention was on me…"

The emotion was too much, building, expanding so his whole body was chocka with it. His little sister had been through *that* so he didn't get a punch? Or as many punches? She'd protected him when it should have been the other way around?

"Don't worry. You can pay me back." She smiled, bright as the proverbial button. "Then we'll be even."

"What is it? I'll do whatever you want." He would, too.

"Whatever? There's a vast amount of things I could ask you to do." She smiled again.

It was the creepy one he didn't care much for, the one she'd had plastered on her face the night of the fire while she'd stared at the flames, and it brought on a shiver. She didn't look right, her eyes glazed, her expression guarded.

"The problem is, I risk a lot by telling you what I want." She leant forward. "I could open my mouth and ruin everything, or you could understand and accept it without judging me."

Puzzled, he tried to work out what she meant. What was she risking? "But isn't it already ruined for you?" He didn't know what she was on about. "I mean, Dad, you loved him, even though he—"

"So I said. I couldn't admit what had happened—not until now anyway. Couldn't tell you how I really felt until I'd done what I planned."

"I'm confused." He glanced at the door in case Jeff came barging in.

They didn't need him around, not when it seemed she was about to open up.

"You have to know that I love you, George, and I did those things for you, as well as...other things."

He had to strain to listen. She wasn't exactly making this easy for him by talking so low. His hearing had never been the same since Dad had walloped him around the head that time.

"What other things?" he whispered, the air tense, seeming to wrap around him, squeezing his chest. His pulse thudded in his ears, and he worried about his blood pressure.

"If I tell you, you can't tell anyone else. You know like when we were kids and we never told? That. You have to do that, no matter what." She flung him one of her glares, the kind that had a hint of danger about it. "But you may want to tell someone else. And if you do, I'll be right in the shit."

This was bewildering as fuck. "Look, whatever it is, I'll stick by you—you *know* that. So just tell me, but make sure *he* can't hear." He jerked his head at the door. "If it's stuff you know about Dad and those girls, Jeff's going to want to hear all about it, being a copper."

"Jeff doesn't need to know *anything*," she sniped. "Helena will do all the work regarding that."

"Okay. Just get on with it." George was arsey now, her going round the houses instead of just saying it.

Rachel inched closer, eyes wide, and stared so hard it was unsettling.

"Rach... Pack it in." A cold trickle of sweat zigzagged down his spine. "You're being weird."

"I killed him."

Three words. So quiet. So brutal. So...welcome yet shocking.

Rachel? *She* did it?

He swallowed. *What the hell do I say to that?* "If...if it wasn't you, it'd have been me eventually, when I grew some balls." It was good to admit it—it'd hopefully make her feel less guilty, except she didn't appear to be feeling that way. "How...why...?"

"It's obvious why," she whisper-shouted and slapped a hand on a cake. The icing oozed between her fingers.

"Not really. Not when you stuck up for him all the time and made me feel like I was wrong for hating him. I thought it was just me who couldn't stand him, but it seems all this time..."

"I hated him, too, except I kept it inside. I *waited*. I pretended...so no one would suspect it was me years down the line when I killed the bastard."

What kind of person was she if she could do that? How could you live for years, planning a murder, knowing it wasn't a fantasy but an eventual reality? George detested their dad, but he'd never...never murder him, even if he did grow balls. He'd thought about it, yes, but wouldn't have done it, despite telling himself he could if he reached his limit.

Where was the lovely Rachel, because she wasn't sitting here?

"So why tell me?" he asked.

"Because I need your help with the next one."

What did she just say? His guts went—he'd need the loo in a minute. He couldn't have heard her right. "Um, that's…that's asking a lot."

"No, it isn't. You said you'd do 'whatever' for me. You *owe* me."

Then she told him what he owed her for, what she'd been through, and it sickened him. It was one thing to suspect what had happened behind her bedroom door, but another to know. She'd been a kid, for fuck's sake, and Mum, had *she* known?

He asked Rachel.

"Yes, she knew." Rachel winced. "But I sorted her as well."

She was so blasé. George's stomach cramped. He needed to be sick. Who the hell was sitting in front of him? Not the sister he knew, but someone else, someone twisted and evil, the snarky sister who showed herself every so often, except more…more demented. Her face didn't look the same at all, twisted with hatred, years of abuse etched into the creases, a woman who was the same as the man he'd strived not to be, bitter and exacting revenge. George had chosen the other route, and he could have sworn she had, too, but…

"And those fucking triplets," she muttered.

"W-what?" He shot up and rushed to the sink, bending over and throwing up on top of breakfast bowls and coffee cups.

The click of the door handle going down, then, "What the hell's going on?" Jeff.

George heaved again. *Shit, he's a fucking copper. How could she have done this knowing she could get caught by her own husband?*

"He had something bad for dinner last night," Rachel said, cool as you like. "Clams. They didn't agree with him."

"But being sick in our *sink*?" Jeff sighed. "That's quite disgusting."

George wanted to apologise, then tell Jeff: *You're married to a killer*. But no words came out, only sick. He couldn't betray her, not after everything she'd been through. His stomach spasmed, and he prepared himself for what was to come.

Out it came.

"Oh, for God's sake." Jeff again.

"It's okay. I'll clean up," Rachel said.

"I'm going out for a new washing-up bowl. We're not using *that* one now." Jeff slammed the kitchen then the front door.

"Oh dear." Rachel tsked. "He gets so upset about the smallest things. Have a drink of water, George, that'll help."

He fumbled in the cupboard for a glass, doing as she'd said, then sat back at the table while she got up and washed the icing off her hands, sorted the mess he'd made by stuffing the bowl and its contents in a black bag and putting it outside in the wheelie bin.

She sat again and smiled. "Now, let's get this plan made before Jeff gets back. We can't have him knowing what's happening, can we."

"Shall we go for a walk?" Rachel tugged on Mum's arm to get her off the bed.

The stupid cow had been crying for the triplets again, wailing loudly until Dad had told her to shut the hell up if she knew what was good for her.

"What's good for you is being on the cliff top." Rachel guided her sobbing parent out of the bedroom and down the stairs. "That's it, get your shoes on."

As if on autopilot, Mum also slid her arms into her coat. "Will I need my brolly?"

"Well, it's raining, but you're going to get wet without the brolly anyway, so what's the point?"

Mum frowned. Was she trying to work out what Nasty meant about getting wet? "Ah. I see. They turn inside out in the wind, don't they." She sounded like a little kid. Lost.

"Yes, they do."

"Where are you two going?" Dad appeared in the living room doorway, hands on hips and his usual scowl in place.

"A walk," Mum said. "If...if that's okay with you. If...if you think I'm allowed."

Dad considered that for a moment. "Right, well, make sure you're back in time to make our dinner. It's sausage and mash night, don't forget."

"I won't forget, Trevor."

"You see you don't."

Nasty led the way out of the house, down the path, and along the street.

It wasn't far to the cliff top, and Nasty made sure she smiled at all the people they knew on the journey. She had to appear happy, just a young girl out for a walk with her grieving mother. Mr Samson from number eleven waved, and Nasty skipped beside Mum, waving back. Yes, just out for a walk.

No one was on the cliff that Nasty could see, the weather too blustery for even the hardiest of people, and she was pleased at the way the wind buffeted them. It could push Mum off, into the sea, instead of Rachel doing it.

They stopped about a metre from the edge, facing the water, Rachel clutching Mum's hand, and she thought about the people who'd jumped off here, into the raging depths. They were on the news a lot, so if Mum did it, she'd just be a statistic. No one would take much notice.

"It's your fault my brothers are dead," Rachel told her.

Mum stared down at her. "W-what?"

"If you'd have taken us away, it wouldn't have happened." Rachel had stolen the words from a neighbour who'd said them just after the fire. She added the rest. "Then you wouldn't have gone out with Dad to watch that film, we wouldn't have gone

to Nanny's, and I wouldn't have seen that fairy and got ideas."

"Do you really think it's my fault?" Mum's words ended on a silly wail.

It got on Nasty's nerves.

"Yes." Rachel nodded. "It's your fault he plays dares with me as well."

"Dares?"

"You know, he dares me to do things, and you listen from your bedroom."

Mum let go of Rachel's hand and covered her mouth. "I'm so sorry. I don't...I don't know what to do about that. He'll hurt me if I tell him to stop."

So it was okay for him to hurt his child instead?

"You can save me and George."

Mum shook her head. "No, he'll find us. We'll never get away."

"If you told a policeman, he'd help us. Policemen keep you safe."

"No police."

Nasty didn't understand why Mum wasn't willing to do anything. Bringing her here had been a test, to see if she'd do the right thing for once. Seemed she wasn't willing to, especially as she'd admitted she'd let Dad hurt Rachel so he didn't do it to her.

What kind of mother saved herself instead of her kid?

"Can you just say sorry?" Nice asked. That was all she wanted, a genuine sorry. "You can write it down if you can't speak it." Nasty took out a piece of paper she'd ripped from Mum's notebook. It fluttered in the wind. On the news, some of the people who'd

jumped off the cliff had written letters, and that was how the police knew they'd killed themselves.

Mum scribbled 'Sorry, I love you', and Nasty got angry.

"If you loved me, you'd take us away. If you loved me, none of this would even have happened." She folded it and tucked it in her pocket with the pen. "You should jump off," Nasty said. "You'll be safe then."

Mum glanced from Rachel to the water, her eyes saying she was hungry to let it swallow her. "But...but what about you?"

It hurt Rachel that there was even a 'but'. It should have been: No, no, I'll never leave you. Not with him... *And since when had she cared about Rachel and George? The triplets? The 'What about you?' was a load of rubbish.*

"You're not a proper mum," Nasty said. "You're a horrible old cow."

Mum shrieked, stared, then jumped.

Nasty smiled.

Nice felt sick.

Nasty forced Nice to scream, and when someone came running, Nasty couldn't see them properly for the tears, but she reckoned they were old, going by their smell—lavender and roses. She handed them the notepaper, the sobs hurting her chest, and managed to tell them who she was.

"Trevor's daughter?" they said. "Blimey, that's a shame."

It was, but Nasty couldn't help being his kid, and she would bide her time.

Until it was his turn.

CHAPTER TWELVE

Helena smiled at Mr Queensley. She hadn't thought she'd be seeing him again after The Child in the Tree case, but here she was, in his living room—and the clutter surprised her. She'd imagined him to be a sparse kind of bloke, minimalist in his decorative approach, and this haphazard room didn't fit her previous perception. If she remembered rightly, he'd been full of bluster last time, clumsy in his approach to the situation, as if he liked order and didn't enjoy disruption. These surroundings didn't match—there was certainly no order here. Knickknacks covered the sideboard and hogged the inside of a dusty display cabinet.

He sat on an uncomfortable-looking chair, the sort with a wing back, the cushions unyielding. She was on the edge of a squishy sofa, while Andy stood by the window, staring out at the tidy street with its equally tidy houses and gardens. The latter for Queensley consisted of overgrown, bent-over grass, dandelions bobbing their banana-yellow heads, and some litter that must have escaped his full-to-bursting wheelie bin that stood beside his front door. All in all, this home was a blot on the landscape, that messy sibling who never cleaned up after themselves.

"As I said when we arrived, sorry to disturb you at the weekend." Helena smiled.

"I can't imagine what you'd need to bother me for," Queensley said. "Surely it could have waited until Monday."

"It can't, I'm afraid." She glanced at Andy.

He turned and faced them, taking his notebook out.

"I need to ask you about a lad called Darwin Gringley." She crossed her ankles. "Specifically, what he was like."

"Ask his mother. Surely she knows him better than anyone."

Helena recalled him not knowing who a student was when she'd asked him before during the other case. "Do you even know who he is?"

"As a matter of fact, I do." Queensley harrumphed as if her question was ridiculous. "He's been the subject of bullying for a while, so he's in my office regularly."

"Bullying... Any particular person doing that?"

"No, it's more of a majority thing, where many students pick on him. He won't say exactly who it is. He's...different, has an imagination—the kids think he's weird, sad to say. We encourage creativity, so I think Darwin gets confused. We're pushing for him to use his brain however he wishes, and the students are telling him not to, laughing at his uniqueness—or weirdness, as they see it. He doesn't even have a friend to support him. I suspect he's given up on trying to find a buddy to hang around with in case they turn on him, too, or they get bullied along with him."

"What's being done about that sort of behaviour?"

"We've had a meeting with his mother. The outcome of that was all teachers look out for him and email one another if there's been an incident. When he tells us he's in a sticky spot, he's usually called upon to do something for the teacher to get him away from the situation. However, we can't be there all the time, like at lunch for example, or breaks, especially if he goes for a walk on the field out of our range. As Darwin won't tell us who the students are, it hinders us somewhat. How can we stop this if he won't allow us to speak to those being cruel? We've had an assembly on it recently, and it was obvious who we referred to—Darwin—but we needed to approach the masses seeing as we didn't have individual names, to make it clear this will not be tolerated."

"Did that help the situation?"

"That assembly was only last week, and I haven't had any reports from teachers saying whether it's had a good effect or not."

"So you're not copied on those emails you mentioned? Surely it's your job to oversee the welfare of a student who has a difficult school life. Wouldn't you need to monitor what's happening to a child?"

"I'll look into that when I go back to work, ask the teachers to add me to the discussions. I should have thought of that before." He fiddled with an ornament on the table beside his chair, a white ceramic ball the size of a grapefruit with cerise feathers sticking out of the top.

Odd.

"Why are you here about bullying?" He curled a feather around his finger.

"Darwin was murdered on his way home from school on Friday." She let that sink in for a moment.

Queensley's face paled then reddened. He let go of the feather, which wavered, and stared at Helena. "P-pardon? He's d-dead?"

"Yes. It's linked to another murder—an older gentleman called Trevor Vakerby. Do you know him?"

"No."

"We need to look further, but perhaps his children went to Smaltern Secondary." *Not to mention his daughter bloody works there.*

"I can certainly find that out, although the name isn't familiar to me."

"Hardly a surprise when so many students go through those doors year after year." *And you don't seem to take any notice of them unless they're brought to your attention.*

"Why would a man and a child be connected in death?" He appeared genuinely perplexed at that. "Unless, of course, they knew each other. What does Darwin's mother have to say about it?"

"Unfortunately, she was in no fit state to answer questions last night. As you can imagine, she was distraught. She was the one to find her son dead. We may go round there today to see if she's up to talking. It's a shame that we can't find out whether there was a bully at school who is so good at it they harassed Darwin when no one else was around, hence no one knowing who it is."

"Are you suggesting a student did this? Killed a boy and a man?"

"Would you say some of your students were around the fourteen stone mark? There has to be some in sixth form, or even in years ten and eleven who are that weight."

"Of course there are, but—"

"To your knowledge, are there any students who can drive?"

"I have no idea. I really don't think a child could kill another child."

You'd be surprised what children can do. "It does sound radical, but it's not unheard of. Let's talk about girls. Are you aware of any who present as troublemakers? As you know, this behaviour can indicate something is wrong in their lives. Or perhaps there are some who are overly withdrawn."

"What does this have to do with Darwin and this Trevor person?"

"Possibly quite a lot."

"I can't think of anyone offhand. Girls are usually the least of our worries at school, apart from the tendency to be bitchy with one another or have a bout of dramatics." He shook his head. "No, now I'm thinking about it, we haven't had any problems with girls for some time."

"Are there any vulnerable ones—those in the social care system, for example, or those with a difficult home life?"

He blushed. She was sure he didn't even know. What kind of headmaster was he?

"Not that I'm aware of," he said.

Clever answer. Absolves him of any responsibility for now. "Let's move on to Rachel Levington."

"What on earth does *she* have to do with this?"

"Her father is Trevor Vakerby."

"Oh my goodness."

"Exactly. You're probably aware her husband is the police chief here?"

"Yes, yes. He came in to do a chat recently, and we were thinking of having him in again regarding bullying."

"Perhaps that could go to the top of the list now, in light of the recent goings-on."

"Absolutely."

"So...there are no students, *that you're aware of*, who may have a tendency to lose it and commit a crime through frustration or any number of other emotions?"

"No."

"We'll undoubtedly be at the school on Monday if we don't catch who did this by then. To speak to the teachers and any children who wish to come forward regarding Darwin. Because of what's happened, some may feel they can't keep the bullies' names to themselves any longer."

"Or they may be more afraid if they think one of their friends is going around murdering people. They may also fear walking to and from school. This is going to disrupt their well-being either way."

"I don't disagree, but there's nothing we can do about that. Murder is as serious as it gets, so if you suddenly recall anything we may need to know, give me a ring." She handed over her card and stood. "We'll leave you to have a think."

She left him stroking the feathers once again and wondered if he used it as a comforter instead of the usual stress ball.

In the car, they buckled up, and she headed for the station.

"What was all that about, with the feathers?" Andy asked.

"No idea. Each to their own."

"Do you think he played with them to calm himself?"

"Probably." She glanced across at him. "Oi, you're not insinuating it's him, are you?"

"No, he's too clumsy, too blunderish."

"Is that even a word?"

"Probably not, but who cares? You know what I meant."

"Good job I do really."

"Hey."

She laughed, then felt guilty about it when a kid had been killed.

At the station, they headed up to the incident room. Olivia and Phil were hard at it, and she called for them to take a break so she could tell them about the visit to Queensley and catch up on what they'd been doing last night and this morning.

Phil sighed. "So some little prat is going round bullying to the degree that Darwin was afraid to say who they are?"

Helena nodded. "Sounds like it, although this 'majority' thing Queensley mentioned—that doesn't sit well with me. Can you imagine going to school day after day with multiple people getting at you? That's got to wear you down eventually."

"Changing the subject," Olivia said. "There have been no reports of sexual abuse that haven't been resolved, so Trevor, if he was messing with girls, was like the bullies—well under the radar. Doesn't mean he wasn't up to something, though, does it. He could have groomed so the girls either thought he was Mr Wonderful or they're too afraid to tell anyone."

"Perhaps we should do a TV appeal," Helena suggested. "Once it's out there that he's dead and no longer a threat, people may come forward. I'll ring the super—I need to let him know what's going on anyway now that the chief is off the case."

She did that in her office, glad Superintendent Yakoshi agreed with her about Levington. He'd be allowed back to work once the shock had worn off but wasn't to have anything to do with this investigation. If he butted in, asked questions, or did anything he shouldn't, Helena was to let Yakoshi know. While she wasn't a fan of grassing anyone up, she'd gladly do so in this instance. Levington was nothing short of an arsehole who'd swept into the station his first day and got everyone's backs up. He was nosy, intrusive, and wanted his finger pressed to every button, even down to how often they took a toilet break.

Well, he could bugger off.

Yakoshi said he'd deal with the TV appeal, so that was one thing she could strike off her list.

She returned to the incident room. "Olivia, Phil, where are you two at?"

Olivia grabbed her notebook. "This is all on the whiteboard, but it's easier to chat about it together, isn't it."

Helena agreed. They sometimes discovered things as a collective they might not have noticed singularly.

Olivia went through a few points. George Vakerby had an alibi, as did Jeff and Rachel

Levington. No one in Trevor's street had been willing to divulge anything, although they seemed relieved he was dead. George's neighbour and boyfriend, Steve Danbury, had confirmed George's alibi. Their phone locations would at least say where their mobiles had been, but that didn't prove the people themselves hadn't left their homes without them.

"Rachel didn't understand what Darwin had to do with anything," Helena said. "What I thought was, after the revelation Trevor had indecent images on his computer, perhaps one of the girls he was involved with told Darwin, but then I remembered Trevor was killed first, so that doesn't make sense."

"And it doesn't gel with what Queensley said." Andy scrubbed his chin. "The lad had no friends."

"But he also said they can't monitor the students all the time," Helena reminded him. "What if Darwin spoke to someone on breaks?"

"True." Andy nodded. "But like you said, it's moot, unless Trevor told someone why he needed Darwin killed, and the killer offed him first because he was a nonce."

"Will we go to the school and speak to the teachers and students?" Phil asked.

"Yes, we'll have to—Monday." Helena sighed. "I'll just give Dave Lund a ring, see if he ended up staying over at Isla's last night." She walked to the corner of the room and dialled him. "Hi, Dave. Are you still with Darwin's mother?"

"Yes. She's only just woken up—well, about an hour ago. A bit groggy from the sedative. Staring into space, that kind of thing."

"Poor woman. So you haven't really been able to get anything out of her?"

"No. I've asked the usual questions, but she's not answering. I haven't even been able to establish any other family members."

"I'll have a chat with Olivia and Phil about it. I'm sure I saw new names on the whiteboard. Okay, if you make any progress, let me know. There's no point in me and Andy coming round if Isla isn't able to speak at the moment. We don't suspect her anyway, but her lack of communication could set us back. At the same time, I don't want to push her. This must be one of the worst things to go through, losing a child."

"I agree. I'll make her something to eat, see if that helps."

"Lovely. Bye." She turned to her team. "Right, Isla isn't with it, so we'll leave her to Dave for now. Family members. Let's chat about them."

Phil clicked his mouse and read off his monitor. "Darwin's father, William Gringley, is currently in Italy—working and living. No movement from him with a passport. I spoke to the authorities there. He was at home when they went round and broke the news. He's remarried—his wife was also in residence. They have two young children, a boy and a girl, ages three and five. William is coming over to the UK later this afternoon."

"Hmm, maybe Isla will start talking once he arrives," Helena said. "Do you know how they parted? Good or bad terms?"

"No idea." Phil shrugged. "There are grandparents. William's mum and dad live in Italy as well, down the road, in fact. They were also home. Isla's are dead—drug overdose, suspected suicide pact. She was brought up with foster parents."

"Interesting."

"Not really." Phil shrugged again. "It wasn't a bad upbringing, on paper anyway. She entered the system at three, was fostered by one set of carers for six months, then moved to another who adopted her. They're also dead now—they were in their sixties when they took her on—and she has no siblings, biological or foster, nor any aunts, uncles and the like. Basically, she's on her own."

"Christ, that's got to be tough." Helena shook her head. "We'll suggest counselling once she's up to listening. She shouldn't have to go through this alone."

CHAPTER THIRTEEN

"Anything else?" Helena asked.
"Digi came back with a few things," Olivia said.
"Go on."
"The images were definitely downloaded onto Trevor's computer from a site called Little

Beauties, although it no longer exists. That's the thing with those types, they risk being found by the authorities, even if they're on the Dark Web, which this one was. Oddly, the downloads were at times he was at work—I've verified the dates with his former secretary, Elizabeth Mackenzie, who was only too pleased to dish any dirt on him. Safe to say she didn't like him and actually laughed when I told her he was dead."

Helena perked up. *Laughed? Christ, Trevor must have been hateful.* "That's weird—the work thing, I mean. He sold his business—he'd retired."

"That's the thing," Olivia said. "The images are old, as in, downloaded four months ago, before the sale of the business, and they were hidden."

"What do you mean?"

"The SOCO found them inside several folders, the final one marked UTILITIES, so like a Russian doll effect."

"Sodding Nora. That's annoying. If we'd known that, we might have had a proper think about it. He was at work, so unless he had that computer in his office there, how was he downloading? He couldn't be in two places at the same time."

"I asked the secretary about that," Olivia said. "He used a laptop at work."

"And she's sure he didn't leave the office during those times?" Helena asked. "He could have nipped home. How could she even be that specific, that sure, after four months have passed?"

"She admitted to being a control freak in that she wanted to know where he was at all times. The reason is, she'd had a few Polish men turn up once, demanding to know where he was. This was before she kept a log of everything. She didn't know what to tell them, and they thought she was lying, covering for Trevor. She told herself she'd never not know where he was again when it was to do with work. If more people came in asking, she'd be able to tell them straight away and not get frightened in the process."

"Polish people? What was that about?"

"Trevor took money from them as rent for a container, and when they came to use it, the bloody thing had been rented to someone else. The men told her they'd beat her up if she didn't say where Trevor was. In the end, Trevor came in and took the blokes outside to chat."

"So we could be looking at those men as potential killers, but that doesn't explain Darwin and why they'd murder him. Did you ask her who they were?"

"Yes, but she said they'd booked as a company, and when she checked it later, it didn't exist. Trevor took any paperwork and computers to do with the business when he sold it, so unless it's in his house, the paper trail of the Polish payment is probably lost—we won't find out who they are."

"What else have you got on the downloads?"

"Each date, Trevor had meetings—Elizabeth still has her diaries she wrote it all in."

"So someone else must have done it." Helena paced. "Someone who possibly knew he had meetings and wouldn't come home and disturb them while they put the pictures on his computer." She frowned. "Why wouldn't he have questioned those folders, opened them to see what they were? You can bet your arse I would if I came across it on mine and knew I hadn't created them. You'd know it wasn't anything you'd done, surely."

Olivia tapped her pad with a pen. "But if it's inside a few others, it's less likely to be found, which begs the question, why would someone bother hiding them? Those images, prior to the SOCO viewing them, were last opened on the days of download, possibly to ensure the images were what had been purchased."

"Blimey," Andy said. "So he might not even have accessed them—probably didn't even know they were there."

"Let's say they *were* planted." Helena stopped pacing. "Someone wanted him caught? That doesn't make sense. If they were downloaded months ago, hidden so deep, how did this person know Trevor would even find them? And if he wasn't that way inclined, into girls, he'd delete them, yes? He wouldn't tell anyone what he'd found in case people thought he was a pervert."

"He might have known they were there but chose not to look for them or say anything," Olivia said.

"What do you mean?"

"One of his credit cards was used to pay for them. Digi sent through some statements he'd kept as PDFs on his computer, although it doesn't say exactly what he'd purchased, just: Wholesome Love/LB, which I assume stands for Little Beauties."

"There's nothing bloody wholesome about that kind of love—it isn't even love." Andy flumped down into his seat. "Disgusting, that's what it is."

Helena huffed in frustration. "So are we to believe Trevor never checked his purchases when his statements came through? Am I the only one who scrutinises them when they arrive in the post?"

"I don't bother with mine much," Andy said. "I just check the monthly amount they want, plus the total, and if it looks right, I pay it."

"Really? When you know how many scammers are out there?" Helena asked.

Andy blushed. "Maybe Trevor did the same." He turned to Olivia. "How much were the images?"

"A tenner for each batch—cheap, considering what they are and the risk the website owner is taking. But maybe they're of a mind that they'll make more money in the long run if they're not expensive."

Phil barked out a laugh. "Those types will pay top prices for that kind of thing."

"True." Helena couldn't argue with that. "Regardless, someone wanted him in trouble."

"Not necessarily." Olivia got up and walked to the whiteboard to jot down what she'd just told them. "What if it was just a warning to Trevor?"

"Explain," Helena said.

"What if they were planted there to warn him that if he continued with whatever he was doing, more of the same could be downloaded, a call to the police could be made, and it'd look exactly how we thought it was—that he's a paedophile?"

"But it seems he didn't even know they existed, so what's the point in that?" Helena asked, exasperated.

"Think about it." Phil swivelled his chair from side to side. "It could be a game. The downloader knows they're there. Then comes the anticipation of Trevor finding the images. Some people get a kick out of that shit, the waiting. Gives them something to get excited about."

"If that person wasn't in Trevor's life as such, you know, a confidant, that exercise is a waste of time." It didn't add up to Helena. "Why download something you might never know the outcome of?"

"Just knowing they're there may be enough for someone to get their kicks," Andy said.

"Or it's worked out exactly as they wanted—we found the images after he was murdered." Olivia sat back at her desk.

"That's plausible." Helena eyed the ceiling, thinking. "Okay, we can sit on this for a few hours or go and speak to George and Rachel again."

"I say we strike now," Andy said. "One of them may have had access to Trevor's place and just hasn't admitted it to us. I don't know, through fear we might suspect them?"

"Fair enough. We'll go now, without warning them," Helena said.

She left Olivia and Phil to it and drove to George's first. He wasn't in, so they checked at Steve Danbury's.

"I don't know where he is." Steve leant on the doorframe. "We're meant to be getting together later for dinner. He said it'd help take his mind off things."

"How is he coping?" Helena asked.

"He's relieved, to be honest. I would be in the same situation." Steve smiled sadly. "That poor man has been through a lot. Maybe he'll tell you everything if you ask him. His father was...well, he's the most unpleasant man I've ever encountered. Didn't agree with George being gay either, although he only found out via rumours. George is happy enough in that regard, so his father's opinion on that doesn't matter, and if you think it's him who's done this, I'd say to look elsewhere. If George wanted to kill him, he'd have done it years ago when everything was still raw. He's come to terms with it all, realised it isn't his fault, and moved on."

"That insight has been very helpful, thank you," Helena said.

They walked down to Rachel's. The chief's car wasn't there, but Rachel's was. Helena knocked, and George answered, his cheeks pale, sweat on his brow.

"Oh, h-hello." He sounded cagey, worried.

"Everything all right, George?" Helena asked.

"Um, yes. Yes, of course it is. Rachel's in the kitchen." He stepped to the side to let them in.

"We're glad you're here," Helena said. "We could do with speaking to both of you. We've already been to yours. Spoke to Steve, too."

George jolted and shut the door.

What's wrong with him?

"Great. Um, come through." He rushed ahead into the kitchen and disappeared to the right.

Helena looked at Andy and mouthed, "What the hell?"

He shrugged, so she followed George and found him and Rachel sitting at the table, two cupcakes on a plate, one with squashed icing. The screwed-up wrappers of some others meant they'd had quite the feast.

"Hello," Rachel said. "Have you found them yet?"

"Sorry, no," Helena said. "Just a quick question. I know you've been asked this before, Rachel, but are you sure you don't have any keys to your father's house?"

Rachel shook her head. "I don't."

"What about you, George?" Helena stared at him.

"No. I left my set on the hallway table the day I moved out. No way would I want to go back there."

He sounded so adamant, Helena believed him.

"Some new information has come to light," she said. "George, we didn't manage to get to you and tell you this, but—"

"If it's about the pervy images, Rachel told me." George flushed. "Revolting."

"We have reason to believe your father wasn't even aware they existed." Helena watched their faces.

Rachel frowned, and George's eyebrows went up.

Helena continued. "They were downloaded while he was at work—his secretary is quite certain your father wasn't at home but in meetings. She has proof in her diaries. The files weren't accessed at any time except on the download day—as in, your father or anyone else hasn't viewed them since. We're concerned someone put them there in order to cause trouble."

George laughed. "That could be anybody. It's common knowledge the old bastard left his key under a stone in the front garden."

SOCO hadn't mentioned finding one—was it still there or had it been taken when he'd been murdered?

"Why didn't you mention this before?" she asked George.

"Only just thought of it." He shrugged.

"Did you know about this?" She looked at Rachel.

"Yes, but I never bothered to check if it was still there. Whenever I visited him, he was in, so there was no reason for me to use the key. I'd never go in there without him knowing anyway—he wouldn't like that."

"No," George said. "He'd likely have ripped her a new one, and just knowing that means she wouldn't have done it. You don't know what he was like, so you can't understand the fear."

"Tell me then, help me to understand," Helena said.

"I can't." George dipped his chin to his chest. "I pushed it all away, forgot about it, and then he died, and everything came back. I'm trying to forget it again."

"But telling us may help the investigation," Helena pressed.

"You just don't get it, do you." George lifted his head. "I don't care that he's dead, so therefore, I don't care about helping you find who did it." He wiped the sweat off his brow. "Unless you force me to, I won't be saying sod all. Just know he was a bastard and he didn't deserve to live, not after what he did to—"

"Don't upset yourself." Rachel rested a hand over his, squeezing. "He isn't worth it."

"That seems like a change of heart, Rachel," Helena said. "You were telling us that no matter what he'd done, he was still your father…"

Rachel narrowed her eyes momentarily, as if she'd let a mask slip, then she schooled her features into something resembling an indication of sorrow. "I've had time to think. Me and George have been going over our childhood this morning. I realise now I'd put our dad on a pedestal to stop myself from admitting who he really was. I see things differently today. I should never have stuck by him. I feel dreadful."

Helena decided to change the subject. "Where's your husband?"

"He went to buy a new washing-up bowl." Rachel rubbed her brother's hand then gave it a harder squeeze. "George was sick earlier. It's all been a bit of a shock."

"I should imagine it has. Okay, well, if you have no idea who may have used the spare key, we'll be off now to find out ourselves. We will catch them, you know." She paused, giving them the once-over in turn. "We always do."

She walked out and waited for Andy in the car.

He got in. "What was that all about?"

She started the engine. "I don't know. Something got my back up. George seemed off at first, didn't he? Jumpy, as if he had something to hide, and Rachel squeezed his hand as if to shut him up—twice."

"Maybe that's because of what they'd been talking about. A return to the past can be traumatising—you should know that."

She drove off, nodding. Yes, whenever she allowed herself to think of *her* past, all the old feelings returned, sending her fidgety. She understood George trying to forget everything, tucking it away so he didn't have to deal with it, face it. "Must be horrible, being forced to acknowledge things again now Trevor's dead."

"Exactly. Same for Rachel. I bet stuff's popping up that they didn't think they'd have to deal with anymore. That's the problem with the past. It's always there, in your head, no matter what you do."

This was getting a bit deep for Helena. "We need to find out who used that bloody key. Can you ring Louise and get her to sort some uniforms? I want a couple in Trevor's street, asking whether they noticed anyone entering his house four months ago on those download dates— tell her to get those off Olivia—although it's a long shot, because who remembers four months ago?" She took a deep breath. "Then ring Olivia and get her and Phil looking into Polish companies that may need to use a storage container."

"Aren't we going back to the station then?"

"No. I want to drop in on Isla Gringley. Maybe she's feeling up to talking by now. If not, we may have to get heavy and make her. I don't want to do that, but we need some answers from somewhere. At the moment, it feels like we're drowning."

CHAPTER FOURTEEN

Nasty wanted to explode. She'd put Helena on a pedestal, like her father, but the woman was coming close to being pushed off it, waltzing round here and asking those questions. Nasty tried to hide her emotions from George—if he thought she'd lost the plot, he might not trust her with the next job, and she needed him to willingly help, to admit his involvement meant he was partly culpable for what had happened to her. He was older, he should have phoned the police and told them his little sister was being treated badly.

But he hadn't.

Calm down, Nice whispered. *It'll be okay.*

But why is Helena being pushy about the key? Nasty said.

Because she needs to know who got into Dad's house. They're just doing their jobs.

Nasty or Nice hadn't thought about the police seeing the images. Rachel had intended to 'find' them on the computer herself, asking Dad what they were doing there, scaring him, forcing him to apologise to her for what he'd done with the dares, but she'd never managed to use the computer while he was there.

He hadn't let her, telling her to use her own at her house.

She'd forgotten about the files until Helena had brought them up, and for a while, she'd convinced herself Dad *had* bought them, that he'd been messing with others, not just her. Jealousy had burrowed deep inside, and it wasn't until George had said 'any girls' that she'd remembered those others didn't exist in Dad's life.

How stupid could she be, forgetting something like that?

She'd have to be careful now. Keep both sides of her straight so she knew what each of them were doing. These little lapses, where she lost sight of one or the other, were becoming more frequent. Yes, she'd planned to kill her father, but Nasty had taken over with Darwin. She'd been insane, so livid, forcing Nice away until the deed had been done.

Rachel worried about her phone information being tracked, pinged. It would show up where she'd left the car at the park.

Shit. Why hadn't Nasty thought about it more? Why had she been a bull at a gate?

"Are you okay, Rach?" George flicked an empty cupcake wrapper back and forth between two fingers.

It was getting right on her nerves. "Stop that, it's bugging me."

He withdrew his hands and placed them in his lap, suitably chastened. "What are we going to do?"

"About what?"

George sighed. "The police keep talking to us. Do you think they suspect you?"

"How can they? I went to Dad's during the night. Jeff was out of it—I told you, I put the powder of one of my sleeping tablets in his tea. No one's windows had lights on. I used the spare key under the rock to get in then ditched it in Steve's garden once I'd dumped Dad at the pub."

She didn't know why Nasty had done that.

"What? You put the bloody key in Steve's *garden*? What if the police, the ones in white suits...what if they extend the search down the street? It could look like Steve had something to do with it."

"But he didn't. You two were together."

"So! They could still think it was him if they find the key. We have to get it." George scraped his chair back. "I'll go. Where exactly did you put it?"

Nasty shrugged. What did she care where it had landed? So long as it wasn't under the rock, that was all that mattered.

You need to care, Nice said. *Because we could get caught. Your fingerprints are on it. For God's sake, think.*

Nasty scrunched her eyes closed, searching her mind, bringing forth the memory of that night. She saw herself throwing it, her manic smile, and experienced once again the flickering of her heart. Excitement, the feeling of retribution. "Um. It landed on his path at one point. I know that because I heard it do a little clang. Maybe it's on the other side, in the grass or something."

"Okay. Right." George moved to the kitchen door, his face pale.

It was weird how it changed colour every so often. Must be something to do with his blood pressure. Nasty wondered if that would be a problem going forward. His heart playing him up would be inconvenient. She needed him to help her so his DNA was left behind, then, when it was time, she'd get rid of him, too, and he could take the blame for everything.

Gullible twat.

He smiled. "I'll text you in about ten minutes. You know, the messages you said I needed to send."

"Make sure you do. Oh, and there's a change of plan on who's next."

What was Nasty playing at? Nice floundered for a moment, worrying what Nasty had in mind.

George shook his head. "God, how many people *are* there on your shit list?"

"Don't worry about it. Your job is just to do what I say."

George walked out, and the front door creaked. "Oh. Hello, Jeff. I'm...I'm just off now."

"See you," Jeff said.

Nice stood, her legs a little wobbly, but she reminded herself that the police kept you safe, and being married to one meant you were even safer. That was why she'd made sure she'd bumped into him all those years ago. Why she'd followed him for months to find out his likes and dislikes so she could make out hers were the same. Why Nasty had allowed Nice to be even nicer, that sickening, simpering side of herself an older man like Jeff seemed to prefer.

Some people got confused when they were out together and thought he was her father. Was that another reason why she'd chosen him? So she had a dad who treated her properly?

He came in and hugged her, albeit stiffly. "Everything okay?"

"Yes, we talked a lot, got a few things out in the open. I feel much better now. And Helena was here..."

He let her go and leant back so he could look at her face. "What did she want?"

"Someone had used a spare key to my dad's. I'd completely forgotten about it, and Helena said someone else had downloaded those horrible pictures on his computer. It wasn't him—he was at work."

"Ah, digital forensics have been on it then. That's somewhat of a relief that he wasn't a paedophile."

But he was, Nasty said. *He was.*

"Yes." Rachel nodded. "But he wasn't a good man, and talking to George today helped me to see I've been denying that. I'll go to Dad's funeral, pay for it even, or go halves with George, but that's the end of it after that. No more sticking up for him."

"Whatever you want, love. I only need you to be happy, you know that."

Happy is killing. Happy is getting rid of them all. "What would make me happy is seeing more of George." She held a hand up to stop him protesting. "I know I told you before that it's best I stay away from him, but I was wrong. He really helped me today. I should never have kept him at arm's length."

"If you're sure…"

Why does he always say that? Nasty said. *As if you don't know your own mind?* She laughed, and it didn't sound good at all.

"I am sure," Nice said, wishing Nasty would just shut up sometimes.

Her phone bleeped on the table. She glanced at it, as did Jeff.

"Do you want me to deal with that?" he asked. "Word might have got out…"

"No, it's fine. I'll do it." She turned from him and smiled, Nasty coming to the fore.

There he is again, trying to look at your phone, to monitor every aspect of your life. When are you going to admit he's a control freak?

She read the message.

George: CAN WE GO OUT FOR LUNCH? I'LL PICK YOU UP IN TEN MINUTES IF YOU WANT.

Rachel: I'LL MEET YOU. WHERE?

George: THE SANDWICH CRUST? WE CAN BUY SOMETHING THERE THEN GO AND EAT IT ON THE CLIFF LIKE WE USED TO AS KIDS.

Rachel: OKAY. GIVE ME FIFTEEN.

She peered at Jeff over her shoulder.

"Who's that?" he asked.

It pissed Nasty off, him asking that. She never nosed into who was contacting him, so why did he think he had the right to do it to her? "George. He's asked me to lunch."

Nasty piped up. *You know what Jeff's going to do when you leave the room, don't you...*

Shh!

She left the messages open and placed the phone on the table. "I'm off to get ready. I'll use your car, shall I? Saves you reversing so I can get mine out."

"Yes, yes, that's fine. But lunch with George? Are you sure that's something you want to do?"

Of course I'm fucking sure, you bloody drip. Nasty wanted to swing round and punch Jeff in his wrinkled face. How dare he question her decisions? Instead, she swivelled towards him. "Yes, very sure."

She left the room, making extra footsteps, as though she'd gone into the living room. She peered through the crack between the frame and the kitchen door, watching Jeff do exactly what Nasty had been about to say he would. He picked up her phone and read the messages.

Told you not to trust him, Nasty said.

Nice tiptoed away, hurt and confused at his lack of trust. Maybe he just wanted to make sure George hadn't forced her into it. Jeff was only interested in her well-being, not anything else.

No, he wants to own you, I've told you that so many times, but will you listen? Will you eff.

Go away.

She ran upstairs, changing into black leggings and a long-sleeved T-shirt. Nasty could go and do one until Nice needed her.

Still, the niggles about Jeff continued. Nice didn't want to face the truth—that Nasty was right and he wasn't good for her.

She thrust those thoughts away and concentrated on George, how he'd sent the message just like she'd asked, the exact words, so they'd have an alibi. There were plenty of places along the cliff they could eat their lunch without being seen. Not that they'd be there for long.

On hands and knees, George ferreted about in the grass beside Steve's path, his stomach in knots.

He couldn't find that bloody key. The police were still at his father's, and he worried one of them would come out and spot him. Or Steve would. How could he explain what he was doing? Maybe he'd say he'd dropped some money, coins, and they'd rolled out of sight.

At least he'd remembered exactly what to put in the messages to Rachel. He got to thinking of what they were going to do next and shivered. But she'd changed her mind, so going to that man's house, the one who lived behind Dad's, didn't seem to be happening now. That was worrying, because they'd gone over her plan a few times to make sure George understood his part in it. Would she use the same plan on the new person? And who was it?

Sunlight glinted off something in the grass, and he pounced on that location, never so pleased to feel metal on his palm. It was the key, *the bloody key*, and he slid it in his pocket, his heart rate slowing. That was a relief. The stupid thing had been pattering way too hard since he'd heard Rachel out. But he couldn't let her down, not again. He'd do what she wanted, however mental it was, and when they'd finished, when everyone was gone, they'd move on in life as if it had never happened.

That was what they'd agreed anyway.

He got up and brushed off his knees, glad Steve wasn't watching him through the window, then went home to change his jeans. Rachel had suggested tracksuit bottoms for ease of movement, so he slipped some on and practised swinging his body around to ensure he was comfortable. Satisfied, he got in his car and drove towards The Sandwich Crust, parking round the back in a residential street like she'd told him to. No one would take any notice of his car there—too many others had been left bumper to bumper.

George walked down the alley into the little street where the sandwich shop was, turning his phone to silent. He entered and ordered what Rachel had suggested—strange fillings that would be remembered—and his sister strolled in just as the server finished wrapping the packages.

"Ready for our picnic?" Rachel asked. "The cliff will be lovely today." She smiled at the server. "Could we have a quick glass of Coke each before we go, please? It's so warm out, I got all hot and bothered."

Once they were poured and everything paid for with George's credit card—Rachel insisted he had to treat her—they headed for the sofa at the back and sat side by side. George's stomach hurt from the nerves, his chest going tight, but he sipped his Coke, splaying his hand on the table in front of them for good measure. Fingerprints. Proof he was there. Rachel hadn't told him to do that, but it was best to have a safeguard.

She'd parked in the same street as George had and drove in Jeff's car to the cliff top by Dad's old business, leaving their phones behind some tall rocks jutting out of the grass in case the police pinged them. George pressed his fingers to one of those rocks, too, desperate to leave confirmation he'd been there. Then Rachel took him to a lone cottage on the outskirts, swerving into the driveway and parking in front of the garage. The garden was beautiful, a riot of colours, the grass well-tended.

"Who lives here?" George didn't feel well. The enormity of what they were about to do hit him, as did the premeditation—the visit to the sandwich shop, the cliff top. He knew what was about to happen, so he couldn't lay the blame solely at his sister's door if they got caught. If he had concerns, now was the time to back out, before anyone got killed.

Killed. He couldn't bloody believe this!

Images of Rachel doing the dares entered his head, and he knew he wouldn't be backing anywhere. Except into a corner. He'd do this. Repay her for what she'd done for him.

"Dad's secretary," Rachel said, her voice weird and tight. "She spoilt things. She let the police know someone else must have downloaded the images."

George's heart sank. "W-was it you?"

She whipped her head round to stare at him, all traces of her kind self gone. "Of course it was me, you stupid fucker. Who else *would* it be?" Then, "Oh God, I'm sorry for shouting. I didn't mean it. That was her, *she* made me say that."

"Who did, the secretary?" George's frown hurt his forehead.

"No, her!" Rachel jerked her thumb at the back seat.

George shifted to peer behind him.

No one was there.

"I don't see anyone," he said.

"You're joking. *Look.* She's right there!" Rachel jabbed her finger in the air as if poking someone in the chest.

"Listen, forget about her." He didn't know what else to say, what else to do except play along. Rachel wasn't right in the head, he got that now, so making her angrier wasn't something he could handle. "Are we doing the same thing to this woman as the man you mentioned?"

"We'll see how it goes."

Rachel got out, so George followed her to the blue front door with the pretty flowers climbing up the buttercream-coloured bricks around it. He wanted to run away and never come back. This wasn't right, what they were doing, but what had happened to Rachel was somehow worse, and someone had to pay, didn't they?

Even if it meant that was a woman who clearly enjoyed gardening.

She won't be doing that again.

Oh fuck. Oh God...

The door opened, and a lady in her late sixties opened up. Grey, curly bobbed hair, black-framed glasses, and was that a slight moustache? She stared at them as if she knew them but couldn't work out where from. Shit, were they even going to tell her who they were? Rachel hadn't said. Floating in limbo, George sensed a panic attack coming on. His head throbbed, and he worried he'd get a nosebleed. High blood pressure sometimes brought those on.

"Yes?" the woman said.

"Elizabeth Mackenzie? We're Trevor's children." Rachel smiled, big and wide and kind. "Sorry to bother you, but we wanted to let you know he passed away. We weren't sure if anyone had told you. Dad said you were very nice to him, so we thought you'd like to know."

Elizabeth lifted a hand to her chest and chortled. "I had no idea he thought that about me. He was always so nasty, I didn't think he was bothered whether I was there or not, except to basically run his business for him. That was all I was handy for."

"He was great at hiding his emotions," Rachel said.

He showed the mean ones often enough. "Yes, that's right," George added. He was in it now he'd spoken. A part of this. *Shit.*

"What do you expect me to do with that information?" Elizabeth asked. "I spent six months being demeaned by him, being told I wasn't up to standard, yet he still kept me on, and quite frankly, I stayed for the money because my husband had died and I only had the one income and had to wait for his life insurance to come through. Whatever you have to say won't make a blind bit of difference to how I feel about that hateful man—he was cruel. Now, please leave. I don't want to talk about him anymore."

"Can't we just come in for a moment?" Rachel asked. "Chat?"

"Why would I want to do that?" Elizabeth asked. "No, you can't come in. If you don't go away, I'll be forced to call the police. I can see you inherited your father's insistent nature and won't take no for an answer. Well, it won't work on me because—"

Rachel snarled.

Then punched Elizabeth in the face.

George's nose bled.

CHAPTER FIFTEEN

"Drag her in there," Rachel ordered.

George shuddered, swiping the blood that had dripped down his moustache and over his lips. He didn't want to drag Elizabeth anywhere, but what choice did he have? Never would he have believed Rachel was capable of punching anyone, let alone killing, but she had, and with some force, too. Enough to knock the old woman out. Or that might have happened when she'd banged her head on the hallway flagstones. They were pretty hard, and the sound of that crack had churned his stomach.

He sniffed to stop the blood falling and bent over, curling his hands beneath Elizabeth's armpits, hating the brush of her blouse on his skin and the heat from where she'd got hot on the doorstep. It was slightly damp. Sweat. God, he'd never touch polyester again. George lifted her a bit. Oh fuck, red liquid was on the floor, and her hair was matted at the back with it. He heaved at the sight, then the smell as his brain engaged with what it actually was—blood—and glanced across at Rachel who stood by the stairs.

"Don't you dare throw up again," she all but snarled. "And wipe your fucking nose."

Christ, what had got into her?

"Well, what are you waiting for?" she snapped.

He used the sleeve at the top of his arm to cuff the area between his nose and top lip.

Rachel nodded. "That's better. Now get that fucking slag in the kitchen. It'll be easier in there. I need to collect my bag."

While Rachel went out the front, George sucked in a deep breath and forced himself to tug Elizabeth along, averting his gaze like he did with Dad's house so he didn't have to acknowledge her and what he was doing. She was heavy, a strain on his heart, and he prayed it didn't give out on him. Rachel would get arsey about it, and the mood she was in, he couldn't risk her having a proper go at him, not now he knew how strong she was. He reckoned she could overpower him, no problem.

While she'd admitted to killing their parents, brothers, and nan, he hadn't quite believed it until she'd launched her fist at Elizabeth, then the certainty that his sister was a killer—one who may well enjoy it, too—walloped him in the gut. Her smile after the old lady had landed gave him the chills even now.

In the kitchen, he let Elizabeth go gently, crapping himself in case she woke up and had a mare. She could scream, but that wouldn't matter—no neighbours—but just seeing her realising what was going to happen would do him in. How could he look her in the eye? How could he live with himself afterwards?

Weakened by the exercise, George leant against the worktop, catching his breath. The skin of his elbow stuck to the Formica—he was sweating. His nose dripped again then finally stopped bleeding, so that was something.

Rachel came to the doorway, and he jumped, momentarily thinking it was someone else. She had a cream boiler suit on, like painters used, and her hair was stuffed inside a black shower cap with pink roses all over it. George had seen them on sale in the new Tesco last week, end aisle, ninety-nine pence. Black rubber gloves covered her hands, sinister things, and he was relieved. It meant she'd be doing the killing, same as the original plan—unless she sent him outside to get dressed up, too.

"Come out here and wait." Rachel stared at him from the hallway. "You don't want to be doing this bit."

Calmed somewhat by her declaration, he did what she'd said and joined her.

"Now." She plonked her hands on his shoulders and looked up at him, glaring like some maniac on drugs. "Watch and learn, okay?"

He nodded, thinking of Steve, ashamed of himself, because if this came out, if they got caught, Steve would be tainted by it. Their father's behaviour had led to two of his children behaving the same as animals, exacting some kind of justice, to what end? To make them feel better? George didn't feel better at all. It was worse, this, than anything he'd ever been through at the hands of Trevor Vakerby. Being hit, being forced to remember every minute of his day, was preferable to standing here looking into his sister's eyes, knowing that soon, the old lady in that kitchen wasn't going to breathe anymore, or plant her flowers, or maybe do a crossword with her morning coffee.

"Rach… Does it have to be this way?"

She narrowed her eyes. Cocked her head. "Yes. Are you getting cold feet?"

He nodded. "This is all a bit much, to be honest."

"Which is why I'm doing this one to show you how it works. Then you'll know and be able to do the man behind Dad's house."

He thought about that man, what Rachel had told George he'd done, and no one round that street and beyond would have done anything about it if the bloke had said something. People were too afraid of Trevor. A phone call would have been good, though, that was what Rachel had said, and she was right. No one would have known it was the man calling the police, especially if he'd used a phone box. They were still around during that time. Anonymous, easily used in the dead of night.

I should have phoned someone, too. I'm just as bad as him.

"Besides, she's seen us," Rachel went on. "She knows it was me who punched her. Do you want me to get nicked for assault? ABH carries some kind of sentence, even if it's only fifteen months or whatever. Jeff told me that."

"No, I don't want you to go to prison."

"So you'll watch and learn?"

"Yes." For now. Maybe he could talk her out of carrying on once this job was over.

"Good."

She picked up her holdall and strutted into the kitchen, placing it on the worktop. Drawing the zip along, she kicked Elizabeth at the same time, maybe to check if she'd wake up. "This..." She withdrew a meat cleaver, bright, shiny silver, and studied it. "This is what I'll use to take out her heart."

She hadn't elaborated as to why it needed to be removed when they'd chatted at her house, and George hadn't pushed for a reason. He imagined the mess, all that blood, and held back another heave. She couldn't be joking about this—Dad and that boy had had their hearts removed.

"Do it now, while she's out of it," he muttered.

"That's the spirit." Rachel beamed at him. "I knew you'd get into it." She paused. "Hmm. I suppose that's sensible—your suggestion, I mean. She won't flail about as much, though she will wake up, most likely after the first chop. I usually hit them a few times with my special bat first."

George's legs threatened to go out from under him, so he reached out to steady himself, hand on the doorframe. "Fucking hell."

"Deep breath, bruv."

Rachel straddled Elizabeth and placed the cleaver on the floor beside them. Using both hands, she ripped open Elizabeth's blouse, then used a knife from beside the cooker to slice the fabric between the bra cups. Saggy old boobs flopped sideways, and Elizabeth appeared flat-chested. George supposed that would make the job easier without all that flesh to hack through. Rachel raised the cleaver over her head with a double-fisted grip, and before he could say *stop, please, just stop*, she brought it down.

Elizabeth's head rose, her eyes wide, her arms curved as if she wanted to cuddle Rachel, hands clawed, her arthritic knuckles large and bulbous. She let out a strange wheeze-groan, and Rachel lifted the weapon once more, slashing it down so it embedded in the chest a few inches from the other messy gash that spewed a tributary of blood.

Elizabeth screamed.

"Shut your fucking face, you old cow," Rachel shouted.

George didn't recognise his sister's profile, the contorted features. Elizabeth's blood had splashed on Rachel's cheek, a teardrop of it hanging off the end of her nose. His pulse hammered so wildly he thought he'd have a heart attack, and he gripped the doorframe harder, wishing he was anywhere but here.

What if he hadn't gone to Rachel's this morning? What if he'd let her be, going through his feelings by himself or perhaps waiting until he met Steve for dinner later? Would Rachel have come round to Elizabeth's anyway once Helena had visited her? George wouldn't be any the wiser, safe at his place, maybe having a nap right now instead of standing in a woman's hallway, watching his sibling kill her.

Another slice of the cleaver, and blood shot out of Elizabeth's mouth. She gargled it, bubbly spume flowing down her chin, and Rachel scooped some up and smeared it on her own cheeks. She turned her head, showing the full horror of what she looked like, smiling, her eyes glinting with what George could only say was malice.

Elizabeth's head thunked to the floor, her lips pulled back, as though she was grinning, her dentures on show. Her grey hair, streaked with crimson, was weighted by blood, flattened to her forehead instead of the curly halo it had been upon their arrival.

Short of breath, George flicked his gaze between Elizabeth and Rachel several times, unable to take in the enormity of this. He was an accomplice, an accessory to murder—*if* he remained here, then left with Rachel and continued his life as if this...this fucking awful shit hadn't happened. But if he walked out now, got in Jeff's car, and drove away to the police station, found Helena Stratton, told her Rachel had forced him, George wouldn't be in prison for too long, would he?

"Don't crap your pants just yet," Rachel said. "There's still one more chop to go. It's the Devil's work getting through these ribs. I have to make a square. Has to be a square."

She wrenched the cleaver out of Elizabeth's chest then quickly whacked it down again. More blood. No more screams from Elizabeth. The woman had gone to wherever people went once their soul split from the body, and wasn't that a weird thing to think? Now? During...this?

"That's lovely." Rachel grinned. "I've just got to dig about a bit with the blade to get this chunk off, then I can cut out the heart."

George watched as if in a dream—or a nightmare—knowing it was happening but unable to fully accept it. His mind refused to soak up the deep implications of this act, perhaps so he didn't break down and make matters worse. A coping mechanism.

"All done." Rachel tossed the cleaver down. It skidded across the floor, coming to rest in front of an undercounter fridge that had fluff just beneath it.

She was being weird and staring at the square she'd made, a creepy smile transforming her face. George didn't like it, and his skin erupted with goosebumps. She'd told him she'd left Dad's square of chest on the windowsill so the man in the house behind could see it. He didn't know how, but she'd been convinced he would.

"Do you see the fox, George?" She leant forward, closer to the square. "Do you see the crow, the woods?"

What was she on about? And what should he say? "Yes, I see them."

"And look at this beauty." She dug her hands into the cavity and gripped the loosened heart, raising it in her black-gloved hands.

"I... I..." George sucked in a big breath. Closed his eyes. Released the air from his lungs. Repeated the action until his heartrate slowed, but his skin was still cold and clammy, his hair sticking to the nape of his neck. "Jesus Christ."

"Keep your eyes shut if you're squeamish while I find some cling film to wrap this up in."

He listened to the opening and closing of drawers and cupboards.

"Damn," Rachel said. "Why do old people only ever use foil? It'll have to do."

George imagined her breaking off a length of it, placing the heart in the middle, then rolling it, scrunching the open ends to secure the little parcel. He let his mind wander to what Elizabeth looked like with a gaping, bloody hole in her chest. He opened one eye. Snapped it shut again. It was too much.

His knees buckled, and he sank into a faint.

Nasty was livid. This had complicated things. George's dramatic faint wasn't in the plan. She rushed out into the hallway to slap his cheek.

"George. George! Wake the fuck up." Nasty was being particularly rough, and her bloodied handprint marred her brother's skin. "I can't be doing with this bullshit. I told you about keeping calm, and you said you could do it." Another slap. "You lied to me, you dumb little fucker."

He was just as thick as Darwin.

She couldn't stand looking at him, being near him, so left him there, returning to the kitchen to wash her gloves then root around in the cupboards for a carrier bag to put the heart parcel in. She did that and placed it in her holdall, ran the cleaver under the tap and packed that away, too.

A scout around the house had her finding Elizabeth's work diaries in a sideboard in the living room. In the garden, she took her boiler suit and gloves off and dropped it all in a pile with the diaries, setting fire to everything, thinking of how cool it was that George had had a nosebleed. Some of his blood must have got somewhere in the house, so him being nailed for this was a given.

Rachel ran inside, stepped over George in the hallway, and washed her hands and face at the kitchen sink. She pulled fresh gloves on and scrubbed the tap, the soap pump dispenser, and any surfaces she may have touched. A spot of blood was on the worktop where George had stood, so she left it there, ready for the police to find.

Back in the hallway, she slid her hand into George's trackie bottoms pocket and pulled out some keys. She left the house bunch in there and took the one for his car, then went to Elizabeth and placed them down the side of the cooker where there was a gap along with some disgusting congealed grease on the floor.

Holdall in hand, she took it out to the car and stowed it in the boot inside a black rubbish bag, adding the shower cap. She'd put it all in her car once she got home and hide it again while Jeff was asleep, although the heart needed to be put in the freezer as soon as possible. She'd take Elizabeth's and Darwin's into school on Monday, defrosted by then, obviously, so two students could work on them.

George groaned, and she moved to the front door to peer inside. He'd sat up and rubbed his eyes. One cheek had a bruise where he must have whacked it on the doorframe as he'd fallen, so maybe some skin particles were attached to the painted wood. Bonus. How was he going to explain that bruise, though? Perhaps she could convince him to say they'd had a row on the cliff and she'd hit him—Steve and Jeff would buy that, seeing as their emotions were all over the place after Dad's death. She'd tell the police a different story. He'd stormed off, returning for her an hour later.

Nasty was so good at this lark.

Nice, however, wasn't. She almost crumpled at what she had to do next, which was getting George into the car. It seemed too much of a feat.

Just do it, you dopey bitch, Nasty shouted. *Get your arses back to the cliff and make sure someone sees you.*

"George," she bit out. "Get up. We have to go."

He stumbled to his feet. Looked in the kitchen. "Oh God, it really happened."

"Of course it did. What, did you think you'd bloody dreamt it?"

He nodded, crying. He'd need to wash that blood off his face and wrist, but the smear on his sleeve…he'd have to tell the truth and say he'd had a nosebleed. That wasn't unusual for his condition. Good job Jeff always kept a packet of wet wipes in the glove box really.

He staggered outside, blinking in the sunlight.

Rachel reached out a gloved hand and closed the front door. "How do you feel?"

"Groggy."

"Well, that's tough. You need to drive us to the cliff so we can pick up our phones. I'm too pumped up to do it. I'll speed, and we risk being caught if I do that."

George obeyed and got in the driver's seat.

On the way, she told him about his bruise and the story he had to tell. He nodded, clearly resigned to the fate she'd mapped out for him.

As always, Nasty smiled.

Rachel stared through the square window in her bedroom while Dad played out the dare behind her. That square had become important to her, something she clung to during these times, a box she pushed herself into, a welcoming void. It was weird how everything disappeared. The frame, what was really beyond that glass—the sky, in whatever form it took at any given moment: bright blue with white puffs; stormy and grey with black-bottomed clouds; maybe an expanse full of sheeting rain, and perhaps a rainbow, too, if the sun managed to squeeze through the drizzle. Instead, she imagined a different world, one at the end of the wooden walkway, a secret forest behind the magical mist, where the fox and his family lived, and the crow from the banister rail sitting on her shoulder as she sat with the animals, her presence shrouded by tree trunks.

She was safe there.

When she was older and killed her father, she'd cut a square in his chest and push herself into that, too, seeking what she'd always wanted—the image of a dad who cared for her as he should, a happy family life where no one had to recite their day down to the last second, just because he wanted to watch them squirm. A scenario where the triplets didn't get treated better than Rachel and George. She'd have a mother who wasn't afraid, one who was present mentally and emotionally and baked cakes and gingerbread men like Nanny, one who smelt of roses, not the stench of a woman defeated.

Squares. They were her haven, her happy zone.

Rachel and George collected their phones and sat with their backs against the rocks.

"I'm scared," George said.

"Maybe you need a Nasty and Nice to help you."

"What? Fuck's sake, talk sense, will you? Christ, my head's banging."

"I have a Nasty and Nice." She gazed at the clouds. "Nasty does all the horrible things, and Nice worries about it. Nasty was the one sitting in the back of the car at Elizabeth's."

That had worried Rachel. She hadn't expected to see herself there, staring back at her, a real person, not just a part of her inside her head. For a moment she'd thought she was mad, totally demented, but then Nasty had vanished from sight, and everything was all right.

She didn't want to see her again.

"I think I know what you mean," George said. "Like a good and bad part of yourself."

"That's it. Nasty is a killer. I'm not."

"But you are, Rach. Doesn't matter which side of you did it."

She bristled at that. Well, Nasty did. Nice had to stop her from grabbing George's throat and squeezing until he couldn't breathe anymore. "We'll agree to differ on that one. So, you have the story straight about your bruise, yes?"

"Yeah, but where did I go when I stormed off?"

"I don't know! I wasn't there." *Dippy bastard.* "You tell people whatever you want, but you went off in Jeff's car, calmed down, then came back to pick me up. Now we're here, making friends again after our argument."

A man approached in the distance, a dog lolloping beside him. Fate was so very kind in sending him to see them. Nasty and Nice smiled, relief winging through them until Rachel felt heavy with it.

"We'll leave soon." *Once that bloke has come close enough to take in our faces.* "And later, we'll go to that man's house. We'll meet round the back of his at midnight."

"Okay," George said, but he didn't sound like he wanted to.

She picked up her egg and gherkin sandwich with fried onions.

Definitely a lunch the server wouldn't forget.

Rachel was pulled out of the world behind the square window, her attention snagging on another opposite. A man stood in one of the bedrooms, hands up ready to close the curtains, staring at her, his mouth open, eyes wide.

Could he see her father and what he was doing?

Maybe he'd ring the police and tell them. Maybe they'd come round and arrest Dad, taking him away so she'd never have to see him again.

The man snapped his curtains together, and she knew help wouldn't come.

She was alone in this, as always.

One day, though, after she'd killed her father, she'd pay The Watcher a visit.

He didn't deserve to live if he wasn't going to save her.

CHAPTER SIXTEEN

At Isla's front door, Helena winced at her stomach growling. It was just after lunchtime, so they'd have to pick something up on the way back to the station. Andy smirked at the noise, and she gave him a glare that told him to behave and be professional.

She clacked the knocker and waited for Dave to answer.

"I fancy a bacon sarnie," Andy said out of the side of his mouth. "With a fried egg on top, runny, so the yolk soaks into the bread. *White* bread."

"You're not meant to be eating stuff like that," she said. "Fried food went to your waistline before, remember."

He didn't grimace at her reminder of his past, when Sarah had ditched him and his world had spiralled. Seemed he really was over it now.

"Yeah, but a small treat wouldn't hurt, and Louise doesn't need to know."

Helena tutted. "Hmm, keeping things from her isn't good."

Andy sighed. "Okay, I'll have ham and brown bread with those annoying seeds in it. A boring sandwich."

"That's better."

Dave opened the door, stepped out, and pulled it to. A Labrador stuck his nose in the gap and peeked out at them.

"How is she?" Helena asked.

"Talking at last, but rather than discuss finding Darwin and helping me picture what his life was like, she's gone off on one about being fostered."

"Anything interesting crop up there?"

"No. There aren't any biological or foster relatives left, so it can't be one of them who did it." Dave closed his eyes for a moment. "The problem is, the minute I try to steer the convo to her son, she starts a new story. I've heard all about her memories with her druggy biologicals, then the happier times with the adoptives."

"She's denying it's happened—her son's death, I mean." Helena had done the same on occasion regarding her own trauma. If you changed the subject, the horrible shit receded, and you felt normal for a short while. "That doesn't help us, though. I'll have a chat with her, see what happens."

"Okay. She's a state…"

"I wouldn't expect anything less."

They entered the house, which was clean and tidy, and Dave led the way to the kitchen, the dog padding along behind. Isla sat on a burgundy velvet sofa in the dining area, hunched over, her feet tucked up, and she hugged her knees. Was she pretending it was Darwin she cuddled?

God, this must be so hard for her.

And she *was* a state. Seemed she hadn't washed since she'd found her son. Blood had dried on her face and hands, although her clothing was unsoiled. Those she'd had on while with Darwin's body would have been taken in as evidence.

"Isla, I'm DI Helena Stratton, and this is my colleague, DS Andy Mald. We need to ask you some questions about Darwin, and while I understand this will be difficult, it's something we have to do in order to catch who murdered him."

She'd been blunt, but Dave coddling the woman hadn't worked. They needed answers, and pandering wasn't going to get them.

"So we'll start with what he liked to do. Hobbies, things like that."

Isla looked up, her eyes watery. "I can't talk about him."

"Do you want someone else killed? Another boy perhaps? Because if we don't get a move on, that's what will happen. Two people have been murdered, Isla, *two*, and another family will be going through exactly what you are if we don't find the killer soon." It had hurt to say that, to sound so harsh. "So, hobbies?"

"He likes chess, on his PlayStation."

"Right. Did he ever go to anyone's house to play it? A friend we're unaware of? A child from this street who doesn't go to Smaltern Secondary?"

"He doesn't have friends except the ones he makes in the summer when they're here on holiday."

"Not even from primary school? Why do you think that is?"

"Because kids think he's silly, childish, but he isn't. He's perfect and funny, kind, and loves making up stories."

"He wrote some?"

"Yes, in all those exercise books he has in his room."

Helena nodded at Dave for him to go up there and have a look. That search should have already been executed, and she'd be having a word with him as to why he perhaps hadn't done it.

But Dave shook his head, came closer, and whispered in her ear, "Already seen them; nothing there we need to know about."

She turned back to Isla, pricked with guilt for thinking Dave hadn't done his job properly. "What sort of stories are they?"

"Animals, forests, magical things."

"That's lovely. So he played chess at home?"

"Yes. In the living room. The computer is the other player. I watch him most evenings in between reading. I'm not much for TV, so it doesn't bother me if he uses that one."

"Did Darwin ever go out after school or at the weekends?"

"Only with me. He has no one else to go out with. I told you. Only friends in the summer."

"Perhaps he had a secret friend, someone he didn't want anyone else to know about."

"No." Isla narrowed her eyes at Helena for daring to say such a thing. "He doesn't keep secrets. He's a good boy."

"Let's talk about the bullying. Why do you think kids picked on him at school?"

"Because he's different. He doesn't think like everyone else. Plus, he was brought up in Italy until me and him moved back here after I split from William. Dar's life was so different there, and he found it difficult to settle here. He speaks fluent Italian, you know, and maybe some children think he's a big head, a know-it-all."

"How long have you lived back in the UK?" Helena asked.

"Six years. We returned when Dar was seven."

"So he still hadn't settled in all that time?"

"No. He misses his dad. Oh God, William... Does he know?"

Ah, the first admittance that she had accepted her son was dead, that she wasn't pretending he was still alive, out there somewhere, and would walk in any second.

"Yes, he's been informed. He'll be arriving in the UK this afternoon. Maybe he even has already." Helena braced herself for the next question, although it was a ridiculous one, considering Trevor had also been killed, but every avenue needed to be travelled. "Was there anyone in Italy who might have wanted to do this to your son?"

Isla choked on air, and the dog scrabbled over to sit by her feet. It had a streak of blood on its flank.

"Of course not. Italy wasn't like it is here. Not the part where we lived. It's a village, quiet, and everyone is nice."

"So no spats with neighbours? You and William didn't fall out with anyone?"

"No. It'll be the bullies, you wait and see." Isla rocked, sucking on her bottom lip.

Was that a comfort thing left over from her early childhood, much like Mr Queensley farting about with that feather?

"We'll need to take a look at Darwin's bedroom." Helena held her breath.

"Don't touch anything. I want it left exactly as it is." Isla leant her head back, closed her eyes, and let the tears fall.

Helena glanced at Dave.

He whispered, "I checked it while she was asleep, so she doesn't know I've been in there."

Helena nodded and left the room with Andy. She collected gloves and booties from the car and handed him his set. Back inside, protective gear on, she poked her head into the living room on her way down the hall—nothing odd in there, just your average family space. She walked upstairs, checking the bathroom first, then Isla's room—again, nothing to report except for a rumpled quilt, the corner folded back where she'd got up.

Helena steeled herself to push Darwin's door open—it had a wooden plaque with his name painted on it. Inside would be the boy's haven, the place where he'd probably cried about the bullies and missing his father and his life in Italy. The bed with its pillow he may have clutched close to him for comfort when things seemed too hard to handle.

"Want me to go first?" Andy asked behind her.

"No, it's okay." It wasn't, but she'd have to get on with it.

She went inside. It was as clean and tidy as the rest of the house, the made bed to the right, his pyjamas folded at the foot. A double wardrobe along with white shelving lined the left wall, bits and bobs placed neatly—the exercise books, a Rubik's cube, a cricket ball, just stuff boys liked. She took one of the books from the start of the row and opened it on the first page.

The Beginning

Owl was sad and wrapped his wings across his belly. The lonely night surrounded him, reaching out through the leaves, weaving over his perch on the branch, cloaking him so he was unseen. Other animals snuffled in the undergrowth far below—a mole, the hedgehog family, mice—and Owl wished he could go down there with them. Play, be a part of something outside his tree, accepted and loved.

But those animals didn't like Owl. He was different. Did they think he'd swoop down and pick them up in his claws, carry them away, up to his branch so he could eat them? They thought he was something he wasn't and hadn't given him the chance to prove otherwise. He just wanted to be friends.

One day, he'd make them see he wasn't weird—he'd heard them laughing about his big eyes, his beak, his clumsy wings, his imagination, his everything. And one day, maybe they'd let him join their circle, and he'd be happy, so very happy, and he'd tell them fantastical stories about magical woodland beings, making *them* happy and glad he was one of them, a welcome creature of the forest.

Tears stung. How could Dave have thought this was nothing? That this story wasn't saying something about Darwin's life? The poor lad had written about himself, Owl, pushed away because he was different. All he'd wanted was to belong, and instead, he was dead, cold in Zach's morgue fridge, mourned by his mother, father, his grandparents, half-siblings, and Helena's team, the SOCOs, but no one else. Not the kids at school who'd ridiculed him, those mice, the mole, and the hedgehogs.

"So fucking unfair," she muttered. "Read this."

Andy did, swallowing a few times, and when he'd finished, she slid the book away and selected another, one lying on its back in front of the rest.

"Christ, Andy, that kid didn't deserve this. He was just a child, for Pete's sake."

He rested his hand on her shoulder. "Deep breath, love."

She turned to the last page, guessing it was his most recent entry.

And the mole shoved him into the corridor wall, digging his elbow in Owl's belly, shouting in his face that Owl was a weirdo and no one liked him. Everyone laughed, especially the many mice, their long teeth exposed in crazy yellow grins, wringing their tiny hands in glee. They were the ones who always watched the mole orchestrating the hedgehogs, staying back to observe but never stepping forward to fully join in.

Owl staggered away, his huge eyes watering, and flew out of the school and into the woods behind, where he soared through then out onto the cliff top. The sea called for him to dive into it: *Come, come, set yourself free in me. I will keep you safe, never to be bullied again.*

Owl shook his head. He spied home in the distance and headed for it, where Mother Owl waited. He dived inside, and she hugged him with her beautiful snowy-white wings and told him he didn't need to have friends, he could manage without them, and he was perfect just the way he was.

"Never change," Mother Owl said. "Be exactly who you are, always."

So Owl did. After many years, he stopped hoping the creatures would be his friends. He lived his life happily alone, being himself despite what the mole and the hedgehogs said, while the mice looked on with their beady eyes. It was just chatter, rubbish, and he didn't need to listen to it.

He'd found his place in the world at last.

The lump in Helena's throat hurt.

"Bloody hell," Andy mumbled, going over to the window and cuffing his eyes. "Those kids have a lot to answer for. If I was allowed to get my hands on them…"

"I feel the same, but there's nothing we can do except ensure they understand that bullying isn't the way to go. Maybe Darwin being dead will be the kick up the arse they need to stop this crap."

"What if one of those creatures killed him? Those fucking mice didn't sound pleasant." Andy stared out into the street. "It's obvious the animals are the bullies."

"I thought the same. There are mice, indicating several, and a family of hedgehogs, again indicating several, but only one mole. Is the mole the instigator?"

"And is the family literally that—a few siblings at the same school?"

"It's a start, something to look into." She took her phone out and rang Olivia. "Hi. Get hold of Mr Queensley for me, a phone call will do. I want to know if there are children at the school who belong to one family. If there is, I need details on who their closest friends are. Bear in mind Queensley might not know. If he doesn't, tell me, and I'll go and visit Rachel. She might have the answers."

"Okay," Olivia said. "I had a thought. Elizabeth Mackenzie's work diaries. We should go and pick them up—evidence. Want me to send Phil?"

"No, I need you both at your desks. Me and Andy will go in a minute. We're just about done here. Speak soon." She shoved her phone away, anger taking over the sorrow.

She'd find out who'd killed Darwin if it meant going without days of sleep to do it. He needed justice, and she could only hope he was flying in Heaven as Owl, happier than he'd ever been in this world, because his school life here certainly hadn't been kind to him.

***

Helena parked on Elizabeth Mackenzie's drive and cut the engine. She needed a moment to compose herself. Speaking to the woman while angry wasn't something she wanted to do. The journey here had been in silence, and she supposed Andy had been thinking about Darwin's stories, how the bullying had affected him so much he'd written a fictional world in order to deal with it.

She'd told Isla the exercise books needed to be taken in case something they could use came to light, and while Isla had protested at first, she'd soon understood that to find her son's killer, his precious tales had to be handed over but would be returned to her as soon as possible. Dave was arranging for someone to pick them up. Olivia or Phil could go through them.

"Okay, let's get this over and done with," she said. "We'll pop the diaries in evidence bags. I've got some in the boot. You never know, something else might be in them that gives us some kind of clue."

"Here's hoping."

They stood on the doorstep, and Helena knocked. She had a nose about while they waited. Nice garden, pretty flowers in neat borders, no weeds in sight. Miniature roses grew around the front door in an arch, one that was clearly kept in check on the regular with shears. A window to the right had a blind pulled halfway down, and a one-armed tap was running into the sink just below the sill.

"Looks like she's about to do the washing up." Helena walked closer, mindful not to trample on the flowerbed beneath the window. She leant closer and peered inside. "Oh. Shitting hell..." She felt sick and immediately moved back.

A body. A square hole in the chest. The heart missing. And blood.

"What is it?" Andy rushed over and stared inside. "Fuck!"

Helena dashed to the boot and grabbed gloves, booties. She threw Andy his, and they tugged them on. Andy rammed the front door with his shoulder, but the bloody thing didn't give way. He smacked into it three more times, then it creaked. Once more, and he was inside. Helena followed, yakking into her phone to Louise, asking for a SOCO team. Then she put her phone in her pocket and joined Andy in the kitchen.

They stood staring at the body.

"Someone found out she'd been spoken to," Andy said. "George? Rachel? Who else?"

"It could be anyone. George could have told Steve, who told whoever. Rachel could have spoken to someone. Word spreads."

"We should find out where the hell those two were after we left them." Andy shook his head. "Jeff was out, remember—shit, was this him? Or the other two could have slipped away while he was gone, come here, then returned home."

"But Jeff only went to buy a bowl—he wouldn't have been long. It would take a while to come all the way here, do this, then drive back without him wondering where they'd been. Not to mention the blood on them. Still, you're right. They need to provide us with alibis. And if they have them, well, we'll have to look elsewhere."

"We can't do anything for Elizabeth. And why hasn't she got the same wounds on her face as Trevor and Darwin?"

"Not enough time?"

"Probably. You take downstairs, I'll go up." Andy left the room.

Helena followed him out, turning right to carry on down the hallway to the living room. One of the French doors was ajar, so maybe Elizabeth had been out the back when the killer had arrived. She glanced around—another door open, fully, in a sideboard. Helena crouched to peer inside. There was a space on the top shelf where something had been, a faint layer of dust in front. Had the diaries been there?

She went outside, checking for a trowel or hoe to show what Elizabeth had been doing out here, but all she spotted was a large patch on the grass where something had been burnt. Moving closer, she hunkered down and held her hand over the area. The centre was ever so faintly warm, or maybe she was imagining that and it was just the sun heating it. There was charred material, a melted black substance, and what she suspected was the spine of a book, the corner of a page, too, which hadn't been affected and bore 2010 in black font.

Someone had come here and got rid of the diaries.

She stood, thinking about Rachel and George. She didn't want it to be them, but given their childhood and how some people grew up warped from being in such a household, and also given the trauma of their mother, brothers, and nan dying, they could be expressing their anger and sadness years later by going on a rampage together. The thing was, neither of them seemed the type, but then she'd met many others who'd appeared 'normal', yet they'd been deranged killers, so the same could apply to those two.

George was odd earlier. Jittery. Sweating.

And what about the chief? Surely he couldn't be in on it. No, he was a stickler for the rules, so hiding the fact his wife was a killer wouldn't be something she thought he'd do.

She returned to the house, meeting Andy in the hallway. "Anything?"

"No. You?"

"Looks like the diaries—or something anyway—have been removed from a sideboard in the living room, then burnt in the garden along with material."

"The smoke from a fire isn't going to get us anywhere. We're out in the bloody sticks," he said. "Not one neighbour for miles to spot it."

"I don't get why Elizabeth was offed, unless the killer was aware she knew something other than what was in the diaries."

"We should also be looking into the other employees."

"Didn't you read the whiteboard? Olivia's already done it. None of them knew Trevor in any other sense apart from him being their boss and that he was a tosser."

"Was that done on the phone?"

"Yes."

"Then maybe we need to see them in person, get a look at their faces when they're talking about him."

"Right. We'll also need to get some lunch somewhere along the line, not that I fancy eating after seeing that"—she jabbed her thumb over her shoulder at the kitchen doorway—"get their names off Olivia, go and speak to Rachel and

George, then make some employee visits. Which reminds me, I need to get hold of Olivia now to let her know what's going on and see what she found out from Queensley, although I'm not holding my bloody breath there."

She stepped outside and walked to the end of the drive where she dialled the incident room.

"Hey," Olivia said. "I was just going to ring you. Queensley knew nothing and said he'd have to go into the school on Monday to find that sort of information, although he didn't sound happy at having to do it."

"Hmm, probably doesn't want to leave his pink feather by doing it today."

"Pardon?"

"Nothing. We'll ask Rachel about the kids. We need an excuse to go and see her anyway. We told them earlier about the diaries, and guess what?"

"What?"

"Elizabeth Mackenzie has been killed at home. Heart missing."

"You're not even kidding, are you?"

"No. Looks like the diaries were set on fire in the garden. Someone doesn't want us poking into what Trevor got up to during his workday."

"Sounds like whoever that is has something they want to keep hidden," Olivia said.

"Exactly my thought, and I'm going to find out what it is."

In the meantime, she had SOCO to wait for and Superintendent Yakoshi to ring and inform of a third murder so he was prepared before the press conference. Balls.

CHAPTER SEVENTEEN

As far as Rachel had been aware, no neighbours had been looking out, spying on her.

She'd put her holdall in her own boot and taken the heart package out, stuffing it in the hood of her sports sweatshirt which she'd found on the back seat of her car. Jeff might wonder what on earth she was doing wearing it in this weather, but she'd make out she had a summer cold coming on and she was a bit chilled.

He hadn't said anything, though, a nap on the sofa had seen to that. She'd crept past into the kitchen, stashed the heart in the freezer with Darwin's, and legged it upstairs to shower. She'd forgotten she'd possibly have blood in her hair, having only washed her hands and face at Elizabeth's, so the fates were smiling on her again, sending her husband to sleep like that.

She'd dried her hair on the low setting with the bedroom door shut so the noise didn't wake him, then popped her clothes in the washing machine. Now, she sat in the garden, which was just as pretty as Elizabeth's, maybe even more so, thanks to Jeff, who had the greenest fingers ever.

She thought about George and how he was faring. He'd promised to go home, get that top of his in the wash, then have a shower himself. Afterwards, he was going to ask Steve round to tell him all about their 'row' on the cliff and how he'd taken Jeff's car to do God knew what. She didn't want to know that part of their lie. If the police came to talk to her about it, her reaction would be genuine—how could she know where he'd gone if she wasn't with him and he hadn't told her?

Everything was working out wonderfully.

She resisted the urge to clap. Good job she hadn't, or it would have scared the crow away. It had landed on the banister rail, cawing at her, so she twittered back, him responding, as though what she'd said was something he understood.

She stared down the wooden pathway, homing in on the square window she'd painted on the bottom fence. It had a different sky in each of the four panes—rainy, snowy, sunny, and overcast. She mentally pushed herself through, into the forest, the crow following her path through the trees.

There was the red fox, its amber eyes glowing in the murkiness, and she walked towards it.

"Rachel?"

Who was that calling her in the woods? No one knew she came here for secret visits. She frowned, glancing around.

"Rachel?"

She blinked, and the fake window came back into view, as did Jeff in her peripheral, standing at the back door, his hair tousled on one side where he'd had his head pressed to a cushion.

"What time did you get back?" He came out and sat at the glass patio table with her.

Nasty didn't like him going straight into questioning, as if she were some suspect in one of his interview rooms. No 'Hello, darling, there you are!' or 'I hope you enjoyed your lunch with George.'

"Oh, ages ago." Rachel waved as if the time didn't matter, when it actually did, but she hadn't checked what it was when she'd arrived home, something she needed to watch herself for. Knowing her stories was important, as was having her facts all lined up in a row.

"Have a nice time with George, did you?" he asked.

There. That was better, wasn't it?

It was what he should have asked the first fucking time, Nasty said. *But instead, he wanted to check up on you. I think he knows what we've done.*

Nice's stomach rolled over.

"Rachel?" Jeff frowned. "Is something wrong?"

"Sorry, I zoned out for a minute there. It's been a trying time. But to answer your question, yes, lunch was lovely. Well, it was until George got upset. We had an argument, and…I'm afraid I punched him."

Jeff stiffened, and his eyes went wide. "That's not like you. He must have really pushed your buttons. I'll go down there now and have a word."

"Please don't." She reached out and touched his hand. "We're brother and sister, we're bound to fight. It's nothing, all sorted now."

The faint peal of the doorbell filtered through, the *ding-dong* ominous.

"I'll get it." Jeff went into the house.

Of course he'll get it. Can't have you opening the door in your own home. He's got a cheek, he has. He doesn't even own any of it, just lives here.

Rachel tuned Nasty out, more worried about who was calling round. If it was George, Jeff wouldn't be able to keep his mouth shut, despite her asking him to leave it. He'd dish out a veiled snipe so George knew Jeff was aware they'd had a spat.

Some copper Jeff is. He'd normally make a comment about your third change of clothes today.

Go the hell away, will you?

Jeff appeared again, Helena and that Andy bloke behind him. Rachel stifled a gasp. What were they doing here? And so soon after what had happened to Elizabeth? Did they know? Did they think it was her?

Nice was all but shitting herself.

Nasty sighed. *You set it up for George to get the blame. Relax.*

"Hello." Rachel held her hand up to shield her eyes from the sun.

Jeff sat, while the other two remained standing. It was unnerving having them looking down on her like that, and she had to stop herself from visibly squirming.

"Sorry to be here yet again," Helena said. "It's hard enough for you as it is without us keep turning up on your doorstep. There's something I need to pick your brains about, though. I'm afraid Mr Queensley wasn't much help."

That's because he's fucking useless. "What's that then?"

"Information has come to light where we're a bit closer to finding out who Darwin's bullies are. Are there any siblings in your school, say, more than two?"

Rachel nodded. "Yes, the Spike family."

"Hedgehogs," Andy muttered.

Helena glared at him.

What? "Um, no, I assure you, they're humans." Nasty thought that was quite funny.

Seemed Helena and Andy didn't.

"Okay, and how many of them are there?" Helena asked.

"Four. In years seven, eight, nine, and ten." She had the year ten kid, Jacob, in her class on Monday, so she'd give him Darwin's heart.

"Thank you, that's been very helpful." Helena smiled. "Who are their closest friends?"

"God, they have so many."

"Perhaps someone who stands out as linked to all of them then."

"That would be their cousin, a year eleven. Mark Spike."

Rachel could have sworn Andy mouthed *Mole*.

"That's great. We'll be off now." Helena made for the back door. "Oh, just another quick question. Have you been anywhere today?"

Her stomach lurched again. "Yes, out to lunch with George in Jeff's car. We nipped to The Sandwich Crust to pick up a picnic, then went to the cliff to eat it. I was just about to tell Jeff exactly what happened, but me and George had an argument, a stupid one about who would pay for Dad's funeral because he didn't want to. He hadn't spoken to him for years, so why should he, that kind of thing. I lost it a little and punched him in the face, then he snatched Jeff's keys and stormed off for about an hour."

Helena's expression darkened. "Where did he go?"

"I have no idea, but he came back, we made up, then I dropped him home with a nice black eye."

"Oh dear. What time did you get home?"

"I can't remember. I didn't check."

"Do you know where Elizabeth Mackenzie lives?"

That had come out of nowhere.

Rachel shrugged, hoping she appeared indifferent. "Why would I?"

"Thanks. We'll be seeing you again at some point."

Helena and Andy entered the house, Jeff scooting after them, no doubt to ask pesky questions. Nasty's hackles went up, and she wished Jeff would just bog off and mind his own business.

Why had Helena asked if she knew where that old bag lived? Couldn't they find it themselves on the database, the lazy sods? And what was that about the Spike children? Was it them who'd bullied Darwin?

Jeff walked back outside and slumped in his chair, a toddler sulking. "They won't tell me anything."

"Of course they won't. You're not on the investigation." She'd snapped that, hadn't meant to, but Nasty was being a bitch and hanging around. "Sorry. I'm tense. This whole thing is a nightmare."

He eyed her oddly. "*Do* you know where Elizabeth lives?"

He was doubting her?

Of all the... "No."

"Okay."

But she did know—she'd found it amongst Dad's old office stuff packed in cardboard boxes during the times she'd poked around his place months ago while he was at work and she was on her lunchbreak. Still, no one needed to know that, did they.

It was another secret she'd be keeping to herself.

"It's fine," George said. "Please don't fuss. It was my fault entirely. I should have just agreed to pay half of the funeral and be done with it."

"No, it *isn't* fine." Steve paced in front of George's living room window. "You have a bruise on your face. You and your father were estranged, he was a bastard to you, so why should you pay? You washed your hands of him years ago, so her expecting you to fork out money on a man who treated you appallingly is pretty damn rude."

It *was* rude, if it were true, but it wasn't. Rachel was stumping up the whole cost, and this was just a horrible lie George hated being a part of, especially bullshitting Steve. It wasn't right and could only create a wedge between them. They'd promised no secrets, and now look at him, collecting more of them, storing them inside him where they'd undoubtedly fester and go rancid, meaning *he'd* be rancid, rotten, someone Steve didn't deserve.

What have I done?

He wished he could wake up and start the day all over again. He wouldn't have gone to Rachel's, and none of this would be happening. He wouldn't know anything.

"She got upset because she doesn't see Dad the same way as me. Well, she didn't, not until I went back to the cliff and chatted with her. Now she sees who he is after I told her a few things, and she feels so guilty for hitting me."

"As well she should," Steve said.

"And she admitted he'd abused her, in *that* way."

"Christ Almighty." Steve craned his neck, gawking down the street. "Ah, bloody hell. The police are here again."

"What?" That word came out as a screech, and George's chest went so tight he couldn't breathe for a moment. What did they want? Did they know he'd been at Elizabeth's? *Fucking hell, fucking hell...* He clutched his chest and wilted into a chair.

"George?" Steve rushed over. "What's the matter?"

"Nothing, just a panic attack coming. It's fine. Go and let them in."

The doorbell chimed, ratcheting up George's discomfort, and for God's sake, he wanted to cry. This wasn't how he'd envisaged his life, an accomplice to a killer, probably the killer himself later, bumping off a man who'd had the misfortune to be standing at his window when Dad had been—

Don't think about that.

Steve backed into the hallway, only turning once he'd reached the front door, as though he didn't want to let George out of his sight in case he carked it. George stared at the cardboard square marks in his curtains, remembering when he'd put them up, how life had been so calm then compared to now. Why hadn't Rachel just let Dad live? Her actions had spoilt everything.

Helena Stratton and Andy Mald came in, staring down at him, appearing as giants ready to stomp his much smaller, scared self beneath their big feet.

"Steve said you're not very well," Helena said, "so we'll keep this brief. Where did you go in Jeff Levington's car after your sister struck you on the cliff top earlier?"

Why were they here about that so soon? Did they know about the old woman already?

"I... I can honestly tell you, I don't know." His voice was strangled, and the panic attack was gearing up to explode. "I was so angry, I had to get away from her."

"Angry enough to confront Elizabeth Mackenzie and burn her diaries?" she asked.

He couldn't remember whether he was supposed to know her name or not. "W-what?"

"Your father's former secretary. Did you drive to her house in Jeff's car?"

Thank God, he didn't have to lie. "No, I did *not* drive to her house in Jeff's car. Absolutely not." *It was my fucking sister!* Should he tell them now, get it out in the open? He thought of Rachel, with her Nasty and Nice side, and her thinking she'd seen herself in the back seat. She was unhinged. Could he let her go to prison or a secure hospital? Could he really grass her up?

"It's fine," Helena said. "We'll look it up on ANPR. We'll soon know where you were." Her smile this time wasn't right. Misshapen.

She suspects me. Fuck.

But the car won't be seen during that time. They'll find out I drove it to the cliffs. They'll see everywhere it went.

His heart palpitated, then seemed to inflate, pushing against his chest wall. His arm went numb, then a pain stabbed his neck. It was worse than his usual panic attack. He concentrated on breathing, finding it a struggle to maintain that he was okay in front of the coppers. Sweat broke out on his brow and beneath his moustache, turning cold.

"He's having one of his attacks," Steve said. "Can you move out of the way a minute?" He brushed past them and knelt between George's knees. "Remember, five things you can see. Look around. Find them now."

George did that—the curtains, the TV, the picture on the wall of a crow that Rachel had painted for him, the ugly gilt frame, the carpet. *Breathe. Breathe.*

"That's it," Steve said. "Almost through it."

It took another couple of minutes, but George pushed past the anxiety and relaxed.

"Do you need an ambulance?" Helena asked. "You've gone extremely pale."

"No, these are par for the course," Steve said. "He's had them since he moved out of his father's house. They started when he worried about leaving Rachel with Trevor."

"And there was me thinking our visit had set him off," Andy said.

It was. It bloody was.

"No, this one was probably on the way before you arrived." Steve stood. "He'd been telling me about the row with Rachel, how he felt guilty about not wanting to pay for his half of the funeral, which I don't believe he should be paying. Anyway, let's not dwell on it. Might cause another attack."

"If you're sure..." Helena didn't look convinced.

"I'm fine," George croaked. "I just need to rest."

"Okay. We'll be in touch, though, if we spot you in Jeff's car going anywhere near Elizabeth's." Helena nodded and showed herself out, Andy right behind her.

The door closed, as did George's eyes. For the first time since he'd been under eighteen, he wanted to go to sleep and not wake up. Finish this once and for all.

Elizabeth's body came to mind, with its square hole and her strange death grin.

He reckoned he'd see it in his mind's eye for the rest of his life.

CHAPTER EIGHTEEN

Helena had let Olivia know she needed Phil on ANPR looking for Levington's car, plus checking in with The Sandwich Crust to see if Rachel and George had really gone there. She also wanted her to round up the Spike kids and get them down to the station. A chat in those surroundings may make them sit up and take notice, show them that the death of a boy they'd possibly bullied wasn't something they could laugh about like they probably did while picking on him. The hedgehog term in Darwin's stories made complete sense coupled with that surname, and she was convinced they had the right children. Whether they were killers or not remained to be seen.

First, though, they had to question Trevor's employees. All of them still worked for the new owner, and Olivia had said they were there today.

The drive up the cliff gave her the usual apprehension, as did turning into the area where the containers were. She held her breath and focused on getting to the Portakabin at the end where the office was.

"You okay?" Andy asked.

"Yep. Coping."

She ignored the fact that the container she'd been in was so close. There. In her rearview if only she took a moment to peek. But she didn't, she carried on, and a sense of winning at life stole over her. *She* was in control, not that past situation.

"Actually, I'm great," she said. "It's really going to be okay."

"Good. You deserve to be able to move on."

"No mushy stuff, because you don't do mushy. We're here." She got out before Andy could offer any sympathy, striding to the Portakabin and knocking on the door, then going in.

A blonde woman in her twenties looked up from behind one of the three desks, and a large grey dog got up from beside her and came over for a sniff.

"Can I help you?" she asked.

Helena smiled and waited for Andy to stand next to her. She glanced at the man sitting farther back, who had his head bent over a magazine. The dog padded to him and flopped down, head on his paws.

Holding up her ID, she said, "DI Helena Stratton and DS Andy Mald. We need to speak to all the employees and the boss, please."

"Oh..." The blonde turned to the man and flapped her hand. "Mr Sanbrook?"

He peered their way and took headphone buds out of his ears. "Sorry, can I help you?"

"We're here about Trevor Vakerby, sir," Helena said. "One of my colleagues spoke to everyone on the phone, but we'd like a little chat face to face. Everyone together would be great."

"Absolutely fine." He stood and picked up a walkie-talkie. "All employees to the office, please." He placed it back down. "They shouldn't be long. Would you like a tea or coffee?"

"Lovely. Coffee, thank you." Helena smiled.

"Cheryl," Mr Sanbrook said. "Can you do the honours."

Cheryl got up and moved to a small kitchenette to the right.

Mr Sanbrook came closer. "Terrible business, him being murdered, although I can't say I'm surprised after what I've been told."

"What's that then?" Helena tilted her head.

"Oh, you know, that he was a bit of a bastard to the staff and people who got in his way or on his nerves. I bought the business off him, you know, and the staff were so unhappy it took a while for them to trust me. Cheryl here is new—the previous secretary was Elizabeth Mackenzie, but she decided it was time to retire."

"Yes, we know of Elizabeth."

Men clattered inside one after the other, filling the small space.

"Okay, I need to make this quick." She introduced herself and Andy. "I know you've spoken to DC Vallier already, but we'd like to do this in person. I assure you that whatever you say about Trevor Vakerby won't matter anymore, as in, how can he affect you when he's dead? His son, George, isn't in any way like his father, so you don't need to worry about him either. Likewise, with his daughter, Rachel. Now, is there anything you can tell me about Trevor that might explain why someone killed him?"

Various answers came: Because he's a wanker; he's a pig; he's a bully who probably pissed the wrong person off—all things she'd worked out for herself prior to now.

"So nothing concrete? No one who needs a finger pointed at them?"

Head shakes.

It had been pointless coming.

"What about Elizabeth Mackenzie? Do you know of anyone who has a problem with her, apart from the Polish men she'd had an encounter with?"

"What are you saying?" a man asked. "Has something happened to her an' all?"

"I'm afraid Elizabeth was murdered earlier today." She waited for the shitstorm.

The workers exploded in a flurry of questions, and Andy took over, seeing as they'd all looked to him for answers. Helena could have been offended, but she wasn't. Mr Sanbrook raised his eyebrows at her. She walked over to him.

"Is it the same person doing this?" Sanbrook puffed out a breath.

"We strongly suspect it is. She was killed in the same manner, albeit with one difference."

"Bloody hell. I only knew her for a month while she worked out her notice, but she was lovely."

"We have an idea why she was murdered, and the reason doesn't warrant her death. It's incredibly sad." She thought about her brief chat with Zach when he'd arrived at the scene—they'd made plans to go out for a meal once this was over. He always understood that she couldn't switch off during a case and it was useless them getting together when her mind was elsewhere. "Do you have any Polish companies on your books?"

"No. Trevor did, though. Elizabeth told me all about a certain incident." He went on to explain what Helena already knew.

"Yes, we heard about that as well. Hopefully, we'll track them down." Though she doubted it. With the company name coming up false, there wasn't much chance of them being found.

Andy came over. "We're finished here."

"Okay." She turned to Mr Sanbrook. "Thanks for letting us interrupt your day. We didn't even get to drink the coffee."

"Don't you worry."

"One more thing." Helena glanced out of the window to check how much of the cliff top could be seen from here. Enough—the Portakabin was on a rise. She addressed the whole room. "Did anyone see a man and a woman having a picnic out there today?"

The men who'd been called in shook their heads, as did Cheryl, but Sanbrook nodded.

"I was walking my dog earlier. Couldn't tell you what time, though."

"Did you get a good look at them?"

"Not really. I was a fair way from them, but they were by the rock outcrop. I got closer, and they walked off and got in a light-coloured car and drove away."

"Who was driving?"

"The woman."

"Do you have any CCTV?"

"Yes, but it's on the blink."

What a surprise. "Thanks."

He showed them out after shaking hands.

Helena got in the car, and with Andy buckled in beside her, she drove away. "Right, what did you make of that lot then?"

"They're just your average blokes."

"Sanbrook seeing a man and woman is a bit of a bugger." She sighed. "It was probably George and Rachel."

"That's just part of the alibi, though, if it was them. George still left on his own for a while and took Levington's car. And Sanbrook didn't know the time. They could have been there before or after the murder for all we know."

"True. And what about his panic attack?"

"Like Steve said, it was on the way before we arrived."

She hmmed. "Would a row with your sister bring one on?"

"Depends. They've had a rough upbringing, don't forget. And some people are prone to them. Their minds are wired differently, and they overthink things, which sets off anxiety."

"Okay. Lunch, albeit a bloody late one, then back to the station to talk to the hedgehogs."

"Will this day ever end?"

"Nope, because after that, we're going back to Elizabeth's to chat with Tom. His team might have found something important."

"Late-night takeaway for dinner then."

"So long as it's a healthy one."

"Spoilsport."

She drew into the station car park. Inside reception, Louise was on the civvy side of the desk, talking to a man and woman along with five kids. It had to be the Spikes. Helena studied the children. The three lads actually had brown spiky hair, and she smiled at the thought of Darwin writing and coming up with his little name for them. Poor boy. The girls looked like something out of a reality show starring children wearing every single top-name brand at once. Their hair was salon straight, silver and dark-grey ombre, and the makeup... Little dolls, the pair of them, women before their time.

"Hi, I'm DI Helena Stratton." She held her hand out to who she assumed was the mother and shook. Then she did the same with the father. "Which parents are you?"

"These four are ours," Mr Spike said. "Mark's my brother's son. We thought we may as well bring him."

"That's fine. It's just an informal chat. And you both are?"

"Derek," Mr Spike said. "And this is Alison."

"Lovely. Okay, this is DS Andy Mald, my partner. We'll all go into the soft interview room for this. It's bigger and more comfortable, like a living room." She leant closer and said quietly, "Puts the kids at ease."

Derek glanced over his shoulder at the children, then at Helena. "This is about bullying, yes?"

Helena nodded.

"Are the kids involved?"

"We don't know, but we'd like to talk to them anyway. They may know who *is* involved. There will be some distressing news, so please be ready in case they become upset."

So he didn't question her about that, she led the way to Soft Interview One. She set the camera to record then explained that they weren't here under caution or anything like that, and the camera was on so they could watch the interview later and take notes.

Everyone sat, the girls either side of their mother on one sofa, two boys by Derek on another, and the eldest lad, Mark, by himself in a comfy chair. Helena and Andy chose the two-seater sofa that faced everyone else so they could clock their facial expressions, mannerisms, and body language.

"Okay, first, I need to ask you if you've ever bullied Darwin Gringley." She expected denials.

Andy held his pen over his notebook.

"It's only ribbing," Mark said. "You know, just jokes."

"Can you give me an example?" she asked.

"Bumping into him, having a laugh at the shit—the stuff he comes out with."

Derek glared at Mark, clearly embarrassed by his language. She imagined he'd be ashamed if his children were involved in harassing Darwin. Alison's cheeks flamed red, as did her daughters'.

"So nothing *major* then?" She'd used that word on purpose. She felt 'just jokes' *was* major if done often enough and with malice, but she had to get Mark on side.

"Nah, just messing about."

The other children remained silent.

"Were you aware that these 'jokes' had a detrimental effect on Darwin? His life has been pretty uncomfortable."

Mark shrugged. "Not our fault he took offence, is it."

"Did you all go to primary with him as well?"

Nods from the three younger siblings.

"Did you mess with him there, too?"

Silence.

"So a good few years then. Can you imagine being got at for that length of time every day when you went to school?" Her blood was threatening to boil at the fact no one apart from the parents seemed to be appalled by this.

"What do you all have to say?" Derek said. "We didn't bring you up to pick on anyone, and your dad didn't either, Mark. What did you hope to get out of this?"

"But he's so thick, though." Mark. "Comes out with a right load of crap. You can't help but laugh at him."

Helena needed to regain control. "Did any of you wish Darwin any harm?"

Mark shrugged. "I've thought about him tripping over and busting his nose or something like that. Well funny. Nothing massive, though."

"Do you know of anyone else who would want to cause him harm?" She stared at the children in turn.

The girls shied away, the younger boys hung their heads, but Mark maintained eye contact.

He's the mole, and they're afraid of him.

"Nope," Mark said.

"Well, someone wanted to hurt him." She nodded at Derek to tell him this was it, the distressing news. "I'm sorry to have to inform you that Darwin was murdered on his way home from school yesterday."

The girls screamed.

The information shook Mark. He shot forward to the edge of his seat, his face pale. "It wasn't us.

Fuck no, we had nothing to do with that. We were playing football on the field, loads of people saw us. We were there until six when Queensley told us to go home."

That was easily checked—if Queensley could even identify who they were.

The girls were crying now, and their brothers, still with their heads down, glanced at each other across their father, one of them shaking his head as if to tell the other to keep his mouth shut.

He didn't.

"I saw someone," he said. "Friday. Straight after school when Darwin climbed over the fence to go into the woods. We were going to follow him, see, but decided not to because of the person."

Helena mirrored Mark, moving to the edge of the sofa. "Did you get a good look at them?"

"No, it was just a shape of someone, and they went after Darwin. I think they were holding something. Like a baseball bat. And...and something else that they put down by a tree."

"Look at the police lady when you're speaking to her, Jacob," Derek ordered, giving him a nudge with his elbow. "Don't be rude."

Jacob raised his head. "They weren't very tall, so could have been a year eleven or something."

"Could you tell if it was a man or a woman?" *Please give us something.*

"No, just someone. I'm sorry. It was a quick glimpse." His eyes filled, and his bottom lip wobbled.

"Thank you, that's been extremely helpful."

"I feel so bad," he said. "If we hadn't bullied him, he wouldn't have walked home through the woods. It's all our fault."

"No, it's the murderer's fault," Helena said, "but I won't deny that all your actions helped us come to this point. You must remember cause and effect. Every action has a consequence, even months or years down the line, like in this case." She wanted to add that all Darwin wanted was to be their friend, but that would be heaping too much guilt on young shoulders, and she was sure Derek would ensure they knew the error of their ways before this day was out.

"This is just awful," Alison said. "I am so sorry the children behaved this way."

Tell that to Mother Owl. Helena's eyes prickled with tears. "The best thing you kids can do now is think before you speak and act. Never, ever bully anyone again. Please wait outside while we speak to the adults."

The girls clung to their mother.

Helena relented. "Derek, it's fine if only you stay. Alison can look after the children in reception." She waited until they'd left. "Derek, I have to warn you that the CPS may well feel the five kids are culpable in some way. I doubt it, but I wanted you aware. I have to include this in my report, and there's nothing I can do if they feel they want to poke into the bullying further."

Derek staggered and leant on the wall. "My God. I swear I had no idea my children were capable of continued bullying—or any bullying. How far did it go?"

"We're not completely sure because Darwin refused to give up the names of his tormentors. We have read some writing he did, though, and we know at one point he was shoved against a corridor wall and everyone laughed at him."

"Bloody disgusting. I'll be having a word—a strong one—once we get home. I'll let Mark's father know, but this hasn't been a surprise regarding him. I've caught him bothering my kids over the years, and there's always the excuse that he's upset because he saw his mother die. She got knocked over by a hit-and-run. But that was years ago, and that kind of behaviour from him isn't on, no matter what he's going through." He took a deep breath. "If I get my kids to talk and it turns out Mark was the ringleader, will that make a difference if the CPS…? Fucking hell. This is a lot to take in. I can't abide bullying."

"It may not even come to that, I was just giving you fair warning." She patted him on the arm. "I'll let you know if anything is being done about the children. Try not to worry in the meantime."

"How can I not?"

She said goodbye, and he left.

Helena and Andy waited for five minutes, taking a break to think and go through what had been said.

"Nasty little mole," Andy muttered.

Helena's sentiments exactly.

CHAPTER NINETEEN

In the incident room, Helena and Andy walked in on Olivia and Phil watching a recording of the press conference, which Superintendent Yakoshi handled expertly, asking for any information regarding the three victims. On the phone earlier, he'd mentioned running the hotline and staff who'd answer any calls so Helena and her team could concentrate on the case.

"Are the murders linked?" a spotty reporter asked.

"We assume so at this point," Yakoshi said.

"What links Trevor Vakerby to the lad?" another wanted to know. "Elizabeth Mackenzie's tie to Trevor is obvious, but a child?"

"We're looking into everything." Yakoshi nodded. "It's our top priority."

"I should hope so!" A woman held up her recording device. "We were promised no one else would get killed in those woods, yet here we are, another young boy dead in that very place."

"We can't ever promise anything like that." Yakoshi's face remained blank. "We said we would *do our best* to see that no one else lost their life there."

"Going to blame the cuts, are you?" she bleated out. "Not enough coppers on patrol? Run off your feet?"

"Next *pertinent* question?" Yakoshi looked around.

He answered three more and called an end to the discussion once it became obvious the reporters thought it was a free-for-all in slagging off the police.

Olivia closed the browser. "Glad we're not dealing with those phone calls. They always draw out the cranks."

"They do indeed." Helena gave the whiteboard a brief check to see what had been added. "So Jeff's car wasn't found on CCTV at all?"

"No," Phil said, "and neither were George's or Rachel's—I checked them anyway to rule them out. Rachel and George were seen entering The Sandwich Crust, though. Both walked into shot separately, so I assumed they hadn't arrived together."

"The Crust has internal CCTV," Olivia said. "I've spoken to the manager, and she's sorting the footage now, although it's a camera mainly concentrated on the till because they've had someone pilfering, so only the torsos of customers are seen."

"We need to go back to Elizabeth's," Andy said. "Fancy nipping into The Crust first, seeing as we never did get any lunch…"

"Yep, let's do that." Helena rubbed her griping stomach. "Phil, I suppose vehicles going towards Elizabeth's got cut off at a certain point because of where she lives."

"It could be any number of cars," he said. "Well, one hundred and seventeen light-coloured ones, two hundred and five in other shades. The cameras stop just outside the town centre. Grainy images, so the techs will need to look at all the number plates and enhance them. Could take a while."

Helena frowned. "If they went to lunch using Jeff's car…was it not parked outside The Crust?"

Phil shook his head. "The camera for that row of shops is opposite, mounted on the bus stop pole, and the width of the shot covers three businesses out of seven. They could have left the car a way along and walked to buy their lunch, but what's bugging me is them not turning up together. They entered about three minutes apart, coming from the left."

"Maybe she was buying a parking ticket," Andy said.

"Could have done." Phil shrugged. "It's still niggling me, though."

"Well, let me know when the light bulb has gone on," Helena said. "Andy, we need to go."

It didn't take long to get to the sandwich place, and Helena drove up the street then back again so they could check out where Jeff's car may have been parked. There wasn't a meter; all cars could stay for free for up to one hour. She squeezed hers between a Kia and a Skoda, then stood at the bus stop, looking left, the direction George and Rachel had come from.

She had a thought and took her phone out, ringing Phil. "What were they wearing when they went into The Crust?"

"Rachel had dark leggings and a long-sleeved T-shirt, also dark. George was in tracksuit bottoms, possibly grey, and a white short-sleeved T-shirt."

"Thanks." She slid her phone into her pocket. "Come on, Andy. Let's see what we can get out of the manager in there." She crossed the street and entered The Crust, a bustling place, the scent of cinnamon prevalent. At the counter, she asked to see the manager.

"That's me," the brunette said.

Helena showed her ID and introduced them. "We're here about the CCTV."

"Ah, okay. I've found the people the policeman asked me for. Come with me." She pulled a laptop out from under the counter and took them to a staffroom. After setting it up, she pressed PLAY on a section of footage she'd previously paused. "You can't see their faces, I'm afraid, but the clothing's right, and I remember them because of the odd sandwiches."

"What do you mean, odd?"

"The woman had egg, fried onions, and gherkins, and the man had Chinese chicken, jalapeños, and um, jam."

"Pardon?"

"I know. Gross. They had a Coke each and went to sit on the big sofa at the back to drink it. Took the sandwiches out with them, though. The lady said she was hot, something like that. Or maybe that it was hot out, I can't remember exactly. Oh, and they were going on a picnic."

"Thanks." Helena checked the time on the footage then started the section again so Andy could write down George's and Rachel's arrivals. "You see he's first, then she joins him. He takes the sandwich packets, she takes the Cokes." She smiled at the manager. "Make sure you save this footage and don't delete it—we may need the original for a case. Can you send me a copy of this section?" She handed her a card. "My email address is on there."

"Yes, no problem."

Helena and Andy went back out the front and ordered a sandwich each; they'd eat them on the way to Elizabeth's.

"Jam in a savoury sandwich, though," Andy said on the way to her car.

"I know. Bloody weird." She thought of the siblings. Had they just had an innocent picnic? Or was there more to this?

Raised voices caught her attention, and she turned around, trying to work out where they were coming from. No one was arguing, just going about their business, but an "Oi, you fucking tosser!" had her swivelling to face an alley.

"Down here." She shoved the sandwiches at Andy and jogged along it, coming out into a residential street.

Two people stood outside a house, shouting the odds about a Honda Civic parked in front of someone's drive.

Helena took her ID out and approached, holding it up. "What's the problem?"

"This dickhead's let his mate leave his car here, and I can't get mine out," one fella said, his cheeks red, long hair greasy.

"I told you, it's nothing to do with me." The other one raised his hands as if that proved his innocence.

Andy strode over and gave Helena the sandwiches back. "Hold up with the gobbing off for a minute. I'll ring this car in, all right? We'll locate the driver." He jabbed at his screen and passed on the details to whoever had answered the call. A pause, then, "Excuse me? Right. Cheers." He stared at Helena and tilted his head for her to step back out of earshot.

"What's up?" she whispered.

"This explains why they turned up to The Crust separately. That car. It's George's."

Andy knocked on George's front door. Helena spotted the closed curtains in the living room. Maybe George was having that rest he'd mentioned earlier.

Steve answered, shaking his head. "Are you going to be leaving him alone any time soon? He's asleep. That attack took a lot out of him."

"We just have a couple of questions." Helena stepped forward to let him know they were coming in whether he stood there or not.

Steve sighed and walked into the living room. Helena and Andy went in there, too. George was asleep on the sofa, his cheeks ruddy, his clothing different to that in the footage.

"Are you aware he has dodgy blood pressure and a dicky heart?" Steve asked. "All this hassle is making it ten times worse."

"Can you wake him up, please?" Helena tapped her foot.

Steve did as she'd asked, and George sat up, clearly disorientated.

"George, why is your car parked in the street behind The Sandwich Crust?" Helena folded her arms.

He blinked. "Um...um, because I left it there?"

"Why?"

"I met Rachel at The Crust. She drove in Jeff's car."

"So why did you just leave it there?"

"We used Jeff's to go to the cliff, then after our row, I wasn't thinking straight and forgot about mine."

"I wondered why it wasn't parked outside here," Steve said.

"Why didn't you drive your own car to the cliff?" Helena asked.

George rubbed his temples. "I don't know. We must have decided to go in Jeff's. I-I can't remember."

"Well, you need to get down there and pick it up, mate," Andy said. "It's blocking someone's driveway. He needs to get to work, and he's late because of you."

"Oh God..." George pushed off the sofa and patted his pockets. "My car keys..."

"Aren't they in the wall box in the hallway?" Steve went out there to have a look. "Nope, only the house ones there."

"I must have left them in my trackie bottoms." George appeared panicked.

"Where are they?" Steve asked.

"In...in the washing machine."

"Changed your clothes today then?" Andy said, eyebrows moving upwards.

"Yes. I had a nosebleed after Rachel thumped me. I got blood on them."

Steve came back in. "He has nosebleeds because of his *heart* issues." He stared at them as if to tell them to back off. "The keys aren't there, George. Where are the spares?"

"In the kitchen drawer with the insurance documents." George shuffled out and stood by the front door, putting on his trainers with jerky movements. "Can you take me, Steve?"

"Yes." Steve turned to Helena and Andy. "Once your guests have left."

"Make sure you're quick," Helena said on her way out. "The house owner isn't a happy chap." She got in the car, knowing something was way off here but unable to work out what. It could be how George had said. She might be suspecting something that wasn't there. Hoping, more like, that this case was coming to an end.

Andy plonked his arse in the passenger seat. "Iffy or what."

"Glad you said that. It'll become clear soon enough. Now, we're going to eat our sandwiches before the heat spoils them."

"They're more or less our dinner." He clicked his seat belt in place.

Helena opened her package and placed it on her lap. "Like you said, late-night takeaway in our future."

She drove them to Elizabeth's, munching along the way, and pulled up behind Zach's car. The SOCO van's back doors were open, so they filched some protectives and got dressed. Log signed at the front door, PC Edwards giving them a grim nod, they entered the property.

"Ah, you're just in time." Tom was on his hands and knees between the body and the cooker. "I've rung in to check this, and Elizabeth doesn't own a car anymore, so why are there keys for one here?"

Helena's stomach lurched. "Does it have the make on the fob?"

Tom nodded. "Honda."

"Fucking hell," Andy said.

"That means something to you then?" Tom bagged the keys.

"Just a bit." Helena's heartrate went up. "We have to go. Explain later."

She shot out of the house, scribbled on the log and, with Andy on her heels, they legged it down the path and flung themselves into the car. Andy took his gloves and booties off as she drove towards the street behind The Crust, her blue lights on.

"This is a turn up," she said. "Is it a stretch to think they're George's keys? Loads of people own Hondas."

"It'd be a sodding shame if they're not." Andy unzipped his suit.

"No wonder he was a bit rattled when he couldn't find his." She clenched her teeth.

"Do you think that panic attack was faked so we didn't think he'd have anything to do with this?"

"Who knows." She zoomed up the street, frowning at an ambulance blocking the way. "What the hell's happened here? Reckon those blokes had a fight?" She came to a stop, undid her seat belt, then rushed towards the commotion ahead.

Steve was on his knees on the path by two paramedics working on someone, their backs to her. The greasy-haired man who'd been blocked in stood by the Civic, arms folded, staring down at the person Helena couldn't see, but she knew who it was. It couldn't be anyone else with those trainers she'd seen so recently. She neared, her body going cold at the unmistakeable sound of a defibrillator going off.

"Don't die on me, George," Steve said. "Don't you bloody die." He caught sight of Helena and got up, rushing towards her, face twisted with rage. "You! This is your fault. George has had a heart attack from the stress of having to come here and collect his bloody car." He shoved her in the chest with both hands.

She staggered backwards, Andy catching her elbow so she didn't go down on her arse.

"Back the hell off," Andy shouted, "before I have you done for assaulting a police officer."

Steve took a few steps in reverse, fists clenched. "If they can't get his heart going again, I'll fucking sue you." He pointed at Helena. "And you." A glare for Andy. "What's the problem with his car being here apart from it blocking the drive? Why did *detectives* need to come and speak to him about it? Why not uniforms?"

Shaken, Helena steadied her breathing. "Please come over here so we can talk privately."

Steve eyed her warily but did as she'd requested.

The defib went off again.

"Oh God…" Steve's eyes filled.

"Trevor's secretary was found dead today," Helena said, her voice gentle. "A set of keys was discovered at her property, near her body. She doesn't own a car. They're for a Honda."

Steve's mouth opened and closed. "No. No, it wasn't him. It can't be him. He went out to lunch with his sister."

Defib.

He turned and raced towards George. "Come on. Beat, you bastard."

Helena imagined Steve spoke to the heart, not George. The paramedics eased back, one packing the defib away, and Steve crumpled to the pavement. The greasy-haired man bowed his head.

"Fuck," Helena whispered.

"Looks like George is gone." Andy put his arm around her.

"What a bloody nightmare this is. Sort Steve while I speak to that bloke." She approached Greasy. "What happened here?"

"He started going all strange," he said.

She stepped closer. "Strange?"

"Yeah. Shouting about leaving his car while he had a picnic and that it wasn't his fault his sister drove him home from the cliff."

"What's your name, sir?"

"Richard Unkley."

"Okay, Richard. When exactly did he go strange?"

"I'd told him he shouldn't have left it here if he knew he was going on a picnic—I mean, come on, who blocks a driveway? I said it was a nasty thing to do, and that's when he clutched his chest. He said, 'Nasty is nothing to do with me. I'm not getting the blame for that.' And I thought: Who else parked it? *You* did, so you *are* to blame. I said, 'You know what, mate, just piss off in your car and don't come back.'" He shook his head. "I'm sick of people using this street when there's ample parking in front of the shops. Hacked off with my neighbour an' all, that bloke who was here before. He's always letting his mates stop in front of my house. He buggered off as soon as you left. Down the alley to the shops."

"What happened then?"

"The Honda fella, he collapsed, didn't he, all dramatic like, and to be honest, I thought he was faking it until his mate started ranting about heart issues. I rang an ambulance, and his friend was guffing on about him not breathing. It was all a bit manic, but the ambulance was here so fast. Must have been in the area."

"And then?"

"They worked on him, and you turned up."

"I'll send an officer round to take a proper statement," she said. "Will you be going to work?"

"Not likely after this. It's shit me up, to be fair."

A sheet had been placed over George, who was now on a stretcher being lifted into the ambulance. Several neighbours had come out to gawk, and Steve sat on a wall, hunched over, crying. Andy stood nearby, looking like he didn't know what to do.

"Best you go inside then," she told Richard. "Sorry you had to witness a death."

"Me, too." He walked off up his drive and into the house.

Helena went to the back of the ambulance and produced her ID.

"Gathered you were a copper in that get-up," one paramedic said, eyeing her protectives. "Stating the obvious, but he's deceased."

"Thanks for the confirmation. I know his next of kin. I'll visit her now." She left them to do their job and went over to Steve. "I'm sorry for your loss."

"You fucking will be." He sat upright and fixed her with a mean stare.

"George is a suspect in his father's murder and those of Darwin Gringley and Elizabeth Mackenzie whether you believe it or not. Suing me won't make that any different. Do you need me to contact anyone to drive you home?"

"No. You know damn well I brought George here." He swiped at tears falling down his cheeks.

"What I meant was, you're in a state, grieving. It'll be better if you don't drive."

He laughed, throwing his head back, a touch of hysteria being added to the mix. "So, *I* can go home with someone else when I've blocked a driveway, but George couldn't? What a joke you are."

She thought of Mark the Mole and 'just jokes'. Anger surged. "If you think I'm a joke for making sure I find the person responsible for killing three people, one of them a *child*, then so be it, but I'd rather be a joke than refuse to see the truth when it's right in front of me."

She stalked to her car, not caring how Steve got home now. He was hurting, needed someone to blame, but when the truth hit him—and it would, hard—she'd bet his attitude changed then.

Finding out you'd been in a relationship with a killer tended to do that.
And don't I bloody know it.

CHAPTER TWENTY

Rachel sat in the woods behind the school, waiting for the fox. She hadn't long married Jeff and should be emotionally secure, but good things like that didn't happen to her. There she was, nervous of what the future held. He'd walked in that evening and asked her what time she'd left *work, what time she'd got home, what she'd done since, and it reminded her of that bastard. She'd felt crowded, wedged into a corner, and had blurted that she needed to go to the library to reserve a book, one she'd use in her class, just so she could get away from him.*

She'd lied. Again. Because she was in the woods, and wasn't her whole self a lie, with Nasty inside her, all the secrets floating about in her head? Wasn't she a bad person?

The ground, damp beneath her bum, would mean she'd have to lie some more if Jeff saw the state of her trousers. Oh, I tripped over and landed in a mud patch. *He'd believe that.*

He was the dad she'd never had, but the caring kind, and she'd thought that was what she'd wanted. Except Jeff asked too many questions, and no matter how much Nice told her it was from him wanting her to be happy, Nasty reminded her it wasn't. It was to control, just like her father.

The crow had followed her. At least that was what she told herself anyway—the creature was her one true friend, a companion from old, but in reality, it had probably been several over the years. Nasty was glad to point that out. It perched on a branch, its beady eyes bigger than usual, its feathers lighter.

She stared at it, frowning, and could have sworn it wasn't a crow at all but an owl, but that was silly, her childish imagination running riot, like that kid, Darwin.

A rustle came from her left, and she slowly turned her head so as not to spook the fox. But the russet animal wasn't there. A person trudged past, a man shape, with a head torch on and a bag slung over his back. What was he doing? He'd stopped at a tree and was fiddling about with it, then he removed a massive piece of bark. A light came on inside the tree, and it took her a moment to believe it was really happening. He stepped in.

Rachel got up and tiptoed along the centre track, hiding behind a trunk so she could watch. Someone else was inside the tree, held up like Jesus on the cross, asleep, and the man was staring into their face.

She shrugged—it was none of her business, although a welcome distraction from her raging thoughts about Jeff—and Nice had the idea that the man had the same demons as Nasty. Whoever was strung up in that tree deserved to be there. They'd probably been horrible, so he'd had no choice but to teach them a lesson.

Would he kill them like she'd killed her brothers? Mum and Nan?

Who cares, *Nasty said*. Go back and wait for the fox.

Rachel crept away, back to her previous spot. She sat on a fallen log, waiting, waiting, and by the time the fox appeared, an hour had gone past. It glared at her, as always, and instead of being comforted, she grew angry. How dare it leave her sitting here when she needed its calming presence.

She reached down and picked up a large rock, using both hands, raising it carefully so as not to spook the creature. Everyone in life let her down in one way or another, her family, Jeff, her work colleagues, even the crow that was now an owl, and this stupid furry beast here, leaving it too late to come and see her, too busy with its foxy business.

She launched the weapon, hard, and went into a frenzy, obliterating her one-time friend.

It was dead, so very dead.

"That'll teach you."

She walked off, stopping short because the man was on his way back, the cone of his headlamp light concentrated ahead. She stood there until he'd disappeared into the darkness, then ran over to the fat tree and stared at padlocks on the trunk.

"Help me!" It was faint, that call. Reedy, childlike.

"No," she said. "No, I won't help you at all. No one helped me."

Dinner had been a takeaway, a Chinese Jeff had ordered to be delivered. Rachel had wanted him to go out and collect it so she could get a bit of space to speak to Nasty, but he'd claimed he was worried about her and she shouldn't be left alone at such a terrible time.

A terrible time? It was bloody glorious.

His concern for her would have been welcome once, but lately, since Nasty had killed her father, it had become stifling. He needed to back the hell off before she went for him with a carving knife or got her trusty cleaver out and sliced his face in half, right down the middle. Or she could suffocate him while he slept, drugged up from her sleeping tablets.

He'd gone up for a bath, so she sat at the table in the blessed peace and went through tonight's plan. George was meeting her at The Watcher's house, then she'd talk him through the murder as they went along. Nasty had her script all worked out, the things she'd say to The Watcher, the way she'd make him feel with her poetry, observing the fear bleed into his features as her brother did his part in paying back what he owed her.

"It's going to be so beautiful," she whispered, Nasty's voice drenching the words. "It'll be over soon, once George is taken care of."

And Jeff.

Rachel ignored that.

The sound of water cascading down the external pipe meant Jeff had pulled the plug. Fucking hell, why didn't he ever have a long soak? She sighed and cleared the table, loading the dishwasher, thinking about what was to come. She'd slip Jeff another pill later, once again ensuring he was none the wiser as to whether she was next to him in bed.

Had the police spotted George's blood on Elizabeth's worktop yet or had they assumed it was the dead woman's? Was it in one of those tubes they used, on its way to a lab to be checked? Jeff had told her earlier he was surprised Helena hadn't asked them all for a DNA sample yet—he said she might think it was one of them who'd been murdering.

"All family members are suspects," he'd said. "So that includes me. Don't worry, though, it's standard procedure."

There he was, bringing work home again, Nasty said. *Ignoring the rules.*

Nasty hated Jeff enough to get him framed for it, but from the start, Nice had insisted he shouldn't be involved. He'd been nothing but good to her their whole relationship, although Nasty would dispute that. She disputed everything positive, hating seeing the bright side, refusing to search for the pot of gold at the end of the rainbow.

She sucked all the happy right out of Rachel.

That horrible noise of a foot slipping on the bottom of an empty wet bath got right on her nellies, and she gritted her teeth, slinging a Finish tablet in the dishwasher. She pressed the ON button and gathered the Chinese cartons, going out into the balmy evening to fling them in the wheelie bin.

It was good to be in her sanctuary, and she wandered down the wooden walkway, smoothing her hands along the banister rails until she came to a stop at her painted window. She sensed someone staring at her and glanced back at the house. Jeff wasn't there, so she cast her gaze about.

The Watcher was at his window down the way—she could just make him out. Was he staring at her old bedroom window, remembering what he'd seen all those years ago? Did he enjoy playing it in his head over and over again, the fucking didn't-call-the-police pervert? Anger burned a path in her veins, her face heating, and she turned to the window on the fence, clawing at the air to get inside.

She stood in the woods, a return visit to see the battered fox, pleased at how mites and other bugs had infiltrated its body. Maggots infested the gashes, even wriggling about on the crepe-like tongue, and flies buzzed, readying themselves to land and feed on the dried-out flesh.

She was a fly, devouring everyone in her path who dared to upset her. The fox was a representation of her bigger prey and what happened if you pissed her off. You got killed, blood all over you, so watch the fuck out.

Knocking rattled. Insistent. Bugging.

She was wrenched out of the woods.

She spun. Jeff stood at the back door, looking at her through the glass, so close to it his breath misted part of the pane. She marched over and smiled through the irritation—*There he is, keeping tabs on you again*—and went to go inside, but he came out, standing beside her.

Crowding her like he'd done earlier.

"What are you doing out here?" he asked.

Questions, so many questions. Can't I just come out for a breather? To think? To be by myself? Do I have to explain every little thing? Why have you turned into my father? Why do I have to account for my movements? Who said a husband needed to know the ins and outs of the cat's arsehole?

"Putting the rubbish in the bin." Thank God Nice had answered. She didn't need Nasty coming out of her mouth. "Let's go inside. There's midges everywhere." She scratched her arms to make her point. *Get out of my bloody way, you loitering moron.*

He followed her into the kitchen, then the living room, right behind her. She swivelled, side-stepping him, and walked to the loo in the hallway. He was there, too, opening the door for her, and she fought back a screech: *Leave me alone!*

"Jeff, what are you doing following me?" She stood with her hand on the doorframe, eyes closed.

"You seem upset."

"I'll be fine—if you don't mollycoddle me." Had that sounded okay? Was it a bit too sharp? "I'm struggling with everything and need to be alone."

He usually understood that, gave her space, but this time he remained, his breath hot on her neck. "I just... I don't know what to do to make this all better."

"It won't get better, it'll always be there, but you can help by backing off."

"You don't seem yourself, Rach."

"Jeff, I'm warning you..." Nasty had popped out. *Shit.*

"Okay, okay."

At last, he left her, and she went in and closed the door. Leant against it.

He'll definitely have to go, too, Nasty said. *We can't have this. He's seriously naffing me off. How can we live like this? Why did you marry someone just like Dad?*

Rachel got ready to reply, but the doorbell went. If that was George, she'd lump him one, blacken his other eye.

Footsteps. Jeff coming to the door. The jangle of the keys, the whine of the handle going down.

"Ah, it's you. Anything new?" Jeff asked, hope in his tone.

"Best if we come in."

It was Helena. What did she want *now*? More footsteps. The front door closing. All of them going through to the kitchen. Rachel stayed put, looking into the square mirror above the little sink. She shoved herself inside and killed the fox again to get rid of some rage, the crow or owl watching her every move. She sensed it was judging her, finding her wanting, so she scrabbled in the undergrowth for a bow and arrow and shot the bastard through the breast. Calmer, satisfied, she retreated from her special place and walked down the hallway.

"God, she's only just got on better terms with him," Jeff said. "This is awful."

What was going on?

She entered the kitchen, a big smile hiding her curiosity and Nasty's madness that lurked, begging to be set free on the lot of them if only she had her spiked bat to hand. Jeff stood at the back door, fingers ruffling his hair. Helena and Andy were by the chest freezer, near the precious hearts. Nasty almost shouted at them to get away from it, get out of the house and not come back or she'd do them some serious damage.

"Oh, hello." Rachel went to the sink, leaning her backside on the cupboard beneath, Nasty twittering on about skating close to the wind.

"Sit down, Rach," Jeff said, and it was an order, him forcing his will on her.

Nasty howled inside her head, same as the fox had when she'd killed it. "I'll stand, thank you."

"Rachel, we're here with bad news, I'm afraid," Helena said.

"So you haven't found the killer?" Rachel twisted her fingers.

"We're not sure at present."

What does that mean, you silly cow? "I don't understand…"

"We were following a lead involving George, and I'm sorry to say he had a heart attack. He died at the scene."

Oh, for fuck's sake. Can this get any worse? I wanted him to kill The Watcher. Now he's got away with not having to do anything to prove he's sorry.

"Pardon?" Rachel blinked away tears of fury. God, she needed to go through a square and into the woods—right this second. She turned and faced the window, seeking out the painted one on the fence, getting ready to run into it.

"He's been taken to the hospital," Helena said. "You can go and view his body tomorrow."

View the body? Mutilate it more like. Hack it with her cleaver until it resembled mush, until all her angst fucked off.

"I…I don't know what to say," she said. "It's all too much. So many things happening. When will it all end? And what did you mean about not being sure at present? Was that about the killer?"

Helena looked at Andy. He shrugged.

"What aren't you telling me?" Rachel held back from diving into her square, again wishing they'd stop…standing…by her…hearts.

"We're following George's movements when he left you on the cliff." Helena glanced at Jeff.

"It might be him, Rach," Jeff said. "His car was parked in the street behind the sandwich place, but his keys...his keys were at Elizabeth Mackenzie's."

Rachel focused on the four different skies in her fence square. This was what she wanted, George in the shit, but not this evening, not when he still had to sort The Watcher. What was she meant to do now? Kill again and frame Jeff? Create a scenario where it looked like the two men in her life had made a pact to get rid of everyone who'd hurt her?

Not a bad idea, Nasty said. *Then Jeff can go to prison instead of being dead. Although, wouldn't it be nice to fake his suicide like you did with Mum?*

"How did the keys get there?" She'd sounded so innocent, so good at lying.

"He may have paid her a visit in Jeff's car, after you punched him." Helena.

"Then afterwards, he came to collect you as if nothing had happened." Jeff.

"We'll have to take your car, sir," Helena said.

"Of course, whatever you need."

"Do you have a key to George's by any chance?"

"No."

Nasty waited for Jeff to come over to her, to annoy her by getting in her face, but he must have thought of what she'd said by the loo because he stayed where he was. Well, at least he'd listened, hadn't overruled her needs. She was still annoyed, though. Still wanted him to cosset her.

Contrary.

She jumped into the square and busied herself in the forest while they chatted. Nasty couldn't be doing with listening to them, instead moaning how George dying had fucked everything up. Nice fretted about any of her DNA being left at Elizabeth's, even though Nasty had cleaned up.

What a jumble it was in her head.

She stared at the dead fox and screamed.

CHAPTER TWENTY-ONE

The chief's vehicle had been picked up for forensics to go over it. Helena and Andy sat in the car and discussed the latest events while waiting for a fresh SOCO team to arrive—a warrant had been obtained to search George's house. Even though he was dead, it was still best to play it by the book, seeing as they were going with the angle that he had killed Elizabeth Mackenzie and most likely had done the same to his father and Darwin Gringley. What they couldn't figure out was the link between the adults and the child.

"Beats me," Andy said.

"I wonder if they'll find the missing hearts in George's place." She clocked a car coming their way. "Looks like that's Steve. Probably went to the hospital after the ambulance. I think we'll stay in here, out of his way. I don't fancy him going for me twice in one day."

"He'll calm down once he realises it wasn't our fault. We're just doing our jobs."

"Might not matter to him."

The car went past, and she looked in the rearview mirror. Steve parked, got out, stood in front of George's, then rushed into his own house, head down.

Poor sod.

Her phone alert chimed, and she accessed the message.

Olivia: WILLIAM GRINGLEY HAS ARRIVED. HE PHONED TO LET ME KNOW AS HE WANTS TO HAVE A CHAT. I TOLD HIM TO GO AND VISIT ISLA FIRST AND COME TO THE STATION ABOUT SEVEN.

Helena: THAT'S FINE. WE'RE WAITING FOR SOCO. NEED TO CHECK GEORGE'S PLACE.

Olivia: HOPEFULLY THERE'LL BE EVIDENCE IN THERE AND THIS CAN ALL BE PUT TO BED.

Helena: YEP. DID ANYTHING REGARDING ELIZABETH COME UP?

Olivia: SHE HAS NO CHILDREN, NO NEXT OF KIN, WHICH IS BLOODY SAD. ALL HER FRIENDS I SPOKE TO—FOUND THEM ON FACEBOOK—SAID SHE WOULDN'T HURT A FLY.

Helena: OKAY, KEEP PLODDING ON.

She told Andy what was said. "So my take on it is that it was the diaries and whatever else she knew about Trevor that got her involved in this. The killer didn't want her opening her mouth. What about?"

"Family secrets?"

"Hmm. Would she know any, unless she earwigged on conversations? I'm going to get Phil to poke into the deaths of the brothers, mother, and nan if he hasn't already, although if George is our man, it'll do nothing but put the blame at his door if anything's found out. Something could have been missed regarding the fire." She phoned Phil, putting it on speaker, and explained what she wanted him to do.

"I've had a brief look at those deaths already, about an hour ago," he said. "Great minds and all that. The fire started with a lit cigarette in a rolled-up rug by the bedroom door. It was assumed the nan accidentally dropped it on her way to bed. The origin of the fire was at the base of the rug, so the cigarette had dropped right down to the floor."

"That sounds off. Isn't it a little fortunate that the cigarette fell down the centre of the roll? And surely it'd have begun smoking before she fell asleep—she'd smell it and get everyone out."

"Maybe she was knackered and dropped off quick."

"I'm not buying that," Andy said.

"Hmm." Phil tapped something. "I've got the report back up. Says the fire spread quickly, so yeah, it's off. She'd have to be asleep to have died from smoke inhalation. They were all burnt to a crisp but found in sleeping positions, so none of them had woken and tried to leave. Rachel woke George, and they left via the back door. Wonder why it wasn't deemed as suss back then?"

"People trying to get their caseloads off their back. You know, file it as an accident and be done with it because the two who got out were children, and who'd suspect them? Or perhaps it really did seem plausible to have happened that way."

"Convenient," Phil said. "As for the mother, it was ruled a suicide. Rachel was with her when it happened. Mother had been inconsolable after the deaths of her sons. She handed Rachel a note that said 'Sorry, I love you'. Then she jumped. A passerby saw it all, albeit from a distance, so Rachel's in the clear, and she was just a child anyway."

"She's had a lot to cope with in her life," Helena said. "We've just informed her George is dead. I'm wondering how much more she can take. Anyway, SOCO are here, so we have to get going. We'll be back in time to meet with William Gringley."

She cut the call and went to meet the van by George's, dreading it in case Steve flew out and had another go. He stood at the living room window, staring out, a hand up to his mouth. His eyes were red.

Tom and Kalvin, looking all kinds of knackered, climbed from the van along with new SOCO. Down the road, a uniform still stood outside Trevor's, another van at the kerb. Neighbours came to view the show again, although some remained indoors, watching from there.

"Here we go," Tom said.

"It's this house." Helena pointed to number twenty-three. "Watch it. George's boyfriend is angry and angling for someone to blame. Namely me, but you never know, it might be your fault next."

A patrol car stopped, and Clive joined them. "I'm on the log."

Helena nodded. Andy slid on protectives then went with Tom to shoulder the door open. While Helena togged up, she briefed Clive on the perils of encountering Steve, then filed into the house with the other SOCOs once Clive had set the log up.

The house appeared the same as it had on previous visits. Everyone spread out to find evidence, and Helena went into the kitchen. The new patch of cement had well and truly dried. What if he'd buried his father's heart under there? She called for SOCO to come and carefully break the cement, then went out into the garden. She wanted to check the shed, see if he'd lied about that roll of transparent plastic being stolen.

Thankfully, there wasn't a padlock, but that would be easily remedied if there was. SOCO would have bolt cutters or something similar. She lifted the flimsy catch and opened the creaking door. The usual paraphernalia greeted her—tins of paint, tools, a lawn mower, even a rolled-up rug, which she found creepy. Had he left it there as a reminder of what he'd done to his brothers and nan? Yes, he could have started that fire, pretending to be asleep when Rachel woke him. He'd begun his murder spree at a young age, and those deaths had calmed his raging thoughts for years until he'd cracked again and killed his father. All supposition at this point.

Sounds of the cement being hit filtered out, and she poked around in the shed until she was satisfied nothing of interest was there. She came out and inspected down the right, which had the dividing fence next to it, Steve's property on the other side. Nothing down there but gravel on the ground and a hoe. Round the back, she peered into the gap between it and the bottom fence, and there, scrunched up, was a bundle of transparent plastic. She reached in and tugged it out. It sprang open from its cluster, revealing a smear of blood.

"Fucking got you." She called out for a SOCO to come and photograph then bag it. "Get that down to the lab. Ask them to compare the blood with Trevor Vakerby's, all right?"

He nodded, and she did a tour of the garden in case anything else had been hidden. Finding nothing, she ventured back into the house, meeting up with Andy in the hallway.

"A sheet of that plastic was down behind the shed," she said. "Blood's on it."

"The lying little shit. I found a key—could be Trevor's. You might want to come and look out here." Andy led her to the front garden where a marquee was being erected.

A SOCO was down on the ground taking swabs off the grass by a hedge. Beneath it was a meat cleaver, blood on the blade.

She stared at Andy. "Why on earth did he put it out here?"

"Easy access? Or he flung it there after he'd done Elizabeth in and didn't have a chance to pick it up later? Maybe Steve came out as George came home from the cliff and he had no choice but to hide it."

Steve wasn't at the window anymore. She was glad. Him seeing a cleaver being bagged would only add to his upset. Then again, it might force him to face the fact he was involved with a killer.

"We're going to have to go next door," she said.

"Hmm. Steve could be in on it."

"Maybe it's even him," she whispered. "No problem for him to drop the cleaver over the hedge or put the plastic down the back of the shed from his side. He could have been so upset over how George had been treated..."

"Why frame George with the plastic and cleaver, though? And we're back to square one with Darwin. The only person linked to all of the victims is Rachel—Jeff at a push."

"Come on."

They left the garden and walked up Steve's path, Helena coaching herself calm so she didn't bite if Steve started on her. She knocked on the door, conscious they were still in their protectives—they'd need to change out of them if they went back into George's. She tugged the hood down and put her gloves in it. Andy did likewise.

Steve opened the door, his glare telling her all she needed to know: he was still so angry, still had her in his crosshairs, and was more than ready to shoot.

"What are you lot doing now, rummaging through his house to pin all this on him?" he said, scowling.

"We need to come in and ask you some questions. No arguing about it either, unless you'd prefer to come to the station."

Whether he was grieving or not, he had no choice, not if it might be him.

"Let's have it then." He stepped back. "See how far you'll go to taint the reputation of an innocent man, even when he's dead."

Helena disguised a sigh and followed him into the living room. Andy got his notebook and pen out.

Steve stood by the window, glaring across into George's garden. "Why is a tent going up?"

Helena dived straight in. "Evidence has been found. A meat cleaver, one that could have been used to chop at the victims' chests so the hearts could be removed. It has blood on it. Do you know how that could have got there?"

He spun to send her an evil look. "No, I fucking well don't."

"What about some plastic sheeting, also with blood on it, behind George's shed? The sheeting George claimed was stolen."

"Excuse me?"

"The dining room floor is in the process of being dug up. Is there anything beneath the new concrete that you're aware of?"

"No! What are you saying? That I've got something to do with this?"

"Do you?"

He reeled off alibis for all the death times she presented to him.

"I'm definitely going to file a complaint about you." Steve gritted his teeth.

"That's your prerogative, but I haven't done anything wrong." She tried to smile but found she couldn't. "If there's anything you need to tell us, now is the time to do it. The cleaver and the plastic sheet will be forensically tested. We'll need a DNA sample..."

Her implication floated in the air between them.

"You can bloody have it," Steve said. "I've got nothing to hide." He sat on a chair, his body sagging. "Fucking hell..."

All the piss and vinegar had gone out of him, leaving behind a man who seemed defeated.

"It's a difficult thing to accept, I know." She did, too. Her ex-boyfriend, Marshall Rogers as she'd known him, real name Franklin Marston, had been a killer, and she hadn't known until it was too late either.

"How could *you* possibly know?" he asked.

"Because I do." She wouldn't go into details. "But it gets easier. It never goes away, but you learn to live with the knowledge."

"I refuse to believe George did any of this. He was a good man, so kind. Broken to some degree, yes, but not to the extent he'd kill people."

She wanted to believe him, but the evidence was stacking up. If Steve hadn't planted it, Rachel and Jeff were the next suspects after George, but if George's DNA was found at Elizabeth's, or on Trevor's and Darwin's bodies, in Trevor's house, a place he'd claimed not to have stepped foot in for years, or on Trevor's computer keyboard from when the images had been downloaded, they basically had their answer. Steve could either believe science or what his heart was telling him.

"I'll arrange for someone to come in and take a swab. We'll be checking those alibis." She walked out, ignoring his retort.

On the pavement, she breathed deeply. The tent was up now, making it clear something big was going on—again. More neighbours had emerged to gawp at the proceedings.

Andy stood beside her. "Back to George's or down the station?"

She sighed. "Time's getting on. We need to speak to William. He might have some idea why Darwin is linked to the other two. Doubtful, but we have to try. With Rachel being the only thread so far, we may as well get her swabbed, too, despite everything pointing to it being George. We don't want to do a shoddy job of it like the investigators did with the fire."

She arranged for that to be done, then popped her head into George's to let Tom know they were off. Protectives placed in an evidence bag and left with Clive, she drove them to the station. Weary beyond words, she had no chance to go up and have a chat with Olivia and Phil because Winston, the new night desk sergeant, called her over and pointed out Mr Gringley, who sat in the waiting area.

She introduced them and offered him her condolences. The man was a wreck, barely holding it together, and she organised for coffees to be brought to the smaller soft interview room. Andy went first down the hallway, and they entered and settled on the comfy chairs.

Helena ran a hand through her hair. It needed washing. "William, sorry to jump straight in, but do you know of anyone who would have wanted to kill your son?"

He shook his head. "No. I've never lived in Smaltern to know anyone. I met Isla at Brookes University in Oxford, and we remained in the city for a good few years afterwards. Once I landed my current job, we moved to Italy. When we split, Isla came back here so Dar was by the sea—he'd been brought up right next to it, and she thought it would be a comfort to him, something familiar."

"I see. So you won't know a Trevor and George Vakerby then? Or Elizabeth Mackenzie?"

"No." He rubbed a palm over his stubbly chin.

"Trevor was killed in the same manner as Darwin. Elizabeth didn't have the head injuries, but her chest was opened up. Evidence is indicating a suspect at the moment, but until forensics come back, giving us solid evidence, we can't announce who it is." She wasn't going to go into an explanation about collecting George's DNA and comparing it to any found on the bodies or at the scenes.

"But you think you know who did it?"

"Yes."

"Thank God. That's something." He paused. "But what if they kill someone else in the meantime?"

"I can't say anything, but I assure you, if it's the person we think it is, no one else will be murdered."

"What I don't get is, why Darwin? What has he got to do with the other people?"

"That's something we're working to establish."

They chatted for a while longer after the coffees had been brought in, him telling them he wanted to take Darwin's body back to Italy, where he'd been born, where he'd been happiest. Isla had apparently agreed to it, so it was just a case of waiting for it to be released.

William left, shoulders slumped, and Helena sighed. The day wasn't over. She still had to have a chat with her team if she got the time, plus there was that takeaway Andy was hankering after.

God, let forensics be in soon.

CHAPTER TWENTY-TWO

Jeff slept soundly, soft snores puffing out, his bottom lip shivering with each exhale. Nasty contemplated using her pillow to smother him—her hands itched with the need to do it—but even she realised that wasn't sensible. There would be no one to blame for The Watcher's death.

Rachel had come to terms with that now: in order to save herself, she'd have to incriminate her husband.

While she'd waited for him to fall asleep, she'd thought about what Nasty had been telling her over the years: Jeff was a controller, and if he asked questions of his team at work like he did her, she understood why they'd been difficult, baulking at his new orders and way of doing things. No one wanted a bossyboots in their life.

He was a pest.

It hurt to admit that. Hurt that she'd got it so wrong at a time when she'd been trying to get everything right for once in her sorry life. She'd hoped for so much more than she currently had—the freedom to do what she wanted without accounting for everything, a partner, not an owner. Was that what the older generation was like or just some of them? She'd made a mistake in picking a father figure. All she'd got was a kinder replacement for her own, and that hadn't been her intention.

You learnt new things every day, didn't you.

And you fixed problems as they arose, just like she was doing.

"Sorry not sorry," she whispered.

His wrinkles stood out in the tunnel of light coming in from the landing. She longed to carve into them with a knife and watch the blood fill the slices then trickle down his face, into his ears. There were so many things she wished she could do but couldn't.

Even now, as an adult, she was prevented by rules, by herself—she was the one who needed Jeff alive so she could move on. She was putting a block on Nasty's needs at the same time as allowing her freedom.

She'd also thought about that policeman coming round earlier to take a swab. Jeff had once again told her it was normal, but unease had still wended through her. It wasn't in the plan, but Nasty had assured her they hadn't messed up along the way. She had to be content with that.

Rachel tiptoed out, even though Jeff wouldn't hear if she stomped. She already had her kill outfit on, now dried from when she'd washed it. It was a new day, five past midnight. No need to stick to the plan she'd made with George by meeting at twelve, seeing as the dead fucker wasn't going to be there now.

Of all the stupid things to do, dying before he'd made amends. How selfish was that? She'd see him in Hell and give him what for.

Until then, she had a job to do.

Leaving via the rear door was the best way, Nasty had said so earlier, so she slung her holdall on her back using the handles over her shoulders to keep it in place. A trot down the wooden walkway had her remembering her childhood, in the garden of the family home, when she'd wished it was a jetty, with a boat at the end of it. She'd imagined getting on it so many times, a pirate, sailing away to better parents, a better life, the crow her parrot, sitting on her shoulder.

Momentarily wishing she could fly into her square window and hide from everything, *be* that pirate on the high seas, she climbed over the bottom fence and jumped down onto the pavement of the street behind. It was still, silent apart from her breathing, the weird buzz from one of the streetlamps where the bulb was on its way out, and the thrum of traffic in the distance.

Some homes had lights on, clotted-cream glows, and the blue tinge of TVs flickered, but all the curtains were closed as far as she could see, people snug inside, oblivious. The Watcher's place stood in darkness, as always at this time. He was an old man now, probably needed his sleep, and she'd heard his wife had snuffed it not long ago, so there would be no one else home to cause any hassle. No one else to kill.

She walked down the street, crossed it, then went along the side of his drive, next to a dividing hedge, keeping to the thick shadows. No security lights on any homes to show her up, no CCTV cameras mounted on the fronts, all things she'd checked using Jeff's telescope in the spare room.

In the back garden, she studied the houses in this row and behind, satisfied no one was nosing out. She used a tool Jeff had told her about, unlocking the door—so scary that someone could enter a house with ease and not too much noise. She stepped inside, her head hot and itchy from the shower cap, her palms damp with sweat, her black gloves a close fit.

The air had a tang to it, maybe beans, burnt toast, the meal of someone who didn't have the energy to cook a proper dinner. And dust, plus the cloying stench of mould. This man hadn't kept up to date with the housework since his wife had died, the lazy git. His daughter—if the woman who visited every Sunday at eleven was his child—would have a nice surprise come the morning.

Bet she won't fancy a roast with all the trimmings once she gets here.

Nasty laughed in Rachel's head and navigated the kitchen, the house a similar layout as hers. Something crunched beneath her trainer in the hallway, the same sound as snails made when you stood on them. She used to enjoy doing that.

You still do.

The living room was empty, as she'd predicted, and she pushed Nice to climb the stairs, imposing her will on her. Sometimes Nice needed persuasion to do things, although her whiny voice of complaint wasn't as often nor as loud these days. Nasty had almost taken her over.

On the landing, she took her holdall off and held it in one hand while she turned the doorknob to the front bedroom with the other. A deep breath in, a long blow out, and she was inside. The Watcher presented as a round lump under the duvet, the glow from a small lamp lighting him up. Aww, was he afraid of the dark? Had childhood demons followed him into the winter of his life?

They had something in common there then.

She walked closer to get a better look, flexing her fingers in readiness for holding the cleaver handle. There he was, on his side, curled like a baby in the womb, safe and secure in his dreams.

Nasty's breathing grew heavier. How could he sleep peacefully knowing what he did about her? How come guilt didn't nip him with its jagged teeth, whispering: *You should have phoned the police and saved her...*

Familiar anger twisted through her, heating her up from the inside, her hair sticking to her head. Her cheeks, so hot, prickled, and Nice worried about sweat dripping onto The Watcher, so she swiped her face with the sleeve of her new boiler suit, the rough material abrasive.

A bedside drawer, ajar, snagged her attention, and she opened it fully. Stared at what it contained. They were spread out higgledy-piggledy, as though he'd shuffled them around in search of the particular one he wanted.

Pictures of her. Of her father.

The dares.

Nasty wasn't sure whether to leave them there or not.

She made up her mind and snatched them, shoving them into the side pocket of her holdall. No one must know how bad it had been, what she'd endured. She found two cameras in the next drawer down, an old-fashioned thing and a digital. There were negatives layered on the bottom, so she took those, too, working quietly so as not to disturb the dirty fucker.

Nasty had an idea then, different from her plan but the same as another. It could wait until afterwards. She wanted to kill first. Needed to.

She dipped into her holdall. Clutched her spiky bat. Walloped him with it so it stuck out of his head. He roused, crying out. She grabbed her other weapon, a second one she'd purchased once Nasty had told her the original could be planted in George's garden. She'd paid cash for them both in a supermarket months ago.

Cleaver in her usual double fist, she brought the edge of the blade down on his cheek, his skull, the metal penetrating his brain a good inch. Blood spurted, a warm splash landing on her face, the wonderful streak of heat that spoke of imminent death. No groan from him, only his body jerking. She wrenched both weapons free, gritting her teeth with the effort, and repeated her action with the cleaver, creating a cross that signified he'd done wrong.

Nasty rolled him onto his back and shoved his old-man white vest up, getting straight to it and cutting out the grey-haired square in his chest. More blood. More anger. This man had violated her with his picture-taking, his spying, had done so much more than keep quiet over the years. Some of the images proved he'd watched more than she'd known, close-ups, where he'd zoomed the lens, getting right inside her bedroom with them, an unseen voyeur.

It reminded her of what she'd done to him using the telescope, coming into this room, noting the layout, him sitting on the edge of his bed, head in his hands, probably missing his wife. Had she known he was a pervert?

Nasty held his heart in her hands, a heart just like her father's, that had no empathy, compassion, or goodness inside it. The warmth of it penetrated her gloves, and she imagined it still pulsed with the beat of a wicked man's pulse. She threw it at The Watcher, and it bounced off his gashed head, coming to rest by his ear.

She admired the blood-spattered walls, sad no one would get to see them. She picked up the heart and put it inside a large Ziploc, placing it out on the landing because she'd need it soon. Then she spat on The Watcher—it didn't matter about DNA, not now she had a new plan.

A Yankee candle and a box of matches sat on the other bedside cabinet, the label proclaiming the scent was lavender, the wax a nice shade of lilac. It had probably belonged to his wife and he hadn't been able to part with it, much like the romance book beside it and the Dame Edna glasses. She took the lid off and lit the wick, rested the jar on its side like it had fallen over, then tugged a free pillow across, feeding one corner inside.

Fire spread, quickly eating up the pillow, and she took the matchbox, sticking it up the long sleeve of her top beneath her suit. She moved to the other side of the bed to grab the photos and negatives, tossing them into the flames that had devoured the top half of the mattress, its tongues licking The Watcher. Did his dead flesh taste good?

She added both cameras to the pyre, then her holdall, and retreated onto the landing, quickly removing her boiler suit, her trainers, and throwing them into the room.

Ziploc in hand, she rushed downstairs, the carpet prickly on her feet, and exited via the back door. In the garden, she took the heart out of the Ziploc and dug her finger in one of the slices she'd accidentally made with the cleaver, drawing a blood square on a patio slab then placing the organ in the middle.

Nasty took off the shower cap and gloves, stuffing them in the front of her leggings. Down the drive, down the street she went, a thief of life in the night, keeping to the shadows again, grit digging into the soles of her feet. She vaulted over the fence, glad she'd had the foresight to leave her trainers behind—she couldn't be doing with worrying about blood transfer. With Jeff asking so many questions lately, he'd be sure to enquire why she was washing the fence in the coming daylight hours.

She streaked along the wooden walkway, stubbing her big toe on a baluster. Her nail lifted, and pain streaked up her foot. She bit her lip to stop a scream coming out.

Indoors, she padded to a dining chair and inspected her toe. The damn thing was bleeding, so she grabbed the first-aid box and put on loads of plasters to stem the flow. Scratches were livid on her ankles where brambles or whatever must have brushed her skin as she'd landed in the garden. They'd soon heal.

She put the first-aid box in the cupboard and hobbled to the hallway where the coats hung on hooks, putting the red-smeared matchbox in Jeff's lightweight jacket pocket. The blood must have come off her gloves, but that was all the better for framing him. Nasty had been quick to think that idea up.

A dash to the kitchen saw her shoving her clothing, the cap, and the gloves in the washing machine, setting it on a hot cycle. She went upstairs to stand in the bedroom doorway, checking on Jeff, her hands still itching, wanting to kill him for tricking her. He wasn't who he'd been at the start of their relationship.

He'd changed.

Or maybe it took me to show you what he's really like, Nasty said. *You wouldn't listen at first. Now look at you, realising I was right. I'm always right.*

She got in the shower, scrubbing herself all over, a smidgen of Nice creeping in through the Nasty haze. Had she covered all her tracks?

Of course I did.

The shouts of people discovering the fire weaved faintly through the patter of the water. She hummed, pissed off she hadn't woken The Watcher to recite her poetry, and that was because of those terrible photos. They'd distracted her, altered her plan.

Things worked out fine in the end, though, didn't they?

Rachel had to agree with Nasty there.

She dried off, put on some pyjamas, and in the spare room, spent a few minutes watching the scene in the street behind through the telescope. People were out in their dressing gowns and slippers, but she wasn't bothered about them. What she wanted to see was the fire, erasing the fact she'd been there, scoffing The Watcher, turning him into a black husk.

It was so like that other fire.

Pretty.

She went to her room and got into bed, wondering how long she should leave it before 'discovering' the matchbox. She'd phone Helena afterwards, whispering, telling her what she'd found and how she was afraid for her life, married to a man who must have set the fire in The Watcher's house. Oh, that poor old boy!

Maybe she'd do it on Monday. After school. She wanted to watch the kids dissecting the two hearts first. Such a shame she'd left The Watcher's behind. She'd had it in mind for one of the girls in her class to open his up, but as she'd learnt early on in life, things didn't always go your way, and besides, it had to be like this to let Helena know the murder was related to the others.

The siren of a fire engine that sounded far away cut through the stillness, Jeff's piggy snores filling the gaps. The wail grew louder and louder, then came the rumble of the engine, the sort that always reminded her of fairground generators.

She loved the fair. Maybe she'd go to one when this was all over. A turn on the Twister was right up her alley.

Rachel's phone alarm tinkled quietly, and she swiped her screen to switch it off. Six a.m. on a Sunday, but she could blame her early rising on grief. She had family to mourn, a certain façade to maintain, and she'd play her part right up until the barred door of Jeff's prison cell clanged shut.

She turned to look at him lying there on his back, catching flies. He snored again, but that was no surprise. She'd given him the contents of three sleeping capsules last night. Maybe he'd wake after noon and think he'd had a tremendous lie-in.

In the spare room at the back, she peeked out onto the street behind. The Watcher's house had no windows anymore, the inner bellies of each room dark shells, and above the open squares, the bricks, blackened with triangles from where the fire had crept out, appeared as eyebrows.

Squares.

She nearly pushed herself into one but stopped.

The front door hung on one hinge at the top, the bottom poking out at an angle over the front path. What a beautiful sight, one she couldn't stand here and stare at any longer. It would appear odd if Jeff came in and saw her using his telescope.

Another shower set her up for the day, and she hung her washed leggings and long-sleeved T-shirt on the line, stowing the gloves in the shed. The shower cap could go in the cupboard under the kitchen sink, right at the back where Jeff wouldn't notice and ask when she'd bought it.

Life would be heavenly without questions.

She busied herself making breakfast, just coffee, and went out into the garden to drink it, wishing she had a big enough knothole in the fence so she could sit and wait for The Watcher's daughter to turn up. See her reaction. Or maybe she'd already been informed her father was dead.

Not for the first time, Nasty wished she could be a fly on the wall. Oh, the fun she'd have witnessing people's devastation.

Another piece of Nice was sheared away.

CHAPTER TWENTY-THREE

Helena had told Olivia and Phil to take today off unless something major happened. At the moment, it was just a matter of getting the forensic results back, which would close the case, proving George was their killer. While Andy wrote up his reports—like Helena, he hadn't had time to do them at the end of Friday and Saturday, and she'd just completed hers—she popped in to see the super.

As far as she knew, the press conference hadn't brought anything to the table except what people had 'thought' they'd seen—a glimpse of someone in the dark; a man acting suspiciously in his garden, miles away from the crime scenes; a teenager slapping his dog to make it behave on the lead. Every call had been followed up, but none of the information had led anywhere. With the exception of one witness, the old lady, Katherine Yeats, who'd watched someone putting Trevor in the hedge, no one had seen anything that helped the investigation.

She sat at Yakoshi's desk and gave him an update.

"So it's looking likely it's George Vakerby," Yakoshi said. "Interesting, considering you swore blind it wasn't him when you spoke to me at the start of the case."

She thought of Steve, how he'd been adamant it wasn't his boyfriend. Yes, she'd have agreed with him once, but... "We follow the evidence, sir, listen to it, and it's saying George was at Elizabeth Mackenzie's. Forensics are doing our tests as top priority—they worked through the night and will continue today to get answers. Zach let me know this morning that he sent the scrapings in from beneath George's fingernails to see if anything is there from the victims. Likewise, each victim has had the same thing done to check if his DNA is there, although I didn't notice any scratches on him on the occasions I spoke to him."

"And if it isn't him? If his DNA *isn't* present in all locations and/or on all victims?"

She knew what he was saying—he wasn't ready to call an end to this yet. The cleaver, key, and plastic could have been planted, like she'd thought, only, her mind had gone to Steve. "Sir...the only other people closely involved are Rachel and Jeff Levington and Steve Danbury—but Steve's alibis have been checked again, and he's out of the picture."

"And? Have you completely ruled the Levingtons out?"

She bit her lip.

"Or," Yakoshi went on, "have you jumped on the George bandwagon and stayed on it for the ride?"

She thought about what she'd said to Steve when he hadn't believed George had done anything. *I'd rather be a joke than refuse to see the truth when it's right in front of me.* Was Yakoshi saying she was doing the same?

He drummed his fingers on the desk. "I'm not turning into Levington here and elbowing my way in—yes, I'm aware of what he's been like and will address it soon—but having read the whiteboard, I've got a feeling this isn't as clear-cut as you think. George possibly didn't know Darwin Gringley, and why would he kill him anyway? That's the sticking point, the lad. The only person with a direct link to all of them is Rachel, and that's a bit of glass in my foot, so to speak. Her alibis..." He held up one finger.

God, he's going to count off points.

"One, she was in bed asleep when her father was killed. Two, she was at the school when Darwin was killed. Three, she was on the cliff when Elizabeth copped it. Have the teachers been contacted? I see no mention of that on the board. Did any teacher get the chance to confirm they'd seen her where she'd said she was on Friday?"

"We were leaving that until tomorrow."

"What about the cliff scenario?" He leant over to read his notebook. "Yes, Mr Sanbrook saw who you think was Rachel on the cliff, but George was with her. With no time for us to go on there, she's safe from suspicion, even with Zach's estimated moment of death, putting Elizabeth's murder in the lunchtime region—she was with George then, and he's dead, so there's no one to dispute where she was."

"She was definitely in The Sandwich Crust and on the cliff."

"She was, but *when* on the cliff? Do you see what I'm getting at? Who's to say she didn't get a taxi to Elizabeth's when George went off in Jeff's car? Get hold of Sanbrook again. He might have remembered something since and thinks it isn't relevant."

She rubbed her forehead. "So we'll look into Rachel today then? Push her for times and whatnot?"

"Yes. Just because she's the chief's wife, doesn't give her a free pass."

Helena almost snapped at him but ensured her voice was even when she said, "She hasn't had a free pass. I've had her in my sights all along, just that the Honda keys naturally meant we went in George's direction, as did the cleaver in his garden, the plastic behind his shed, and the key, which turned out to be Trevor's. Any police officer would have done the same."

"Then reverse, go back to before then. Yes, it seems obvious it's him, but what if it isn't? What if we get egg on our faces at some point?" Yakoshi smiled, maybe to take the sting out of his implied scenario—that she'd dropped the ball as soon as she thought the game was over. "We have to make sure we've covered everything before closing this off, even if it seems obvious it's George. It could be both of them."

"I had the same thought at one point."

"Then why discard it?"

"Okay, I get it. I've jumped the gun, too eager to come to a final conclusion."

"You may well be right and it's George, but with how the press vilify the police when we fuck up, it's best to tie off all loose ends, especially because of Levington."

"Is this just because of how it'd look if we're wrong, sir, or are you seeing something I'm not?"

"I don't know what it is. I'm not prepared to ignore it, though. Things seem too orchestrated. Oh, would you look at that, all evidence indicates George, a man who seemed to have got out of an abusive household and moved on with his life for years, not letting his past turn him into a monster."

"The same could be said for Rachel," she admitted.

"Not if she started that fire."

"The statements said she woke George up that night and—" *Shit. Rachel was awake first.* "Okay, I see it now. But she was a young *kid*. Really? A little girl doing *that*? Burning her brothers and nan alive? And why not kill George, too? Why not wait for the fire to come downstairs then run outside, and by the time anything could be done, George would have died from smoke inhalation? Can someone that age be so devious as to set a fire?" She recalled another thought she'd had. *You'd be surprised what children can do.*

"There are studies on kids being cunning from a young age. She was also with her mother on the cliff."

"But someone saw her jump. Rachel didn't push her or anything."

"Words are good for making someone do things, think things. Look at us now. We're talking, and what I've said has got *you* thinking. I didn't know what was wrong until we started chatting, and now I do. Rachel is bothering me. I met her when Levington came for his interview for the chief's job, and I have to say, I didn't like her."

Maybe this would have been hashed out last night if Helena had had a team talk, but everyone was so tired, and she'd been convinced they had their man. And as for Yakoshi saying he didn't like Rachel…the woman seemed okay to Helena for the most part, and dislike wasn't a reason to go after her.

But some people are chameleons.

Her email alert chimed. "Excuse me a second, sir." She read a forensic report regarding Jeff's car. Looked up at Yakoshi. "George's fingerprints are on Jeff's steering wheel. His blood is on the left-hand side of the driver's seat, where the top of his arm would be—probably from his nosebleed." She sighed. "But there's blood on the passenger seat."

Yakoshi raised his eyebrows. "And...?"

"It's Elizabeth's."

"Right. That could be from George if Rachel took him home from the cliff once he'd returned from his sulk. However..."

"It could be from Rachel if he drove them from Elizabeth's. They could both have been there."

"Correct."

Her phone pinged again, and she closed the first email and opened the second. Her stomach flipped, and her heart lost a beat. "George's blood was found on Elizabeth's worktop—again, it must have been the nosebleed. His skin cells and a sweaty handprint are on the kitchen doorframe, head height, skin cells on the worktop. Two strands of his hair in the hallway." She took a moment to digest the next bit. "Okay, bear in mind uniforms went round to Rachel's yesterday and took elimination swabs..."

Yakoshi sat upright. "Go on."

"A strand of *her* hair was found on Elizabeth, stuck to the blood and mess of her chest."

The super nodded as if he'd predicted that all along. "Two scenarios. Rachel's hair transfer to George—she'd given him a wallop on the cliff; they'd had contact. Or she was there, at

Elizabeth's, with George. This is where you tread carefully. She may not have been there. The chief is involved just by being married to her. If we get this wrong, he could cause a lot of problems for us."

He was doing her head in with the swings and roundabouts. "But you're the one pushing for me to still suspect her, sir, so I have to investigate it whether he's the chief or not. I've worked this case as if he's a citizen. I've treated him no differently to any other husband. I haven't even given him information unless he needs to know it."

"I'm just saying be careful. Yes, I'm pushing you, but go about it sensibly. Ask her if, at any time, she sat in the passenger seat while George drove. Put it to her that because of the trauma she's been through regarding her father's death, and the death of one of her students, she may have got things mixed up around the time of the picnic. Assure her it's nothing personal. Make her feel like you're on her side."

"I know how it works, sir." She resisted rolling her eyes.

"You do, so therefore, go back to work. Oh, and get those other teachers spoken to today. Tomorrow may be too late."

"Surely she won't kill again, not now George isn't here to take the blame. I bet him dying really threw things off."

Yakoshi's eyebrows shot up again. "You know as well as I do that killers don't always make sense with their actions."

She did, but Rachel committing another murder was senseless. As it stood, if her alibis were still solid after another check, she was free as a bird because her hairs could be classed as transfer onto George, flimsy evidence which CPS may throw out, and if it went to court, jurors might dismiss it. Unless her rage and trauma drive were such that she *needed* to kill another person, why bother?

"I'll be off then, sir." She said goodbye and walked to the incident room.

Andy glanced up. "You look like you've been slapped round the face. What's up?"

She told him everything, her throat strained by the time she'd finished. Then, "Yakoshi didn't come out and say it, but he's got a feeling Rachel's not innocent in all this."

Andy slammed his pen down. "But we've both kept her in mind throughout. We're not stupid!"

"I know, but he's right. We need to be sure she isn't in on it before we close the case."

"Hmm, this stinks of Yakoshi being worried because the chief's her husband. Any other investigation, and it'd just be George, as the evidence suggests."

She blew out a ragged breath. "Ring Olivia and Phil for me, will you? Give them the teachers' names and addresses. Tell them to go and visit the lot of them at their homes, providing they're even in. Being a Sunday, people might be out for the day."

"Why don't we do it?"

"Because we need to visit Rachel."

"Bloody hell. Not something I wanted to do again so soon. The chief's going to get pissed off."

"Not our problem."

Her email alert tinkled.

"Oh my word," she said. "Trevor's blood has been found in the chief's car boot."

"Pissing Nora…"

Helena's phone rang. Louise's name came up on the screen. "For fuck's sake…" She answered. "Yep."

"Hi. Got something you might be interested in. While it isn't the same as the other murders, it's still a murder, and it's iffy."

"Just what we need, a new case right at the end of the current one." She could have kicked herself. It wasn't Louise's fault. "Sorry. Carry on."

"Okay. First and foremost, it's a house fire."

If hearts and stomachs could drop down to toes, Helena's would have. "Right…"

"And while that's not unusual, a heart placed on a patio slab inside a square drawn with what appears to be blood, is."

"Shit, the killer's at it again."

"That's what I thought. Heart removal kind of says it all, doesn't it."

"Where was the fire?"

"In the street behind Blagden. Directly to the rear of Trevor Vakerby's. The deceased is an elderly man, Peter Alton, seventy-two."

"We're on our way." She swiped to end the call and stared at Andy. "Yakoshi's right. This isn't over. There's been another murder."

The heart sat inside a blood square, just like Louise had said. Helena stared down at the organ, which had only been found recently by the fire inspector. The patio slab in question was to the far right, so any firefighters tackling the blaze from this side, in the dark, wouldn't have seen it.

Daylight showed it in all its hideous glory, and SOCO swarmed the outside of the property, looking for evidence of who had been here to set the fire and leave the heart. The inside of the house was deemed unsafe to enter for now, and fire officers trained to spot arson were inside, working diligently. Peter Alton's burnt remains had been removed for Zach to do a PM and try to determine, despite the state of the body, how he'd died.

"Why leave the heart out here?" Andy said.

"I don't know, but what I find creepy is the fact it's in a square. They're carved into the chests—the squares, I mean—and the heart removed. This time, the heart is *in* a square. Does that mean anything? Am I looking into it too much?"

"God knows." Andy's protective suit rustled from a stout breeze that had picked up since they'd arrived. "Might rain." He pointed to the sky. "Grey clouds."

"Tom?" Helena called. "Can we bag this up—the heart and the slab, please? The weather's on the turn."

Tom and a SOCO came over, and Helena left them to it, indicating with a tilt of her head for Andy to follow her. They walked to the front, where some neighbours spoke to uniforms. The police had already been out during the night asking questions, but since the discovery of the heart, Helena felt everyone needed speaking to again.

A fire investigator stepped out of the front doorway. "You the SIO?"

Helena fumbled for her ID and showed him. "DI Helena Stratton—this is DS Andy Mald."

"Okay, given that a heart has been found, this is arson, therefore murder. Had a heart not been present, I'd still have ruled murder. The head had a weapon embedded in it. Some kind of stick with nails in it. As for the arson, a candle in a jar. Although the glass exploded into pieces and the wax melted, there have been enough candle fires for me to know what I'm talking about. The candle could have fallen over. You can work out the rest. I saw the body during the night—what's left of it anyway. Significant dip in the heart area of the chest." He nodded. "I see by your face you were expecting that."

"Yes. We believe this is related to the recent murders you may have heard about."

"I did catch something on the news, yes. Nasty business."

"Well, it isn't nice, is it," Andy griped.

Helena cast him a look that told him to shut up if he didn't have anything productive to say. He was tired, she understood that, but so was she and this fire fella here, and *they* weren't being sarcastic. "When can our people go inside?"

"Tomorrow. I still have a fair bit to do before I can sign it off. I just came out for some fresh air."

"Okay, thanks." She turned her attention to the street as he trudged back inside.

Opposite was a row of fencing, the bottoms of the gardens in Blagden. She counted the houses from seventeen, Trevor's, to the left, where Steve lived. He'd have had a good view of the fire if he'd looked out of his window. Then she cast her gaze to number one, Rachel's. While it was a way down, she could probably still see Peter Alton's place from upstairs. Trevor's was the house she was interested in, though. Directly ahead, all windows aligned perfectly with Peter's—he'd have had an excellent view into Trevor's garden and home and vice versa.

Had he been a friend of Trevor's? An enemy?

She phoned Louise, as Olivia and Phil were out with the teachers. "Hello, it's me. Can you look on the system and tell me whether Peter Alton was spoken to regarding Trevor when door-to-door was done the other day. Also get a couple of uniforms in Blagden. I want to know if anyone there saw anything suspicious last night."

"Two secs." The clicking of a keyboard tapped. "Yes, here we are. He said he didn't know Trevor or the family, even though he's lived there over forty years. Reckons him and his wife, who's deceased, kept to themselves. Although...he was cautioned back in the nineties about exposing himself to a little girl in the park. He denied it, but a couple of days later, the child ended up saying she'd made a mistake, and nothing else was done."

That brought the indecent images on Trevor's computer to mind. "If he didn't do anything since, it could just be a genuine case of mistaken identity."

"Hmm, but he did do something. He was asked not to take any photos of girls at the park as well. His excuse was that he didn't have kids of his own and wished he had one, so looking at the pictures comforted him."

"I'd like to say poor sod, but coupling that with the supposed exposure… Wonder why the police back then didn't spot a potential link there? Both incidents involved children. And why only take pictures of girls? I'd have been straight on that as suspicious."

"It was different back then. People might not have been as cautious about perverts like they are today—it seems there's a paedo around every corner now. It was only just being spoken about openly in the nineties, wasn't it?"

"True. So, we have a possible nonce, who lived behind Trevor, also implied as a nonce, so that could be the link between them. Cheers for that. Chat soon." She slid her phone away and told Andy the latest. "What if this is like the Tracy Collier case and two friends were perving on kids? What if one of the kids killed Trevor and Peter because of abuse? What if Elizabeth Mackenzie knew about what they were up to from eavesdropping and kept silent?"

"But that still leaves Darwin, who's a boy. Unless Trevor and Peter changed their tastes as they got older…"

"This is officially doing my head in now."

She moved to the pavement and took her protectives off. Andy did the same, and she bagged them, passing the stuff to Edwards, who stood at the edge of Peter's garden. One of the uniforms doing house-to-house approached from the right, and she met him in the middle of the road.

"Got something," he said.

He might be Pearson, might not. He was new.

"What is it?" she asked.

"Someone up there at number six saw a woman climbing over the back fence of a Blagden house."

Helena's legs weakened. "When?"

"About half twelve in the morning."

"Which fence did they climb?"

"Number one."

She whipped her head round to Andy. "Fucking hell's bells." Then to the man who may or may not be Pearson, "What was she wearing? Did they spot that?"

"Yep, there's a lamppost outside number three. The light was enough to see. Black clothing—a long-sleeved top and what looked like leggings."

"The same as she had on at The Crust," Andy said.

"Um, she had no shoes on." Might Be Pearson shrugged.

"That's just bloody weird," she said.

"He has her on CCTV—that's when he spotted her after he'd checked the footage about fifteen minutes ago because of the fire. Hidden camera in his front door. Looks like a peephole."

"Oh my God, that's brilliant."

She headed straight to the man's place, and the resident let her in to show her the clip. There was no question. It was Rachel.

"Thank you, sir. I'll arrange for someone to come and collect the footage." Back outside, she said to Andy, "Right, we'll go to her house now."

She jogged to the car, and they got in.

There was no other reason for Rachel to be out at that time. She *must* have set the fire.

Helena's email alert twanged, but she'd have to ignore it. There was no time to waste.

She started the engine and sped off. "Get on the phone for a warrant. I want Rachel's house searched from top to bottom."

CHAPTER TWENTY-FOUR

In the garden, Nasty stared at Jeff across the patio table. *What* had he just said?

"Can you repeat that?" she asked, toying with the stem of her wine glass. Yes, it was early for alcohol, but so what? She'd already told Jeff to mind his own business about it.

Nice had cringed when Nasty had said that, and Jeff had stormed inside, only to return a couple of minutes ago and say what he'd said, his phone in hand.

He narrowed his eyes. "I *said*, your hair was found on Elizabeth Mackenzie's chest wound."

Oh God. "And you know this how? You're not even working the case." Her mouth went dry, and her skin chilled. She'd been so careful, had kept the shower cap on throughout the murder. Shit. What else had she done or not done that would get her in trouble?

He eyed her as if he didn't know her anymore, like they were strangers, her the suspect and him the formidable chief. "Forensics obviously weren't told not to copy me on emails. They probably haven't been informed that I'm not on the investigation."

She couldn't work out whether he was angry with her or what. His face blanked and showed no emotion she could discern, so how could she react accordingly? How could she gauge what path to take? If she admitted it all, did he love her enough to cover for her?

No. Once a copper, always a copper.

She'd have to stick to her story. "Then it's from George." That was her best angle. Blaming it on him. Especially because he wasn't around to refute it. "You know hair falls out all the time. I was with him yesterday, for goodness sake, *near* him. We sat next to each other in the car and on the cliff top."

"That's what I *hoped* happened." He sounded sceptical.

"What's that supposed to mean?"

"It's just that your hair was also found on Darwin."

No time to pause and think about it. "Obviously! I taught him on Friday, last lesson. You *know* this. I had to bend close to look at the heart when he was prattling on about it being human, which as you're aware, is utterly ridiculous."

"That's the thing which has been bothering me since his death, though." He raked a hand through his hair, still clutching his phone with the other.

"What, me bending bothered you?" Christ, wasn't she allowed near her students now? What else did he have up his sleeve? A list showing what she could and couldn't do?

"No, Darwin saying it was a human heart." He took a deep breath. "Hearts have been removed from the victims."

"I know that, and didn't I say how weird that was?"

"You did. I was listening when George was round. Heard you talking about using human hearts. I can't keep it quiet any longer. Rachel, there's something else. I've also got blood in my—"

The doorbell dinged, followed by a series of harsh, urgent knocks. Jeff got up and went inside. Nasty lifted her wine, pretending to be calm when she was anything but. If this plan got messed up by *hairs*, she'd lose her bloody shit.

Jeff returned with Helena and Andy, and Rachel almost buckled. All owned grim expressions, although Jeff's eyes were watery, red, and he sniffed, remaining by the back door while Helena and Andy walked forward. Had they told him something?

"Just a few questions," Helena said.

"Of course." Nasty bustled in and smiled as best she could. The slither of Nice that remained cowered. "Would you like to sit down?"

Andy stayed standing, notebook and pen out, full of officialdom. His ruddy cheeks gave the impression he'd been running or had got himself all het up. Maybe he'd seen the email about the hairs, too. Nasty imagined that sort of information got a copper excited. Jeff had said stuff like that got the adrenaline flowing.

Helena took Jeff's seat, her glance at the wine reproachful.

Don't judge me, bitch. I'm three sheets to the wind, and what of it?

"Where were you from, say, half eleven last night?" Helena asked.

"That's easy. In bed." Nasty smiled. *Prove I wasn't.*

Helena perused the washing line, her eyes narrowing. "Can you explain why a neighbour from the street out the back saw you climbing over your bottom fence in clothing just like those on your line there?"

"Climbing the fence!" The consumption of wine forced a wretched titter out of her. "They must have been dreaming. Like I said, I was in bed. And why would I be out at that time anyway?"

"Do you know Peter Alton?"

"Who?" *Maybe it's The Watcher.*

"A gentleman who lived behind your father's house."

"That name's news to me." Nasty took a large gulp of her drink.

"So you don't know him from when you were little then?"

Heat flushed Nasty's cheeks. "Why would I?"

"We wondered if he was a friend of your father's, seeing as they both seemed to like young girls."

Her guts churned. This was getting too close to the truth. How did they find out these things? Was Helena about to spill Rachel's hideous secret?

"I don't understand what you mean," Nice said.

"The images on your father's computer, although possibly downloaded by someone else, may have been put there to let him know the downloader was aware of his proclivities. Mr Alton is on our records as a man who might have had the same penchants. It was first logged in the nineties."

"And he's been allowed to roam free to spy on girls?" Nasty blurted, angry that The Watcher could have been stopped before he'd even set eyes on her.

Nice whined. *Why didn't you think before you made me say that?*

"Who said he was spying?" Helena cocked her eyebrow. "I certainly didn't."

"Well, you know what I mean. Fancying them, preying on them, or whatever it was you implied." Nasty flapped her hand as if the error was nothing.

"Did a man ever approach you as a child? His home is behind what was once yours. Did anyone ever expose themselves to you through the window? I'm trying to work out whether Mr Alton had done things to girls other than what's in his file, and as you were the only female child in your home where he had direct access to watch, he may have tried to groom you."

The window. She mentioned the window... "Why would he watch me? There was nothing to see in my bedroom. Nothing at all." Nasty protested too much, and Nice panicked. "If he did watch me, I didn't notice."

"Why do you think your hair was on Elizabeth Mackenzie?" Helena asked. "Jeff said it was on Darwin Gringley as well. I've yet to check my email to confirm that, but I don't doubt your husband."

Why did he tell her that? How come he wasn't hiding it? He was on Helena's side, not Rachel's?

I should have smothered him when I had the chance.

Nasty told her what she'd told Jeff—hair transferred so easily. "So it's obvious why, isn't it?"

"That is plausible. However, Jeff also mentioned that the forensic report states your DNA is on your father's computer keyboard. Just a speck, but it's there. I recall you specifically saying you didn't go near that when we discussed the images."

"Not when he was there, no. I remember now, I was by it when I went into his cubby office to get a piece of paper and a pen. He wanted a bit of shopping, so I needed to make a list. Maybe my fingerprints were from that. Yes, I touched some keys as I leant over—I'd dropped the pen and needed to pick it up."

"I didn't say fingerprints, although of course, we'll have to take your prints to cross-check them with those on the keyboard."

Fuck. *Fuck!* "That's fine by me." Had she sounded calm enough?

"Let's go back to the neighbour seeing you climb the fence. Can you state, once more, where you were? I just want to be sure I heard you correctly the first time."

"In bed."

"In bed. Right. So if I told you your activity was caught on CCTV, what would you say to that?"

"That there's no CCTV in that street." She'd put her foot in it, she knew it. Blabbed again without thinking.

"How would you know that unless you were looking for it?"

"Well...well...there just isn't. I nose out of the back window sometimes."

"Rachel, why were you in the street behind? Why did you climb over the fence? You were in those clothes on your washing line, the same clothes as when you went to The Sandwich Crust, and you had no shoes on." Helena stared at Rachel's foot.

The plaster on her toe. The scratches on her ankle.

"How did you hurt yourself?" Helena asked.

"I stubbed my toe on that." She pointed to the walkway. "The nail lifted and bled, so I bet there's blood on there. You can check it. That'll prove I'm telling the truth."

"What about the scratches?"

Nasty shrugged. "Must have been from the garden this morning."

Helena narrowed her eyes. "Depends what time this morning. The scratches have scabbed."

Will you just fuck off, woman?

Helena's phone beeped. "Please excuse me." She read her screen.

Tension and silence stretched between them all. Andy stared at his pad. Jeff found the patio interesting. Nasty watched Helena, who looked up and fixed Rachel with a penetrating stare.

"On Friday, you implied you stayed at school for a while." Helena paused. "A teacher has said you left at the same time as him. A Mr Nichols. He remembers because you flew out of the parking area just after the final bell and almost collided with a student."

"He's lying. He's the other science teacher and has always been funny with me."

"In what way?"

"Keeps coming into my classes and taking over. He's just…annoying." He'd almost made her kill list, but she'd scrubbed him off, planning to find something to sack him over when she became headmistress.

"He mentioned CCTV at the school."

Nasty stared at the painted window on the fence. "It's not me you should be asking questions. It's him."

"Who, Mr Nichols?"

"No!" *Is she thick?* "Jeff. Ask him why he has a box of matches in his jacket pocket with blood on it."

"What?" Jeff snapped his head up to stare at her. "I don't even have a use for matches. Why would I need them?"

"You tell me." Nasty turned her gaze to him. "I found them this morning when you were asleep. I was looking for some loose change—a pound, to be exact, for the supermarket trolley. I'd intended to get a bit of shopping in." The lies came so easily.

Helena's phone jangled yet again. She read the message and stood. "Jeff and Rachel, please remain in the garden. I've been issued a warrant to search your property. An officer will arrive with it shortly. We'll stay out here in the meantime."

Nasty got up, her attention fixed on the fence window. She wandered towards it, down the walkway, ignoring Helena asking her what she was doing. Frightened, Nice headed for the only thing that had given her peace—the sanctuary of what was beyond the four skies. She launched herself at it, eager to get into the woods, but she smacked into the fence, staggering back. She clutched her forehead. Why hadn't she gone through? Why wasn't she with the fox so she could kill it again?

A crow cawed, mocking her.

"Rach, are you okay?"

Jeff, always there with his bloody questions.

"Fuck off," she said. "You're a killer. I know you are."

"It's not me, Rachel, it's you." It sounded as if he'd struggled to say that, his voice croaky.

"Not Rachel," she whispered. "Never her. It's Nasty, don't you see that?"

"Yes, this whole situation is nasty."

She faced him, her head throbbing from the bang. "You've seen her? You've really seen her living with us?"

Jeff frowned. "Who?"

"Nasty, you dopey bastard!" And she flew at him, reaching him quickly, raking her nails down his face. "I hate you. Why did she marry you? Why didn't she listen to me? You're just like *him*."

Hands gripped her arms from behind, and she was dragged away from the man she'd married. Andy was on one side, Helena the other, police bookends to her, the shelf full of stories that held heavy burdens.

"It was the dares," Nice said. "He made me play dares, and I didn't really want to." She shivered.

"Shut up!" Nasty bit out. "Don't ever tell anyone what he did. Shameful!"

"Rachel, talk to me," Helena said. "Tell me. What are the dares?"

Nice struggled to hold Nasty back. "I can't. She won't let me."

"Who?" Helena glanced around.

"Her!" Nice pointed at Nasty, who stood between them and Jeff. "She's right there. Always there. She did it. All of it."

"What's her name?" Helena asked.
"Nasty Levington. She's the one you need."

"Truth," Rachel said, trembling. She was sick of dares, so this time was prepared to take a beating or a grilling, whichever he chose, then the twenty-four-hour starve. Nasty was growing stronger with every passing year, egging her on to defy him, and while it was scary, it felt good.

"Truth?" Dad said. "Okay. What happened on the cliff with your mother?"

Why was he bringing that up now when so much time had passed?

She had to tell the truth. That was the nature of the game. He'd find out if she was lying, so what was the point?

"I made her jump off."

Dad's laugh hurt her ears it was that loud. "Oh, that's classic, that is. Why did you do that?"

"Because she didn't care enough to... She didn't care."

"Enough to what?"

"Save me from the dares."

"Ah. Those. Have you ever wanted to tell anyone?"

She shook her head. "No."

"If you ever think about doing that, princess, I'll tell them what you just told me," he said. "That you're a murderer. They'll take you away, put you in

a home for naughty kids, and all the male nurses will also play dares with you. Then they'll kill you, make out you hanged yourself or cut your wrists. And when you're gone, I'll find someone to play dares with George. How about that, eh?"

She shook from the fear of it, Nasty nowhere to be found, just Nice standing there by herself with the beast who was her father in front of her. "I won't tell."

"Good girl."

Nasty appeared then, standing beside Nice. You'll definitely have to kill him to stop this. There's no just imagining it now.

I know. You'll do it when we're bigger, won't you?

Nasty smiled. With pleasure.

CHAPTER TWENTY-FIVE

Rachel had been declared unfit for trial. Helena had suspected as much. During their time of waiting for the officer to arrive with the warrant two days ago, Rachel had babbled incoherently, a stream of nonsense that had them scratching their heads. Then distinct words had filtered out: plans, murder, the window, safe there, fox, crow, owl.

That had snatched Helena's attention immediately. What about the owl? Had Darwin told Rachel about his stories? Turned out it was just a coincidence, and Rachel had imagined an owl instead of a crow that was apparently her best friend for years.

The psychologist had wheedled the whole story out of her—well, out of Nice, who was apparently the real Rachel. Nasty was the one who'd committed the crimes, an alter ego Rachel had devised so she didn't get the blame. Her twisted mind hadn't believed she would be held accountable, as Nasty was another, sinister side of her who had murdered all those people. Nasty had appeared when Rachel was a child, a personality born from trauma and a fairy who had set fire to a forest.

Perhaps that was why she had an obsession with going to the woods.

She'd seen a fox there in real life and had latched on to it, pretending they were friends, the fox's family becoming a replacement for hers. It begged the question as to why Nasty had repeatedly killed that fox, something Rachel hadn't been prepared to explain.

She'd admitted to setting the fire at the nan's house, to forcing her mother off the cliff, and in the intervening years, she'd planned her father's murder. Elizabeth had been silenced for nothing more than exposing Rachel as the one who had downloaded the images, and Darwin's death was a result of her panicking that she'd get caught for using a human heart.

And those missing hearts... They'd been discovered in the small chest freezer, and Helena had recalled Rachel acting uneasy when Helena had stood by it.

The window and square explanation had just about done Helena in. How terrible that a child had to 'push' herself into another world in order to cope with what was happening to her. Trevor Vakerby had sent his daughter mad, although she'd been able to hide that well. Peter Alton also had a hand in that, just by standing at his window, and then later, Rachel finding the photos and negatives had nudged her a little more into insanity, desperate to hide her secret, one she'd carried alone for too long.

George's stolen roll of transparent plastic had been found in Rachel's shed, as had a pair of black gloves she'd admitted to putting there. A shower cap was under the kitchen sink. The boots she'd had on while killing Trevor were at the back of her wardrobe—she hadn't had time to clean off the blood—and a rounders bat with nails in it was in Peter Alton's head.

Mr Queensley had had a close shave. He was going to be next, on the Monday, and Rachel's goal of becoming headmistress would have been sooner.

An investigation had started into whether Peter Alton had gone a step further in his sexual depravity. A press conference had gone on air yesterday to ask any victims to come forward so they could get the help they needed, mentally and emotionally.

Helena could only hope that by telling her story, the real side of Rachel found a measure of peace. While her trauma didn't justify her actions, Helena couldn't help but think of the girl she'd been, how life in the Vakerby household had moulded her into a woman who, on the outside, had appeared nice and kind, when inside, Nasty lived and breathed, forcing her to right the wrongs.

As to why she'd left it so many years to kill her father... Nice had explained that she'd waited for him to express sorrow for what he'd done, and they could rebuild their relationship, start again. But he'd been just as rotten to her in adulthood, so she'd found Jeff, an older man who could take her father's place.

That hadn't worked out as well as she'd hoped.

As for George, the same thing applied. Rachel longed for him to say sorry for letting her play the dares, for knowing about them and doing nothing, the same as their mother. George had apologised, but by then, Nasty felt it was too late. She'd use him as a scapegoat, had planned to kill him after The Watcher, Peter Alton, had been killed. Except George had died, ruining the plan, and Nasty had settled on Jeff to take the blame for Peter—and Mr Queensley, who had no idea how lucky he was to have escaped death. There were plenty more years ahead where he could play with his feathers.

The matchbox had Alton's blood on it, plus hers from when she'd stubbed her toe.

Helena sighed. Thinking about all this had worn her out, and she rose from her desk to peer out of the window at normality. People walking or driving past the station. A blue sky with a bright sun. A murder of crows swooping.

That picture in George's house came to mind. The one of the crow. Then there was the one at Rachel's of the fox. How deep that must have been ingrained in her psyche to come out in her paintings. She'd painted one for Trevor—it had been found stashed away in a bedroom cupboard. And that was significant. She was telling them, in her own way, what she had to envisage in order to get by, what she had to grab on to because of them. The same as Darwin had done with his stories.

How awful. Sad.

A knock came at her door, and she turned.

Andy entered. "Um, Levington's here for you."

"Okay, send him in."

She braced herself for seeing him, a man who'd been nothing short of abrasive and bossy at work but one who'd changed his tune once that gibberish had burbled out of his wife's mouth. What would he be like now he'd had time to digest it all? He'd been advised by Yakoshi to take time off to recover from the ordeal. So why was he here?

She remained standing, wanting to have some control, the upper hand. Childish, perhaps, but she was done with men walking all over her, acting superior. First Uthway, then Marshall, and to a degree Yakoshi, though she'd admit he'd been right in pushing her to take a closer look at Rachel. And Levington had tried to bulldoze how she ran her team, and she'd resisted all the way.

Yes, it was time for her to stand up and be counted as an equal.

Levington entered, somewhat sheepish, and she supposed he would be, considering his wife was a killer and he hadn't spotted any signs. He'd lived with a woman who'd perfected the art of deception. Rachel had been a master at disguising Nasty, so the chief could hardly be blamed. Okay, he'd admitted he'd been asking her a lot of questions lately because she'd seemed off, but never in a million years had he pegged her as a killer.

"Hello, sir." She smiled and gestured to the seat in front of her desk.

He sank into it, diminutive in stature now, as if all the bluster his body had contained had hissed out of him, leaving him deflated. "I came to apologise."

She widened her eyes at that. "Oh. Really? What for?"

"Coming here like I did, barging into things, wanting to change stuff when it's clear you know what you're doing. This case showed me that."

"I see. That's…" She was about to say 'big of you' but changed her mind. "That's kind of you. You made things a bit difficult, I have to say."

"I had it in mind to create a strong team, one unparalleled, and didn't notice it was already at that level. Blinkered, that's what I was, despite reading up on your track record. And Rachel…" He fixed her with a watery stare. "She...she wouldn't have meant it, any of it. She was kind. I know that's hard to believe, but she was."

"It must be difficult to get your head around that, sir, but you know all about people with multiple personalities, surely."

He nodded. "Doesn't make me feel any better, just worse. To know she was suffering as Nasty, and I didn't have a clue. What must it be like to have a part of you controlling the rest for most of your life? Nice was all but obliterated until she came through in the end and exposed Nasty, not realising she'd still be in trouble for it."

"Yes, I think she really believed Nasty would be punished, not her, as though Nasty is a separate entity."

Levington broke down and sobbed, a fractured man, and despite him being an arsehole, Helena couldn't stand there and let him suffer on his own. She went over and crouched beside his chair, held his hand, and waited for him to finish.

"It'll get better, sir," she assured him. "You've read my personal file, so I'm not talking out of my arse, giving you empty promises."

He nodded, took his hand from hers, and wiped the tears away. "You're a strong woman, Stratton. I just wish Rachel could have been the same."

"But she had no chance. Nasty appeared while she was a child and didn't know any better. I was an adult, able to cope, to understand what happened to me wasn't my fault. Rachel must have thought she'd done something wrong, especially because the triplets were treated so well compared to her and George. Imagine your whole family against you, no support. It's no wonder she created a new self and the worlds behind the square windows."

"I've had the fence painted. Couldn't bear to look at it. I'll be moving, too. It's her house, the exact one she wanted right from a little girl."

"To be number one. I found that part of her story incredibly sad." Helena moved to her chair and sat opposite him. "Will you remain in Smaltern?"

He shook his head. "No. A new chief has already been appointed. Yakoshi's been dealing with it for me. I can't stay here, not now."

"Where will you go?"

"No idea at present."

She'd leave it at that. He clearly didn't want to talk about it. "Thanks for coming in, sir."

He stood, wiped his face again. "I'll go and apologise to your team, then I'll be off." He gave an awkward wave and walked out.

Helena stared at the closed door. She wouldn't go out there to witness his humiliation all over again. A glance at her desk reminded her she had paperwork to do, loose ends to tie off. What else was there but work for now anyway? She wasn't meeting Zach for dinner until tonight.

She pulled a form towards her and picked up a pen. Dived in, wanting to wrap this case up before another came in. Hope filled her heart that the next chief would be kinder, someone they could all get along with.

Because without hope, life was dour, and she wasn't signing up for any of that depressing rubbish anymore. It was time to let go of the past and welcome the future.

A future that had sunshine instead of rain.

And no versions of her own square window.

Printed in Great Britain
by Amazon